THE
COLUMBIA EAGLE
INCIDENT

The untold story behind the U.S. Army's
incursion into Cambodia during the Vietnam War

A NOVEL

LEO SULLIVAN

The Columbia Eagle Incident

Copyright © 2021 Leo Sullivan
All rights reserved.

Published by Edith Lane Publishers
PO Box 6379
San Diego, CA 92166

columbiaeagle@coxbusiness.net

Published 2021
Printed in the United States of America

ISBN: 978-0-578-83871-7

To Eileen, the English Teacher,
and Cate, the Veterinarian,
with Love

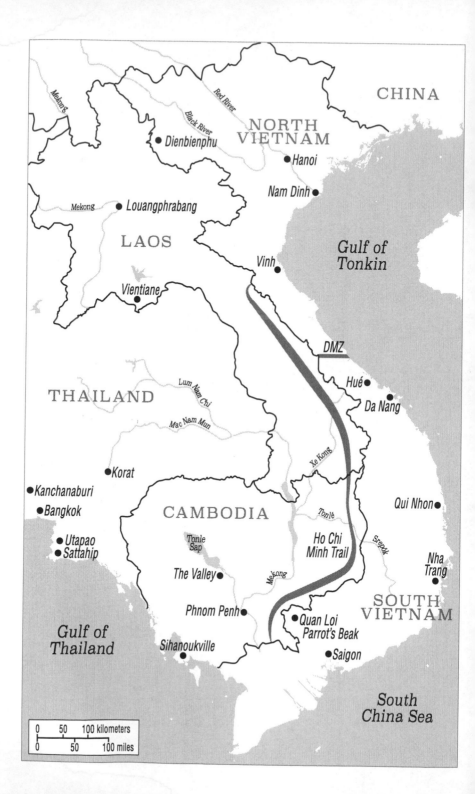

AUTHOR'S NOTE

The hijacking of the *Columbia Eagle*, the coup d'état in Cambodia, the incursion of the American army into Cambodia, and the campus unrest that followed are historical events that occurred in 1970. The military, political, and economic situations in Cambodia and Vietnam at the time are accurately described. The newspaper quotations of the hijackers and of Prince Norodom Sihanouk and General Lon Nol, the Cambodian leaders, are taken from the historical record.

The U.S. Army posts and Air Force bases in Thailand and Vietnam existed at the time and served the purposes indicated. The 501st Field Depot, the 558th Supply and Service Company, and the First of the Seventh Battalion of the First Cavalry Division were actual units stationed, for the most part, at the locations indicated.

Otherwise, this is a work of fiction. The references to military units, political leaders, and historical events are intended only to give the fiction a setting in historical reality. The incidents described and the names, descriptions, and actions of the characters are products of the author's imagination. The names of some of the characters may appear similar to the names of actual persons, but they are used fictitiously and any such similarity or resemblance to real-life counterparts is entirely coincidental and unintentional.

The author gratefully acknowledges the *New York Times* and Associated Press for the use of newspaper articles published in 1970 that were used as the basis for newspaper articles in the book.

PART ONE
The *Columbia Eagle*

CHAPTER 1
Cambodia
OCTOBER 12, 1969

SERGEANT DAVID CANEDO SAT CROSS-LEGGED on the ground at the edge of the jungle clearing and studied his boots. They were shiny black above the ankles where the fatigues were tucked in, but the soles were caked with mud, and mud had splashed over the toes. They had come a long way, those boots. Probably started out in a factory somewhere in the Northeast, a factory like one where he might be working if it wasn't for the army, where he would get off at five o'clock and have a beer with his friends and maybe take his girlfriend to the movies on a Friday night. He'd worn the boots since they were new, issued to him in basic training. He'd hoped they would last until he got home so he could wear them hiking and fishing, but now he wasn't so sure, they were in such bad shape.

Canedo ran the U.S. Army laundry at the Air Force base at Utapao, Thailand, fifty miles west of the Cambodian border and more than a hundred miles west of where he sat on the damp earth with Privates Ramos and Greenwald, who worked for him at the laundry. When it rained in Utapao and the streets were wet and muddy, they stayed inside, dry and comfortable. Here in the jungle, they were wet, cold, and miserable. But it was their own fault, letting the colonel surprise them like that, half-smoked joints lying in the open and beer cans littering the floor. The colonel hadn't chewed them out, and Canedo knew he wouldn't if they didn't make a fuss about helping him with the rifles piled at the edge of the clearing.

Still, he wished he'd begged off when the colonel said he needed their help taking the rifles into Cambodia. American military weren't supposed to be in Cambodia—even he knew that, although he couldn't be sure because he was just a three-striper and three-stripers weren't privy to the big picture. But one thing he *did* know was never to volunteer for anything, and here he was volunteered by the colonel to risk his neck in the middle of the jungle. If he got killed, no one would know where to look for him, and his parents would never know what happened to him.

If it wasn't for the war in Vietnam and the draft that came with it, he'd be home in San Diego with his mother and father. The summer weather would be lingering—warm days and cool evenings, but no rain, not yet; it would still be dry as toast. On Sunday his mother would take his grandmother to mass at St. Patrick's and then cook breakfast—huevos rancheros and homemade corn tortillas—for his sister and her kids and the aunts, uncles, and cousins who would drop by. After breakfast they might drive to Tijuana to visit relatives or hang out in the backyard taking it easy, his dad telling stories about their Mexican and Spanish ancestors. They'd heard the stories many times, but the younger kids would still hang on every word; they couldn't get enough of it, just like him when he was little.

In a few weeks, the weather in San Diego would turn damp and overcast, and nightfall would come earlier, fitting for Día de los Muertos—the Day of the Dead—in November. His family would dress in colorful costumes and parade around the neighborhood wearing skeleton masks and holding photos of their ancestors. He wished he could be there to join in the celebration, not in Southeast Asia where so many of the dead were now coming from, and especially not in Cambodia where he could be dead and missing at the same time.

Canedo looked around the clearing, a small patch of mud hemmed in by thick, green, dripping jungle. He wasn't sure where they were, only that they were in Cambodia. The colonel had insisted on driving, and Canedo and his men had sat in the back of the truck, the canvas flap pulled tight across the opening. They hadn't been stopped at any checkpoints or the border, but he figured the colonel would have taken care of that before they left.

The drizzle started up again and drops of water dribbled down Canedo's neck. He dragged a poncho over his head, leaving a crack just wide enough to keep an eye on the colonel, standing by himself on the other side of the clearing. The colonel seemed at ease, poised and self-assured, exuding an aura of confidence that said he wasn't one to be messed with. He looked like he stepped out of a recruiting poster, a soldier's soldier—short, graying hair; tanned, weather-beaten face; square jaw. And he dressed the part, wearing a camouflage-mottled scarf around his neck, jungle fatigues so starched they held their form against the dampness, and spit-shined tanker boots secured with leather straps. Two nine-millimeter pearl-handled revolvers hung in holsters from his webbed belt.

This guy's too much, Canedo thought. He thinks he's the second coming of Patton.

Canedo snapped out of his reverie when a Cambodian soldier stepped from the jungle not ten yards from where the colonel stood. The man was short, about five feet six, and heavy, with a paunch hanging over his belt. The skin of his hands and face was soft and puffy, his oily black hair cut short and slicked to one side. He was forty or fifty years old and dressed in GI-issue jungle fatigues. The man stared at the colonel through cold, unfriendly eyes.

"Where are guns?" he demanded, his high-pitched whine slicing through the silence.

The colonel didn't move, though a faint smile played at the corners of his mouth. Canedo glanced at his rifle leaning against a nearby tree, within easy reach if things didn't go the way the colonel expected.

"Where are guns?" the stranger asked again, louder this time, more insistent. "I come for guns."

Without taking his eyes off the man, the colonel raised an arm and signaled to Canedo, who shook off the poncho and scrambled to his feet. He lifted an M16 from the pile of rifles and cautiously approached the Cambodian with the weapon lying across his outstretched palms like a priest making an offering. The Cambodian studied the rifle a moment, then snatched it from Canedo's hands and held it up for closer inspection.

Canedo removed a clip of cartridges from his belt and handed it to the Cambodian, then backed away to rejoin Ramos and Greenwald. The Cambodian pulled the charging handle back and inspected the firing chamber, then inserted the magazine and moved the selector switch to fully automatic. With a crooked, mischievous grin, he swung the barrel toward the colonel and fired a burst over his shoulder. The colonel didn't flinch.

"You bring more," the Cambodian said, patting the rifle in satisfaction. "You bring more, many more. You, me, we fight!" The Cambodian cackled happily and disappeared into the jungle.

Canedo wondered who the man was and why they were giving him weapons, but those things weren't his concern. His concern was to get back to the laundry and finish putting in his time in the army so he could go home to his family.

CHAPTER 2

Washington, D.C.

OCTOBER 15, 1969

"YOU SURE WE SHOULDN'T TELL HIM?" CIA DIREC-
tor Sharee Fish nervously fingered the gold key hanging
from a brooch on her blazer. "It's the first time we've done
anything like this in Cambodia."

Fish stood by the window of John Lynch's office in the
West Wing, watching the evening thicken over the White
House lawn. Behind her, discarded newspapers littered
the carpet and news clippings hung haphazardly from
the gumwood mantle above the fireplace. Photographs
of Lynch with the president lined bookshelves along one
wall, showcasing his long association with the man who
now occupied the Oval Office.

Lynch sat stiffly at his desk and stared at the director's
back, wishing he didn't have to deal with the woman and
the unsavory matters she brought to the White House.
He'd played football for the Pittsburgh Steelers—getting
beat up on the gridiron was easier than dealing with
Sharee Fish. But he was the president's national security
advisor, and it was his job to put up with her so the president wouldn't have to.

"We haven't 'done anything,'" Lynch replied wearily.
"What's a few rifles? Christ, Sharee, the president's honor
guard loses that many in a month."

"Well, I don't like it," insisted Fish. "We're out on a limb. I think the president should be told."

Lynch eased himself lower in the chair, his rumpled suit coat tugging at the buttons across his bulging belly. He knew it wouldn't do any good for the director to see the president. The president wouldn't grasp the significance of the situation, and he'd be annoyed that Lynch had allowed her to bother him with such a trivial matter. The president wouldn't make a decision one way or the other anyway, and Lynch wasn't sure he should. What's done was done, and even the president couldn't undo it.

Fish was too much a politician for Lynch's taste, appointed from the Senate by a president grateful for her support during the election. Lynch thought she was a bad fit at the CIA, a Navy captain before entering politics—a ship driver—with no intelligence experience. She was more concerned about her personal reputation than the agency's, spending more time managing her Rolodex than managing the department. Unwilling to take responsibility for even the most trivial decisions, she was constantly running to the White House to get the president's okay. Lynch's job was to insulate the president from people like her and from the unpleasantness they brought with them. He had to eat a lot of shit to keep it off the president's plate, and here she was serving up another meal.

He wondered if she really wanted to see the president or if she was just looking for someone to take the blame if things went wrong. That was her modus operandi, and making him the scapegoat for this Cambodia affair would fit the bill. He decided to call her bluff.

"Sharee, you want to tell the president? You tell him."

He made no effort to hide his annoyance. "But before you do, let me ask you this: What good will it do? It's too late to ask him whether you should or shouldn't do it. You're already in this thing up to your eyeballs, and you got there without his help. Why involve him now?"

Fish turned from the window and looked at him with a grave expression. "John, the United States has supplied arms to the Cambodians. The president should be told. I assume he would want to know."

"They're not 'the Cambodians,'" Lynch countered lamely, frustrated by her intransigence. "You said yourself they're a splinter group—a tribe, really—operating near the Vietnamese border. No connection to the government. I bet if you asked them, they wouldn't even know they were Cambodians. They could just as easily be Vietnamese. A mere accident of geography that they happen to be on the Cambodian side of the border."

"You underestimate the seriousness of the situation," Fish replied. "They are not a 'tribe,' and you are not familiar with them. They are not Montagnards, primitive faces staring pitifully from the pages of *LIFE* magazine. They're sophisticated soldiers, at least by Southeast Asia standards. Our man over there thinks they may soon be strong enough to take over the entire country. And, John, the fact remains"—she rested her knuckles on Lynch's desk and leaned forward to underscore the message—"they're on the wrong side of the border. We're supposed to be in Vietnam. We're not supposed to be in Cambodia."

Lynch pushed himself up from the desk and walked to the fireplace to avoid the director's gaze. He stood with his hands clasped behind his back and stared into the small fire crackling on the hearth. He wished she wouldn't lean over his desk like that—she was always showing off her tits. He found her attractive for her age—indeed, they spent time together on occasion—but there was something unseemly about getting aroused by a member of the president's cabinet, especially in the West Wing of the White House.

"Sharee, there aren't any borders out there, only jungle," he said, a hint of pleading in his voice. "It's not likely to come back on us. Nobody knows. Let's drop it for now, okay? Let's wait and see what happens."

"Okay, John," she said, her sudden capitulation catching him by surprise. He'd expected to spend another half hour twisting her arm and maybe negotiating a budget increase to get her to back off. Worse, he might have had to take her to dinner, although the thought of another post-dinner tryst had some appeal.

"I'll keep it to myself for now," she continued. "But the next time I come knocking on the president's door, you'd better let me in."

After Fish left, Lynch sat quietly in the gathering gloom and reflected on the visit. She'd been bluffing all along, he knew. He didn't like getting played by her, but, still, he had done his job. The president would not, for the time being at least, get caught up in what could become a very messy affair. This was just the sort of two-bit operation that could blow up in their faces, and if it did, he would be the one to take the blame—Fish had just made sure of that.

"Are you going to keep it up?" he'd asked as he ushered her to the door. "Send them more arms?"

"Yes, I think we will, John." Lynch sensed the relief

in her voice now that she had laid the responsibility in his lap. "A bit at a time. It could work out quite well indeed."

"Sharee, if anybody gets wind of this, it could spell trouble," he cautioned. "The press would have a field day."

"I know, John. But my man's reliable. He'll keep a lid on it."

"I hope so. The president was elected to get us out of Vietnam, and we still have four hundred thousand troops there. And they're still dying every day. If the press finds out we might be widening the war—even in an effort to end it—the shit will hit the fan."

CHAPTER 3

San Francisco
OCTOBER 19, 1969

FRANK SCHANIEL GINGERLY RAISED HIS HEAD from the pillow and squinted at the clock. Nine o'clock. Only five hours' sleep, but Joanna would be waiting, sitting impatiently at the kitchen table, sipping coffee and pretending to read the Sunday *Herald*. He wished he didn't have to face her, not so early on a Sunday morning after a Saturday night like the night before.

He rolled onto his back and rubbed the sleep from his eyes. If Joanna knew he'd been with another woman, there'd be hell to pay. Not that she had a claim on him; they were just roommates, after all. But they usually slept together when she was in town, and she was becoming possessive.

Frank pulled his clothes on and ran his fingers through his hair, wincing at the reflection in the mirror. His hair was oily and mussed and dark fatigue pouches hung under his eyes. He considered taking a shower to wash away the evidence, but he didn't have the energy, not yet.

He walked into the kitchen and greeted Joanna with a smile he didn't feel. "Hi," he said brightly. "How was the trip?"

"Fine, thank you," she replied, not looking up from the newspaper. Frank slipped into a chair and poured a cup of coffee. "I was out late last night, huh?" He tried to gauge how angry she was. "Mike Reidy and I tied one on. His last night out on the town, you know. He leaves for Thailand tomorrow."

"Yes, I know." Joanna's Chinese accent was thicker than usual, a sign her anger had not yet dissipated. The inflection in her voice changed with her mood, and Frank had learned to interpret the slight variations. She'd come to the United States for high school, too late to lose the accent, and now it served as a window to her emotions.

"It was a long flight from Hong Kong. I had to work coach and I'm very tired and the whole time I thought about getting home and being with you." Tears welled in her eyes. "And you weren't here. Maybe you were with another girl."

Not for the first time Frank wondered what Joanna saw in him. He was just a punk kid, barely four months out of college, chubby and still struggling with pimples. Half the time he cut himself shaving, coming out of the bathroom with pieces of toilet paper stuck to his face. He still worked part-time as a grocery clerk at the Marina Safeway, his college job, and could barely afford his half of the rent, let alone taking her to a decent restaurant or out on the town.

Joanna was two years older, smart, and employed. She was slim and always made up and dressed right out of *Vogue*. She flew all over the world with Pan Am, visiting places that to him were just pictures in *National Geographic*. She spoke three languages, for Christ's sake. She could have any guy she wanted, any one of those suit-and-tie guys who worked downtown and had a lot of money to throw around. Who wouldn't want to screw a good-looking Chinese chick? Still, he wasn't complaining; he just couldn't understand why she seemed so smitten with him.

"Joanna, I'm sorry I was out late. I really am. But with Mike leaving, we got a little carried away is all. Nothing happened."

"It better not have, Frank." She looked at him appraisingly. "I find out, maybe I kill you."

Frank's laugh broke the tension, and Joanna reluctantly joined in. He reached over and took her hand. "No need to kill me, Joanna. I'll be a good boy. I promise."

"I know, Frank," she said. "But we used to make love when I come home. Now, not so often. I think maybe you don't love me anymore."

Maybe that was it—he was good in bed. He doubted he was any better than the next guy, but what did he know? He'd been with only one other girl before Joanna, a prostitute he picked up in North Beach after having too much to drink. He noticed the girl waiting for a bus and asked her if she wanted a date. He didn't know what he was getting into until she took him to a by-the-hour hotel and told him to pay for the room. And it didn't go well—he was so nervous his half hour was up before he finished.

So if he didn't have the experience, maybe he had a big pecker? It was big enough to get the job done, but he had no idea how he compared to other men Joanna may have been with. The guys in the dorm never lined up and compared their units, and *Playboy* ran pictures of women with big breasts, not male genitalia.

"It's not you, Joanna," he assured her, his thoughts wandering to Eileen McClellan, the girl from the night before. "It's just that I'm worried about things. Reidy's going overseas tomorrow, Ming's leaving in a few days, and I'm not far behind. I'm uptight, is all."

"Everyone's leaving," Joanna said, self-pity in her voice. "It's that fucking army, that fucking war." The way she said "fucking" it sounded like "fooking." He suppressed a smile. He didn't want to tick her off; he'd learned from experience how quickly her anger could erupt. She was volatile and her temper unpredictable, one reason he wouldn't mind some time away.

"I'll be around awhile," he said. "I still have a few months before I join Reidy in Thailand, and we'll be back before you know it."

Joanna rose to clear the dishes. "Okay, a few months. I'll pretend you're not leaving."

"It's a beautiful day," Frank said. "Ming will be over in a bit. Let's go to the park. What do you say?"

The apartment was carved out of an old Victorian house on Cole Street, between the university and the panhandle of Golden Gate Park. On Sundays, rock bands played from the back of a flatbed truck, covering songs from the Grateful Dead, Jefferson Airplane, or one of the other rock groups that emerged from Haight-Ashbury. Hippies turned out in force wearing flowers in their hair and bell-bottom trousers, the girls braless in sheer linen blouses. With his short hair, creased trousers, and Converse low-cut Chuck Taylors—his standard footwear since grade school—he would never blend in, but he could still look, and he liked nothing better than a Sunday in the park.

Promptly at ten, Ming Chu rang the doorbell. Joanna met him at the door with a warm hug.

"Hi, Ming," Frank said cheerily, waving him to a chair at the table. "Make yourself at home."

Frank had met Ming four years earlier, when Ming was in his last year of law school and a resident assistant in the dorm where Frank shared a room with Mike Reidy. He was now in army intelligence, a major already, home on leave on his way to Vietnam. Ming had met Joanna on one of his overseas trips and introduced her to Frank when Frank was looking for a place to stay while waiting to go on active duty. Joanna had an extra bedroom and he jumped at it, never expecting he'd be jumping on her as well.

Joanna busied herself in the kitchen, putting together a plate of bacon and eggs for Ming. "Frank," she called out, "why don't you shower and get ready?"

Frank feigned the look of a henpecked husband for Ming's benefit, then dutifully retired to the bedroom and slipped out of his clothes. He looked down at his flaccid penis in mock disgust. "You little devil you," he said in reprimand. "You almost got me in real trouble this time."

Frank winked at himself in the mirror and climbed into the shower, allowing the stream of water to cool the memory of Eileen McClellan. He was feeling his oats, living the life—a new college grad, an officer and a gentleman by act of Congress. He knew he couldn't be a kid forever, that eventually he'd have to settle down, but why rush it? Anyway, when the time came, it wouldn't be with Joanna, he was pretty sure of that; she was more than he could handle. But Eileen McClellan might fit the bill, if he ever got to know her for more than a one-night stand.

He met Eileen the night before when Mike Reidy dragged him to The Sturch and Thistle, a loud, raucous, wood-paneled English pub draped with Union Jacks. Normally Mike wouldn't go near an English bar—he resented all things English because of their long history of screwing over the Irish—but he gave The Sturch and Thistle a pass because they served Harp Lager and allowed Irish music from time to time, even tolerating rebel songs as long as the crowd didn't get too rowdy.

Eileen was sitting at the next table, singing "Roddy McCorley" at the top of her lungs, inching into rowdy territory. He recognized her from college and started up a conversation, shouting to be heard above the music. She was out with a girlfriend, blowing off steam after a dreary day at the rewrite desk of a local newspaper; judging from the empty glasses on the table, they were making good progress. He bought her a Harp and soon cajoled her into ditching her friend for an Irish coffee at the Imwalle Lodge, a college hangout near the campus, and then took her home to her apartment. Only after an alcohol-besotted, sweaty coupling did he remember Joanna was due back from a flight to Asia. In the early hours of the morning he slipped out of Eileen's bed, quietly pulled on his clothes, and tiptoed out of the apartment, leaving Eileen snoring with her nose in the pillow.

THEY TRAILED INTO THE PANHANDLE AMONG knots of young people drifting toward the band, Joanna between Frank and Ming, her arms linked in theirs. Summer had turned to fall, and brown-speckled leaves crunched underfoot. Joanna spotted Mike Reidy standing near the bandstand and propelled them in his direction, but Frank begged off. He was still feeling sheepish about sleeping with Eileen and piqued with Mike for letting things get out of hand.

"I've said my goodbyes," he said. "I think I'll just enjoy the music."

Frank sat on the lawn some distance from the band and idly watched the hippies dancing among the picnic blankets spread on the grass. It was all Reidy's fault, he told himself, assuaging his guilt. It was always Reidy's fault. He was fun to hang out with, but too often there was a price to pay.

Born and raised in Ireland, Reidy came to the United States to study at the university. They'd been roommates, fraternity brothers, went through ROTC together. Now they were newly minted second lieutenants, and by happenstance would both be stationed in Thailand—a near occasion of sin if there ever was one. Mike would have plenty of opportunities to satiate his cravings—and to get Frank into trouble at the same time.

His thoughts turned back to Eileen. He wondered if he would ever see her again. He wouldn't have much of a chance, being out of the country for a year. He was off to war—at least, that's what he'd led her to believe, playing the patriotic card to get her between the sheets. If truth were told, Thailand was a quiet backwater of the war in Vietnam, but it sounded romantic, like the GIs in the Second World War kissing their young brides goodbye at the train station. Or he was Rick from *Casablanca* and Eileen was Ilsa.

He wasn't for or against the war—he didn't know much about it, really. He was just doing what was expected of him. The flower children dancing around him wouldn't understand, with their peace symbols and their protests, burning draft cards and smoking pot. But he was a middle-class Catholic boy, and middle-class Catholic boys did what they were told—at least, until guys like Mike Reidy led them astray. And now that he would be stationed in Thailand, the war in Vietnam was not his concern.

Mike was opposed to the war, Frank knew, although he was careful to guard his views. He was an army officer, and army officers were expected to toe the warmongering line. More important, the army was Mike's ticket to U.S. citizenship, and that was number one on his list of priorities. And regardless of his views about the war, Mike would never let his political beliefs get in the way of having a good time—and dragging Frank along to share in the fun.

Frank looked over at Mike, who was huddled with Ming and Joanna and talking to a Chinese man in a dark business suit with a black patch over one eye. The man's clothes looked expensive, but he wore them sloppily, his narrow tie pulled loose at the neck, a shirttail hanging out of his pants. Frank wondered who the man was, but he didn't give it another thought, not until later. Not until Cambodia.

CHAPTER 4
Bangkok
JANUARY 12, 1970

BOB MACNAMARA, FOREIGN CORRESPONDENT for the *San Francisco Herald*, sat on the bed with his feet pulled tight under his thighs, elbows resting on his knees, chin supported in the hollows of his cupped hands. He stared out the window of the hotel room at the dingy gray buildings across the street and the patch of sooty sky above them, thinking about what to write.

He hated thinking about what to write. He liked writing the stories, but he didn't like thinking about them before he wrote them. He wished he could just compose an article in his head and then put it down on paper, but his thinking about the story always got jumbled up with how much he hated the pressure of having to write it—the panicky feeling that he wouldn't be able to come up with something, or that it wouldn't be any good, or that he wouldn't finish it on time.

He closed his eyes for a moment and took a deep breath, then pushed himself to the edge of the bed and leaned over the typewriter precariously balanced on an upended suitcase. He flexed his fingers above the keyboard like a maestro about to conduct an orchestra.

Dateline: Bangkok. He pecked at the keys with two fingers, the maestro settling for a small combo in a cabaret.

Though he could type properly with all ten fingers, he used only two because that's the way the old-timers did it. It didn't matter that it was slower because he couldn't think any faster than his two fingers could type. Hunting and pecking gave him something to do while he thought about what to write, and it was easier to think about what to write once he started typing. Starting—that was the hard part.

He pulled the paper from the typewriter and wadded it into a tight ball. Who wants to read a story from Bangkok? All the action was to the east, in Cambodia and Vietnam. He tossed the wad into a corner and watched it settle on the floor, then watched it some more, anything to postpone the agony of starting the article.

Turning back to the typewriter, he inserted a fresh sheet of paper.

Dateline: Phnom Penh. What the hell, he'd lie a little. Chuck Fox, his editor, didn't know where he was, and most of what he was about to write came from Phnom Penh. Some of it may have been thirdhand before he picked it up in Bangkok, but it was good stuff nevertheless.

Dateline: Phnom Penh, Cambodia
Jan. 12, 1970

The war in neighboring Vietnam is slowly and inexorably spilling over into Cambodia. The sporadic bombings and occasional firefights near the border are less noticeable than the pervasive influence of American goods pirated from supplies intended for the GIs in Vietnam. Many Cambodians routinely smoke American cigarettes, wear American fatigues, and fry their rice in American soybean oil. They treat themselves to Schlitz beer and their children to Tootsie Rolls. There is no disguising the fact that great quantities of American supplies intended for American soldiers in Vietnam are smuggled into Cambodia and sold on the black market.

He was pleased with the opening, his little part in supporting the war protests at home. Americans had become immune to the daily reports of young soldiers dying in Vietnam. Maybe he could help re-ignite their outrage with news of misspent tax dollars. Although the war protests ebbed and flowed, they mostly ebbed in the last year. They needed new fuel to keep the heat on the administration.

The Cambodians also sell locally sourced rice, meat, and poultry to North Vietnamese soldiers along the Ho Chi Minh Trail in exchange for Cambodian riels. The Cambodian government is attempting to stem the flow of Cambodian currency into the country in anticipation of issuing new bank notes, but business remains brisk.

Cambodia was suffering from horrific inflation. North Vietnam was spending huge amounts of riels it had stockpiled abroad to buy food on the local economy for its troops sheltered in sanctuaries on the Cambodian side of the border with Vietnam. The Cambodian government hoped to solve the problem by swapping old currency for new, which would make riels held outside the country worthless.

> There are also reports of a steady flow of military supplies to North Vietnamese troops—arms and equipment that arrive surreptitiously through the Cambodian port of Sihanoukville. Knowledgeable sources report that General Lon Nol, a rival of Prince Norodom Sihanouk, Cambodia's chief of state, is also receiving military equipment and supplies through Sihanoukville and that he is preparing an army to challenge Sihanouk. His only other possible source of supplies is over the border from Thailand; however, Thai military hardware is supplied by the United States, and the Americans keep a watchful eye on its use. The U.S. military has a series of installations along the highway that connects Bangkok to Cambodia that are well-positioned to seal off any significant flow of arms into Cambodia.

MacNamara didn't know much about Lon Nol, but he thought it a long shot that Sihanouk could be deposed. He was royalty in Cambodia—his mother had been queen—and the people revered him. Whether they revered him enough to let him drag the country into the Communist camp was yet to be seen.

MacNamara straightened his back and looked at the pitcher of water resting on the nightstand beside the bed. He never drank the water because there was no telling what might be in it. He jiggled the table and watched the water slosh weakly back and forth, then glanced at the wad of paper in the corner. But with the article finished, he didn't need any more distractions. What he needed was to find Mike Reidy and have a drink.

Reidy had become a welcome distraction in the few months since they met at the Bangkok officers' club. They shared a disdain for all things military and a love of Irish history and the rebel songs that came with it. And they shared an appetite for a drink or two after work—enough to relieve the boredom of the day and warm up for the evening's activities.

Still, Reidy was an enigma to MacNamara. They were both graduates of liberal California universities, both opposed to the war. But Reidy volunteered for Army ROTC even though, as an Irish citizen, he was immune from the draft, while MacNamara was determined to avoid the draft any way he could. When he failed his draft physical because of bone spurs his family doctor had conveniently discovered, he was elated. Now Reidy was in the army that was fighting the war, and MacNamara was doing his part to undermine it—harping in his articles about the expense of the war, the rising death toll, the endemic corruption, anything his editor would let him get away with.

MacNamara wondered why Reidy hadn't just gone home to County Clare. Was American citizenship so important he would support a war he didn't believe in? A war in which he could be killed if he was sent to Vietnam? The war, the draft—they unsettled an entire generation. Maybe Mike was just another casualty.

He folded the pages of the article and stuffed them into an envelope. He would walk them to the post office and cable the story to San Francisco. Tonight one of the rewrite people—probably that Eileen McClellan—would take a whack at it. Tomorrow afternoon subscribers to the *Herald* would read it, and while they were reading it, he would be trying to think up something new to write. The cycle never ended—and he wouldn't give it up for anything.

MACNAMARA SAT WITH REIDY OVER DRINKS ON the patio of the Mandarin Oriental Hotel, overlooking the Chao Phraya River. Both would have preferred a pint of Guinness, but Guinness didn't travel well and never tasted as good as it tasted in Ireland. They settled for dry martinis; each had quaffed a quick one and was now leisurely sipping a second. Before long they would switch to Tullamore Irish whiskey, and it would go downhill from there.

"I finished that article I told you about," Bob said.

"Which one was that?" Mike was only half listening, concentrating on the olive he was swishing through his cocktail. A waiter placed a lobster tail in front of him.

"The one about American stuff ending up in Cambodia. You know, PX goods and stuff like that."

"Well, it doesn't surprise me." Mike picked up the lobster and began to crack off pieces of the shell. "A lot of our stuff goes where it's not supposed to."

Bob looked at Mike thoughtfully, wondering if he might have some idea where Lon Nol was getting his arms. "Mike, you ever hear about any weapons going to Cambodia?"

"No, but I know there's a lot of stuff missing from the depot, stolen by the locals. But how would it get to Cambodia? There's only one road, and there's roadblocks all over the place."

"Look, Mike, I don't want you to tell me anything you feel you shouldn't, but there's an army general over there, a rabid anti-Communist. General Lon Nol. He's getting military hardware from somewhere. You don't think the Americans could be supplying him, do you?"

Mike looked up from his plate and shook his head. "No way, man. If it's coming from Thailand, I'd know about it."

MacNamara knew Reidy was right. Everything the Americans brought into Thailand came through Reidy's warehouses. He ran the Bangkok port operations of the 501st Field Depot, which supplied the American forces in Thailand, mostly the Air Force which made bombing runs from Thailand over Vietnam. If Reidy said Lon Nol wasn't getting anything from the Americans out of Thailand, then he wasn't. MacNamara would have to look elsewhere for the answer.

CHAPTER 5
Bangkok
FEBRUARY 1, 1970

FRANK SURVEYED THE ROOM REFLECTED IN THE mirror behind the bar, the cocktail lounge of the Chao Phraya Hotel, a way station run by the U.S. government for military officers passing through Bangkok. Dark, cool, and comfortable. No windows to let in the afternoon glare or the cacophonous noise of the bustling street. Soldiers on leave from Vietnam sprawled in soft leather chairs, drinking rum cocktails from crystal glasses served by thin Thai waiters wearing tuxedos and pasted-on smiles.

Frank swirled a swizzle stick through a rum and Coke and silently toasted his good fortune. He missed Joanna, more than he thought he would. And he missed Eileen McClellan, not that he'd been able to spend more time with her. He missed it all—San Francisco, his friends, the carefree college life—but it could have been worse, a lot worse. It could have been Vietnam.

Two obviously hung-over Americans played tired rock tunes from a small stage in the corner. *The In Case Brothers*. Probably schoolteachers from the States, earning extra bucks entertaining the troops. He grimaced at their half-hearted attempts to mimic songs broadcast on Armed Forces Radio. They butchered "We've Gotta Get Out of This Place," the anthem of the American soldiers fighting in Vietnam, and their rendition of "If You're Going to San Francisco" was barely recognizable.

They should get Mike Reidy to back them up on piano, he mused. *The In Case Trio*. Even without the use of one thumb Reidy would be an improvement. His mother Margaret taught him to play, but young Michael couldn't get his right thumb to cooperate; it would hang by itself off the keyboard, refusing to participate.

Maybe *he* should join them. *The In Case Quartet*. His voice wasn't any worse than Bob Dylan's, and he'd sung enough of those Irish songs with Reidy, having learned them at his mother's knee.

And even if he *couldn't* sing, he would be a better fit with The In Case Brothers than with the army. Why the army had ever taken him was still a mystery. He'd never been an athlete, never made much of an effort to get into shape, never seriously tried to lose the extra twenty pounds he carried. He drank too much. He smoked too much. He was nearsighted and mildly color blind and had back problems from stocking shelves.

He had none of the skills one would think the army would be looking for. He wasn't an outdoorsman. He'd never been hunting, never even fired a rifle before the army. The only camping he'd done was a few weekend trips with the Boy Scouts. He didn't know how to read a map or talk on the radio beyond "over and out," and he'd picked that up from watching television.

In normal times, the army wouldn't have given him a second look. But these weren't normal times. The army was fighting an unpopular war and relied on the draft to fill its ranks. If the draft hadn't been breathing down his neck, he never would have stayed in ROTC beyond the two years the university mandated. He'd counted on the war being over by the time he graduated, and if it wasn't, he figured he'd be better off going in as an officer than being drafted as a private.

The army recognized the reality of the situation and tried to find something suitable for officers like him to do. They assigned him to the Adjutant General Corps, the administrative branch of the army, to make use of his limited talents: drafting orders, writing daily bulletins, making sure the mail got delivered. Personnel, duty rosters, awards and decorations. It was desultory office work, and if he made mistakes, at least they wouldn't have life-and-death consequences.

Frank studied his reflection in the mirror. His face was puffy from the five pounds he'd put on since graduation, and the horn-rimmed glasses made him look too much like a librarian to be taken seriously as a soldier. No matter. He would manage. Once the clerk-typists working for him at the headquarters of the 501st Field Depot understood he wouldn't push them any harder than he pushed himself—which wasn't very hard—they wouldn't give him any trouble. And no need to worry about female companionship. He'd done okay with Joanna—though he still wondered why she bothered with him—and any guy could buy a girlfriend in Thailand.

Frank caught sight of Mike Reidy walking toward him across the lounge. He was dressed in olive-drab jungle fatigues and wore his hair the same as he did in college—short on the sides with a tangle of prematurely white curls on top. At the university Frank would sometimes accompany Mike to the barber—Blue Fogg, the Fogg Cutter of San Francisco—and Blue would invariably get into an argument with Mike over how he should wear his hair. But no matter how hard Blue argued, Mike would leave the shop with an unruly white mop on the top of his head.

A wide grin split Reidy's face when their eyes met, and he raised his arms above his head like a prizefighter who had just won a bout. You made it, pal, his expression said, and boy, are we gonna have some fun!

MIKE SWUNG THE JEEP ONTO CHAO PHRAYA Boulevard, dodging pedestrians and swerving around clattering pedicabs and sputtering Toyotas. He drove like a local, with little regard for other vehicles on the road. Frank used both hands to brace against the dashboard and still jerked with each twist of the wheel. They drove by gold-encrusted pagodas guarded by stern-faced lions and chipped unicorns, broken-down shacks squeezed between modern concrete-and-glass office buildings, and shops and restaurants climbing on top of one another, some hanging precariously over the street. An occasional park relieved the tedious press of the buildings, gray trees struggling to shade small boys kicking soccer balls across sparse patches of brown grass.

"Well, this is it, man," Mike said proudly. "Bangkok, the jewel of the Orient. It's got everything a man could want." He looked over at Frank with a devilish grin. "Even a man of your exotic tastes."

"Where are we going?" Frank asked above the din, ignoring the intended insult. "I'm hungry."

"Not to worry. I have an errand to run, then we'll get some chow."

Mike merged the jeep into the endless flood of vehicles on King Rama Road. A huge statue of Rama himself overlooked the busy roundabout, staring down at the passing traffic with a disapproving frown, an aging father glaring at the frenetic pace of his children.

"This is the main intersection of Bangkok," Mike said. "The main intersection of the whole country, really. That way," he said, pointing west, "you go to Kanchana-buri on the River Kwai and into Burma. About a hundred miles up the road we're on, you'd get to Korat—that's where you'll be stationed. To the east, the road goes past Sattahip and Utapao and eventually crosses southern Cambodia into 'Nam, not that you'd get that far with-out getting killed first. Distances are deceptive—Saigon is only three hundred miles from here."

They drove past the central market, a huge square covered with hundreds of multicolored tents braced hap-hazardly against one another. Dried squid and other delicacies hung from the rafters, and fruits and vegetables lined the packed-dirt floors. Afternoon shoppers with bas-kets dangling from their arms crowded into the stalls and elbowed each other to get a better look at the selection.

Mike left the crowded boulevard and drove through thinning traffic into an industrial area beside a broad expanse of water dotted with river taxis and flat-bottomed canal boats.

"The Chao Phraya River," Mike explained, "from which everything gets its name. My warehouses are on the river, next to the docks where the military ships from the U.S. unload."

THE TWO LIEUTENANTS CROUCHED BEHIND A crate of machinery on a wharf beside the river, watch-ing a group of men gathered by a column of six-wheeled, five-ton military trucks parked outside the gate of the warehouse complex. Afternoon had turned into evening, and the men were obscured by darkness and a light drizzle.

Mike wanted to check on the security of his warehouses, he told Frank, but he wanted to do it without anyone knowing. Frank shifted his position uncomfortably. He'd been looking forward to an early dinner and a visit to a local brothel, not an evening in the rain beside a smelly river. He was an administrative officer, not a detective. He wasn't cut out for this sort of thing.

"Take it easy," Mike whispered. "We'll be out of here in a flash. Anyway, your sense of duty to the 501st Field Depot demands that you be here."

"Good try, Mike, but it won't work." Frank winced as he straightened a cramped leg.

"And," Mike continued, "because I promise to take you to Niddrie's, the best restaurant in Bangkok. Kobe steak smothered in mushrooms, and fresh, broiled pineapple, and lots of steamed rice."

"That's better," Frank said, somewhat mollified. Still, he wished Mike would conclude his business so he could get out of the dampness which was beginning to penetrate his light summer clothing.

"Look, Mike, we came here to catch people stealing from your warehouses, or so you said, and there's a whole passel of people out there either stealing or discouraging other potential stealers. So why don't you just go out there and apprehend them or something, and I'll go back to the jeep and keep dry?"

"Well, that's the problem," Mike replied, rubbing his chin fretfully. "They look like Americans, and those are American vehicles, although they could belong to the Thai army now." He peered uncertainly at the men through the mist. "But I didn't expect to find any Americans here. And I can't just go out there and ask them who they are and what they're up to because if Colonel Neil finds out I was spying on my own warehouses after he told me to stick to business . . ." His voice trailed off.

"Well, maybe you can't, but I can." Frank got to his feet and, ignoring Mike's protests, strode purposely toward the men waiting by the gate. When he was close enough to make out their uniforms, he was relieved to confirm they were American soldiers.

"Uh, Captain," Frank called out, addressing a pint-sized officer with close-cropped hair and matching mustache who appeared to be in charge. He was wearing the insignia of the Quartermaster Corps on the collar of his fatigues.

"Yeah?" The officer was startled by Frank's sudden appearance.

"You mind telling me what you're doing here?" Frank asked politely.

The captain's eyes narrowed, and he stuck out his chin pugnaciously. "As a matter of fact, mister, I *do* fucking mind. What's it to you?"

Frank sensed the captain suffered from a short-man complex, a bantamweight trying to play above his class. Another marginal officer struggling to meet the army's expectations.

"Uh, nothing," Frank replied diffidently, ignoring the captain's hostility. He noted the insignia of the 558th Supply and Service Company on his shoulder patch and the corresponding emblem on the bumper of the nearest truck.

"Nothing at all," Frank continued, shifting his focus

to three soldiers who had detached themselves from the group and were edging behind him. "I'm the new depot adjutant. I'm on my way to dinner—thought I'd stop by and check on a few things." He was stretching the truth a bit since he hadn't yet reported for duty at the depot headquarters in Korat.

"Well, why didn't you say so?" The captain's demeanor instantly improved. He smiled ingratiatingly and extended his hand. "I'm Captain Broderick, Laurence G. With a U. The boys and I are down from Kanchanaburi for supplies. We're bivouacking here 'til the warehouse opens in the morning. Thought we'd come down a bit early to enjoy the night life." The captain winked. "Won't turn us in, will ya?"

"Of course not," Frank replied, shaking the man's hand, relieved to be included in the conspiracy. "No sweat off my back. But, with a U what?"

"That's how you spell it. Laurence, with a U."

"Oh, I get it," Frank said, playing along—he sensed it wouldn't help the situation to ridicule the man's eccentricities. "Like Laurence Olivier, the actor."

"More like Saint Laurence, killed by the Romans for doing his duty."

"Okay, if you say so," Frank said. He excused himself and walked back to where Reidy was waiting, still concealed behind the crates.

"Well, friend, it looks innocent enough to me," Frank said. "Just some supply guys from Kanchanaburi waiting for your warehouse to open in the morning. Their Captain Broderick is a weirdo, by the way, a typical career guy. Let's go find that Kobe steak you were talking about. I'm starved."

CHAPTER 6

Bangkok

FEBRUARY 1, 1970

FRANK SHOVELED A FORKFUL OF STEAK AND mushrooms into his mouth, then looked up at Mike. "What's this between you and Colonel Neil?" he asked between bites, noting Mike's untouched plate. They were sitting in the crowded restaurant beneath bright fluorescent lights, surrounded by Thais eating with one hand and holding a lit cigarette in the other. Niddrie's was inexplicably named after a village in Scotland. A coat of arms hung behind the hostess stand, and the waitresses wore short plaid kilts that barely covered their bottoms.

"You'll understand when you meet him. He's an asshole. First in his class at San Diego State. A Rhodes Scholar, which is hard to do from a state college. Law degree from UC Berkeley, first in his class again. He's already a legend in his own mind. He routinely flips the bird at the West Pointers."

"Why's a man like that assigned to a supply depot?"

"Makes you wonder, doesn't it? Maybe he got in trouble somewhere along the line. Maybe the higher-ups realize he's an asshole too. Maybe he's here to give guys like you and me a hard time. He's very good at that."

Frank was mildly alarmed at Mike's description of

Colonel Neil. He would be working for the colonel as his adjutant, his desk just outside the colonel's office. But Mike was probably exaggerating—a personality quirk Frank was familiar with—and even if he wasn't, Frank knew how to kiss butt enough to get on anyone's good side. That was one thing he learned in college.

"Still, why does he care if you check on the warehouses? He's the commanding officer of the 501st, isn't he? And they're 501st warehouses, aren't they?"

"He says I'm not using my time effectively. Whenever I complain about stuff being stolen—and we've been losing a lot—he says we have too much stuff to begin with, and that I should worry more about getting my requisitions straight than about a few missing crates."

"What's wrong with the requisitions?"

Mike winced. "Well, we did screw up—once. One of my NCOs ordered M16 ammo by the crate when he meant to order individual cartridge boxes. We ended up with a shipload of bullets—a bit more than the depot needed, considering there's no war going on here."

"What'd you do with it?"

"We gave it to the Thai Black Panther Division. They're getting ready to go to Vietnam, part of the president's effort to get more allies involved in the war. The extra bullets turned out not to be a problem, although to hear Neil talk, you'd think it was worse than Pearl Harbor."

Frank scraped the last of the dinner from his plate and started picking at Mike's. "I wouldn't worry about it. Neil will get over it."

Mike pushed his plate over to Frank. "Don't count on it. And even if he does, that doesn't solve the real problem—the Thais are robbing us blind. Judging from the latest inventories, they're taking it out by the truckload, everything from canteens to rifles."

"You explained that to Neil?"

"Sure I did. That's what started it all. He said I was exaggerating, and even if I wasn't, he didn't think it was worth pissing the Thais off by making a big deal over a few missing supplies." Mike looked at Frank in embarrassment. "And I can't really prove the stuff is gone. That's the worst part. The warehouse records are all screwed up—my predecessor's fault, not mine—and I can't tell exactly what's missing. It's a lot of something, though. I'm sure of that."

When Frank finished the last of Mike's meal, the waiter replaced the dinner plates with fresh strawberries and snifters of brandy. Frank looked out the window as he sipped his drink. The passing traffic was rushed and chaotic, the din audible through the thick glass. Neon lights flickered on a movie marquee across the street advertising *The Good, the Bad and the Ugly*, a Clint Eastwood film that opened in the States four years earlier.

He wondered what he was getting into in Korat, working for Neil. It didn't sound like the easy assignment he'd been expecting—more like Neil was the Bad and he might soon become the Ugly.

"What say we hit the road, Mike? If I have to report to Colonel Neil tomorrow, from what you're telling me, I'd better get my fun in tonight."

MIKE TOOK FRANK TO THE ROSE HOUSE CAFÉ, one of the hundreds of massage parlors for which Bangkok was famous. They entered through ornate wooden doors, leaving the jarring noise of the city and the humid stench of the drainage canals behind. When Frank's eyes adjusted to the gloom, he found himself standing in the middle of a small, dimly lit room surrounded by scantily clad women sitting demurely on wooden benches along the walls. Following Mike's instructions, he pointed to an especially attractive girl sitting by herself in a corner, who, with feigned shyness, took his hand and led him to a cubicle in the back.

"I'm Frank," he started uncertainly, unsure of the protocol. "What's your name?"

"Laurel my name," she replied with a practiced smile, efficiently laying out towels on a narrow, cushioned table, which, together with a bathtub, all but filled the small room. She turned on the spigots to fill the tub with hot water.

"Laurel? They have laurel bushes in Thailand?"

"Laurel a summer flower."

"That's a nice name. Laurel. I like that name. Laurel, how long have you—"

She silenced him with a finger to his lips, studying his face with expressionless, almond-shaped eyes. She unbuttoned his shirt and pulled it from his pants, giggling softly at the thick hair on his chest. She ran her fingers through the tangle, lightly pinching his surprisingly sensitive nipples.

"Hairy," she observed.

Frank's body tingled in response to her soft touches. He kicked off his shoes and pulled off his socks and trousers, then straightened self-consciously. Laurel smiled at his discomfort and indicated that he should remove his shorts as well. He obediently slipped them off and stepped naked into the bath, settling back against the cold porcelain.

Laurel knelt beside the tub and bathed him with a soapy sponge, maintaining an aura of detached dignity. When his stiffening penis peeked out of the water he wondered again if that was what attracted Joanna. Wishful thinking, he decided.

After the bath, as Laurel dried him with a threadbare towel, Frank gamely attempted to slip a hand down the front of her tight bodice, but she firmly removed it and gently pushed him onto the massage table. She poured lotion onto his chest and rubbed it through the matted hair, spreading it down over his abdomen, slowly working her hand back and forth. She added more lotion and quickened the pace, stroking him until he experienced the happy ending he had heard so much about.

Frank lay still for a moment, breathing heavily, then pushed himself to his feet and began to dress. "May I see you again?" he asked hoarsely, buttoning his shirt. "You here all the time?"

"You have five dollar?" she asked, ignoring the question. "Five dollar for me?"

Frank reached into his pocket and took out a wad of baht. "Here, take this," he said, thrusting two hundred-baht bills into her outstretched hand, the equivalent of five dollars plus a generous tip. "I'll see you again. I promise."

CHAPTER 7
Korat
FEBRUARY 2, 1970

FRANK WAITED PATIENTLY FOR COLONEL NEIL to look up from the papers on his desk. Recalling Reidy's critical description of the colonel, he fidgeted nervously, perspiration staining his new, ill-fitting jungle fatigues.

"Goddammit, Lieutenant," the colonel growled, raising his head and fixing Frank with a steely gaze. "I told Reidy to stick to business, to stop acting like a policeman."

Neil slammed his fist down on the desk, jerking Frank to a semblance of attention.

"And now I find out that a goddamn wet-behind-the-ears green second lieutenant conspires with that incompetent Reidy to subvert my orders the first goddamn day he's in the fucking country. Now what the hell was Reidy doing sneaking around that warehouse last night when he can't even do what he's supposed to be doing during the day? And you—you're supposed to be here in Korat, doing whatever you administrative assholes are supposed to do, not in Bangkok playing footsie with your lieutenant pal."

"Yes, sir," Frank replied. His first meeting with the colonel wasn't going well, and he didn't see any benefit in prolonging it with an explanation of their activities the night before.

Colonel Neil glared at him through cold blue eyes, then his lips curled into a thin smile. "What I want from you, Lieutenant," he continued in a friendlier tone, "is a first-class job in the admin department. Personnel, daily bulletins, cutting orders, duty rosters, that bullshit stuff you admin people take care of. I don't want any screw-ups with the paperwork. You run the office and I'll run the depot."

He rose from behind the desk and took Frank by the arm, steering him toward the door. "Forget about Lieutenant Reidy and his imaginary concerns. Take care of your job here, and you'll leave with a record you can be proud of."

Frank sighed with relief when the door closed behind him. How did Neil learn of their visit to the warehouse? From Captain Broderick, most likely. The colonel probably had a network of people who kept him informed. Still, it seemed odd that such a trivial incident would merit his attention. Well, no matter. He wouldn't cross the colonel again. He would be the obedient officer the colonel wanted, and he would stay away from Mike Reidy, who once again was the cause of his grief.

THE COLONEL SUMMONED FRANK BACK TO HIS office the following morning. Frank braced for another chewing out, but Neil was in a conciliatory mood.

"Lieutenant, I have a job for you," he said with a forced smile. "I want you to know I don't hold grudges, that I let bygones be bygones. And to prove my trust in you, I've decided to give you a little responsibility right off the bat. I want you to go down to Utapao and check on the laundry."

"Laundry?" Frank asked in surprise. "What laundry?"

"Well, our laundry, of course." The colonel strained to keep the smile on his face. "The depot's got a number of laundries around the country. Somebody's got to wash the sheets. Who do you think does it, the Special Forces?"

Frank laughed involuntarily. "No, sir. I just never thought about it."

"Well, I wish more people would think about it. The 501st does an important job here in Thailand, providing food and supplies to the troops and everything else they need. It's all without glory, that's for sure. But I wish we'd at least get a little credit."

"Yes, sir," Frank agreed dutifully. "Where's Utapao?"

"It's an Air Force base, not far from the Cambodian border. They run bombing missions from Utapao over Vietnam. It's pretty quiet. You won't have any trouble getting there."

"And once I'm there?"

"Check on the laundry. See how the men are doing. There's a young buck sergeant in charge. He's Mexican, does a good job with the wash. Let him know that we consider his operation an integral part of the 501st."

"That's all?"

"Find out if he needs anything." The colonel held a hand up in warning. "But don't make any promises. He'd ask for the kitchen sink if he thought he could get it."

The colonel lifted a bulky canvas bag from the desk. "As long as you're there, I want you to deliver this pouch to our embassy in Phnom Penh. It's not far from Utapao. The Air Force will fly you in."

The pouch was made of heavy gray canvas trimmed in brown leather. A thin chain with a handcuff affixed to one end dangled from a padlock that sealed the opening. A white eagle and the words *United States of America* were emblazoned on the side.

"What is it?"

"Oh, just diplomatic mail. We help the State Department move their stuff around this part of the world."

Frank took the pouch from the colonel. It was surprisingly heavy.

"Here's your orders," the colonel added, handing Frank a mimeographed sheet of paper. "They'll get you over the border. And don't forget your official passport."

The mention of a passport set off an alarm. "Phnom Penh, sir? In Cambodia?"

"Where did you think it was, California?" The colonel's meager patience evaporated. "We don't have any troops stationed there, but they're used to seeing these pouches come through. You won't have any trouble."

The colonel reached across the desk and fastened the handcuff to Frank's wrist. "Now don't screw this up, Lieutenant," he warned, "or I'll string your ass up alongside Reidy's."

Frank looked at the pouch accusingly, as if it was the pouch's fault that he had to go to Cambodia. Then he remembered the promise he made the day before. "Okay, Colonel, whatever you say. If you want me to go to Cambodia, I'm happy to go to Cambodia."

"Now that's the attitude," Neil said, escorting Frank to the door. "We all have to pitch in around here to get the job done. I'm glad to see you're part of the team."

WITHIN AN HOUR, FRANK WAS STRAPPED INTO A seat on an Air Force C-130 on the daily milk run to

Utapao. Neil had greased the skids, and he had no trouble getting a seat, even though a group of Air Force technicians with a pile of electronic gear had been waiting two days to catch a hop. The plane bounced down the runway and flopped into the air like a pregnant cow, but he wasn't worried—he knew the C-130 to be one of the most reliable planes in the Air Force inventory.

He relaxed to enjoy the ride. The terrain below was an endless expanse of rice paddies carved into irregular rectangles by earthen dikes topped with footpaths and occasional clumps of trees. Eventually, the paddies gave way to thick, green jungle, broken now and then by scattered clearings and small villages.

Utapao appeared on the horizon, a huge scar on the verdant carpet, a few miles from the seaside resort of Sattahip visible in the distance. The Utapao runway cut a wide asphalt swath between a narrow river and clusters of wooden buildings lining a series of intersecting streets. A half-dozen B-52s sat on the apron, wings drooping to the ground. The C-130 landed on the tarmac and lowered the ramp to let off the passengers.

Frank had difficulty locating the laundry. He crisscrossed the base, hitching rides from airmen who tried to be helpful but had no clue where the laundry was. Their fatigues, it seemed, were washed by their mamasans, local women who came onto the base each morning to attend to their personal needs.

He eventually stumbled onto a dilapidated slat-and-chicken-wire hooch in a remote corner of the base, a faded sign bearing the insignia of the 501st Field Depot tacked over the door. The building housed three huge washing machines hooked by a tangle of pipes and valves to a fifty-gallon drum that served as a hot water heater. In one corner stood a gas-fed dryer attached to a propane tank, a mass of wet but apparently clean sheets and towels piled nearby. Beside it stood the shell of a disassembled dryer, its parts strewn about the floor. Two shirtless GIs sat on the floor sorting through the mess.

"Sergeant Canedo here?"

"He's out back," replied one of the soldiers. Neither looked up.

What happened to the practice of calling a room to attention when an officer entered? he wondered. Another sign that military discipline was going to hell, that the draft was taking its toll. No matter—they were just putting in their time, the same as he was.

Frank gingerly picked his way across the room, pushed open a screen door hanging from one hinge, and stepped into a fenced yard. An elderly mamasan, squatting next to a cooking fire, looked up at him with a toothless grin. A soldier smoking a marijuana cigarette reclined languidly in a hammock slung between the hooch and a lone rubber tree.

"You Sergeant Canedo?" Frank asked.

"Yeah, that's me."

"I'm Lieutenant—"

"I know who you are," interrupted Canedo, propping himself up on one elbow to get a better look at the visitor, pinching the joint between two fingers. "You're lieutenant somebody or other and the colonel sent you here to see how we're all getting along."

"Yeah, were you expecting me?"

"No, but you're the third one in as many weeks. The

other two never came through with the stuff we need, so I figure they're full of shit and so are you."

Frank was curious about the previous visitors. "Were the other two carrying pouches?"

"Yeah, just like you."

"What'd you tell them you wanted?"

"A new dryer is all. Or parts to fix the one that's broken. There's three of us here, and we can get the laundry done, no sweat. But we're not goddamn engineers, and that dryer needs a lot of work."

"Okay, I'll see what I can do."

"Yeah, you do that, Lieutenant." Canedo slumped back on the hammock, taking a long drag on the joint. Frank briefly considered upbraiding him for his insolence but decided to let it pass. He was new to the country—what did he know? Maybe that was the norm in the boondocks, less formality away from the larger installations where the senior officers hung out.

Frank crossed the yard and circled the building to the street, then caught a lift back to the airstrip. Hassled by Colonel Neil in Korat and now by a punk three-striper in Utapao, he'd be almost relieved to get to Cambodia in the morning.

CHAPTER 8

Phnom Penh

FEBRUARY 4, 1970

FRENCH COLONIAL MANSIONS IN VARIOUS STATES
of disrepair, with ornate balconies overlooking manicured
lawns, lined the broad boulevard on which Frank rode
to the American Embassy in the back seat of a gleaming
black limousine. Next to him sat Charge d'Affaires David
E. Monahan, the senior American diplomat in Cambodia,
who had secured his release at the airport.

Frank's reception at the airport had been less than
cordial. He wasn't waved through customs with a cursory inspection, as Neil had assured him would be the
case. Rather, he was unceremoniously ushered into a
dimly lit, windowless room by two rough-looking Cambodian soldiers who proceeded to poke at the pouch
chained to his wrist. Frank refused to release the pouch
for what he hoped was a credible reason—he didn't have
the key. He explained that the key was at the embassy,
although Neil hadn't covered that point. The thought
of a bow-tied, pinstriped foreign service officer sever-
ing his hand to liberate the pouch flashed through his
mind.

Frank was equally confident in deflecting questions
hurled by the Cambodians about the contents of the
pouch. He didn't have the slightest idea, he explained.

Nobody had told him what was in it, and he hadn't asked. It was none of his business. He was just the courier.

After twenty minutes of awkward jousting, the disposition of his inquisitors visibly deteriorated, and Frank grew concerned that things might take a turn for the worse. He assumed brief detainments at the Phnom Penh airport were nothing unusual, that interrogation of a foreign military officer in jungle fatigues dropping in on an unscheduled flight could be expected. But they'd had plenty of time to check his passport and confirm his identity with the embassy. Assuming, of course, that Neil had bothered to tell the embassy he was coming.

He also assumed a code of conduct governed diplomatic couriers, but Neil hadn't filled him in on that either. To what lengths was he expected to go to protect the pouch? Was there anything important in it anyway? Or was it a matter of principle that he not give it up regardless of the contents?

The soldiers had not yet attempted to remove the pouch from his wrist. If they were serious, he told himself, they would dispense with the preliminaries and simply cut it off. The thought was interrupted by the entrance of a third soldier with a rusted but serviceable pair of bolt cutters. Frank's initial alarm turned to relief—no one could fault him for failing to resist three burly soldiers possessing the equipment to get the job done.

A ruckus ensued in the hallway outside the room, momentarily distracting the soldiers. The door banged open and in strutted a very diplomatic-looking American of medium height impeccably dressed in a gray, vested suit. A gaggle of worried-looking customs officials tumbled in behind him.

"What is the meaning of this?" demanded the American in a haughty New England accent. "You are interfering with a diplomatic courier, protected from this sort of harassment by international law. And if you intend to use those large scissors to breach the integrity of this gentleman's pouch, I should advise you that such intent alone is sufficient to bring upon you the full wrath of the United States government. Now release this man so that we may be on our way."

The three soldiers looked from the intruder to one another and commenced arguing among themselves in Khmer, gesturing from Frank to the diplomat. The customs officials joined in the heated discussion.

"Enough of this, I say," interrupted the diplomat, his voice rising to a dignified shout. "In the name of the United States of America, I demand that you release this man without further delay."

The soldier with the bolt cutters looked at the diplomat with open hostility, then shrugged as if to say the pouch was no longer of concern. The diplomat didn't hesitate— he took Frank by the arm and ushered him quickly from the room and through the terminal to the limousine waiting at the curb. He didn't speak again until they passed through the embassy gates, then turned to Frank with a small brass key pinched firmly between his fingers.

"Young man," he said, "if you will be good enough to extend your wrist, I shall relieve you of this burden. Your transport home awaits you at the airport."

MONAHAN SAT AT HIS DESK, HIS HEAD RESTING in his hands, a glum expression on his face. He'd barely been able to maintain his composure at the airport. The burden of managing an understaffed mission in a strife-torn country was taking its toll. Washington didn't understand the responsibility he had, the pressure he was under. And now this, dealing with some off-the-wall army colonel and a hairbrained CIA scheme to make an ally out of Lon Nol. Of all the stupid ideas, that had to take the cake. He reached for a bottle of Scotch in a lower desk drawer and slopped another half inch into his glass, draining it in one gulp.

Christ, even the booze doesn't help anymore.

He was unsettled by the confrontation at the airport. He hadn't been confident he could get the pouch through. If those soldiers had opened the pouch and found all those riels, he and that lieutenant would have been in deep shit. How stupid was that, sending Cambodian currency into the country in the face of a crackdown on just that sort of thing? But those CIA boys didn't care. It wouldn't have been their necks in a sling. No, it would have been his neck—the neck of Charge d'Affaires David Emory Monahan, twenty years in the State Department and hoping to be reassigned any day now to a cushy desk job in Washington.

He walked to the window and stared, unseeing, at the garden. If he could just hold on. If he could just keep the CIA from bollixing things up a bit longer, maybe he'd make it back to Washington with his reputation—and his neck—intact.

He sat back at the desk and encoded a cable to Colonel Neil. "Pouch received with difficulty. Dispatch no more pouches. Too dangerous. Suggest cease intervention in Cambodia. Little chance of success. Risk too great."

He folded and sealed the cable. He wished he could

simply order the CIA to keep its hands off Cambodia, but it was no secret he didn't control his own mission. He had to do whatever Colonel Neil and the CIA wanted him to do—the president himself had given him that directive.

He looked pensively at the portrait of the president hanging on the wall. At least he assumed the directive had come from the president. The message instructing him to cooperate with the CIA was signed by John Lynch, the president's national security advisor. If he didn't speak for the president, who did?

Maybe he would have a chance to clear the air if Lynch ever made his promised visit to Bangkok. If he could get Lynch and Neil in the same room, he was certain he could convince them of their folly. The political situation in Cambodia was volatile. Their little conspiracy could blow sky high, and they could all get badly burned.

CHAPTER 9
Bangkok
FEBRUARY 23, 1970

THE PAN AMERICAN CLIPPER CARRYING JOHN Lynch back to Washington took off from Bangkok's Don Muang airport and leveled off over the Gulf of Siam. Lynch settled wearily into his seat, his rumpled suit and unshaven face reflecting his exhaustion.

He smiled. He'd pulled another one over the president, modest payback for giving him the thankless task of managing the fucked-up Cambodia situation. Well, he'd turned the tables, prolonging a two-hour meeting with the CIA director's man and the Cambodian charge d'affaires into a weekend holiday in one of the pleasure capitals of the world, a discreet dalliance with a hotel waitress highlighting the visit.

The smile faded. As happened more and more often, the perverse satisfaction he took from outfoxing the president—mostly, he reminded himself, for the president's own good—was ruined by a sense of overwhelming responsibility. He no longer served a two-bit politician. He was no longer a campaign manager trying to keep the candidate out of trouble during what everyone assumed was a doomed bid for the White House. The candidate had unexpectedly won, and now Lynch served a president—a president with whom he shared the responsibility of the office, having helped wrest it from other and perhaps better qualified men.

Lynch was good at what he did, but maybe no one was good enough to keep the president out of trouble this time. The situation in Southeast Asia was a goddamn mess, an absolute disaster. Keeping things from getting any worse until the secretary of state could negotiate a way out of the war in Vietnam seemed an impossible task. Well, thank God the CIA's man seemed to know what he was doing, even if he had miscalculated a thing or two.

A call from Secretary of State William Noel Hall on a cold, drizzly Washington morning precipitated Lynch's visit to Thailand. The secretary wanted the president to know that the Cambodians were opening diplomatic pouches—a breach of the Vienna Accords, he said, but nothing to worry about. They weren't sending anything sensitive in the pouches anyway. The American Embassy in Phnom Penh was a backwater outpost with a skeletal staff, in the eye of the hurricane, so to speak, but untouched by the storm swirling around it.

As the secretary spoke, Lynch's thoughts drifted back to the CIA director's visit in October, when he first learned of the arms shipments to Cambodia. A dim but persistent alarm flashed in the back of his mind.

"What are they looking for?" he asked.

"Currency, mostly," Secretary Hall said. "The Cambodians think one of the embassies is importing Cambodian currency stockpiled outside the country to buy supplies for North Vietnamese troops along the border. They pay three times the going rate on the Cambodian market, causing a frightening inflation problem."

"Which embassy?"

"One of the Communist ones, presumably." Hall sounded irritated, unaccustomed to being cross-examined. "Red China, I suppose. But just tell the president about the inspections, that they're a breach of the conventions but that I don't think we should make a big deal of it. We're holding our mail in Bangkok for the time being anyway, until it blows over."

Lynch called the CIA director as soon as Secretary Hall hung up.

"Well, now that you mention it," Fish said, "the pouch inspections did cause a bit of a stir over here. Seems our man has been accumulating riels at the embassy in Phnom Penh to buy on the economy what he can't get for General Lon Nol through the port in Bangkok. But the Cambodians didn't catch him—the embassy people were able to bluff the last one through."

"Jesus Christ," exploded Lynch. "Aren't weapons enough? Do we have to buy food and boots for these guys too? Can't they do anything for themselves?"

He decided to fly to Bangkok to find out.

"Good idea," agreed the president when Lynch told him about the inspections and suggested he find out first-hand what was going on. "Go over and make sure we're not caught with our pants down. Our relations with those Cambodians are shaky enough. I don't want anything this insignificant to jeopardize it."

The president sat back and looked at Lynch reflectively. "And John, as long as you're getting involved, you may as well go all in." A cynical smile spread across his face. "How about being our point man on Cambodia?

Our major domo. Our *numero uno*. Keep things on an even keel. We can't afford any trouble there. We've got our hands full with Vietnam."

Lynch knew exactly what the president meant—if anything went wrong in Cambodia, his ass would be grass. He was boxed in, first by the CIA director and now by the president.

LYNCH FLICKED OFF THE OVERHEAD LIGHT AND reclined his seat. He was impressed with the CIA's man. Colonel Neil didn't try to hide the fact that he'd made a mistake. He didn't know how the Cambodians got wind of the riels, he said. Yes, he had hoped to solve some of the logistical problems of supplying Lon Nol's small but growing army by purchasing provisions and equipment on the local economy, but now he would simply increase the deliveries from Thailand or try to find a way through the Cambodian port at Sihanoukville.

The charge d'affaires was another story. A prissy little worm. One of those Eastern schoolboy types who looked the part but lacked the backbone for the dirty work. He probably got where he was by dressing in whites and playing tennis with the right people in Virginia. At first, Monahan insisted that the CIA keep its nose out of Cambodia, but he quickly backed down when Colonel Neil agreed not to go through the embassy again. Monahan was more concerned with his own neck than America's interests in Southeast Asia.

Lynch closed his eyes for a nap. No harm done. Things were back under control. Still, he decided, it was time to tell the president what they were up to in Cambodia.

CHAPTER 10

Bangkok

MACNAMARA STARED AT THE TYPEWRITER. THE keys seemed to undulate in front of him, dipping down and rising up in a wave, the letters lifting off the keyboard, the swell dissipating among the commas and semicolons on the margin. He shifted his gaze to the window to break the tedium, but he was sick of looking at the nondescript buildings across the street.

He inserted a fresh sheet of paper. *Dateline: Bangkok.*

He was troubled by the story he was about to write. It was too much conjecture, but what else could he do? Once he got past the daily handouts of the military spokesmen, he had to resort to bribing low-level officials, taxicab drivers, massage girls, anybody who might have a snippet of information. After overcoming the language barrier and discarding the most obvious fabrications, he was left with what might or might not be a story with no way to confirm it. He sometimes ran it by Mike Reidy or another of his American friends, but they rarely knew what was going on outside their own little domains.

He had two stories, and he was reasonably sure both were accurate. The problem was he thought they might be connected, but he couldn't tie them together. He knew the Cambodians were inspecting diplomatic pouches. Reidy had tipped him off, telling him about a friend who was stopped at the Phnom Penh airport, and he confirmed it with the American Embassy in Bangkok. The embassy was reluctant to talk at first but agreed to cooperate for the sake of accuracy once he threatened to print the disjointed bits and pieces he had already accumulated.

And he knew John Lynch had visited Bangkok. A Pan Am clerk told him, a young woman he met at a reception hosted by the airline. The embassy confirmed that Lynch had been in Bangkok for a brief stopover on his way back to Washington after a visit to Vietnam, but MacNamara had already learned that Lynch had been in Bangkok a full two days, staying at the Siam Intercontinental. Two days was a significant amount of time for the national security adviser to carve out of his schedule. Something big had to be going on.

He decided to visit the Siam Intercontinental to see what else he could find out. Though he struggled to write the articles, he enjoyed ferreting out the information to put in them. For all his whining about having to bribe his sources and sort through the lies and half-truths they sold him, he wouldn't have it any other way.

What to wear to the hotel was the big decision. He was young for a foreign correspondent—only three years out of college—and he took his lead from the veteran reporters at the press club. A sand-colored safari jacket with lots of pockets was standard reporter attire, but if he wanted to be inconspicuous in the dignified atmosphere of the Intercontinental, his one pair of dress slacks and a clean, short-sleeve Filipino barong shirt would be better.

He timed the visit for midday, when most of the guests would be out and new arrivals would not yet be checking in, a slow time for the staff. He took a seat in the lobby on a settee partly obscured by a potted elephant ear tree, a suitable spot from which to observe the reception desk. He watched as one of the clerks, an especially attractive girl with long, silky black hair, picked up her purse and walked through the lobby to the garden. He stood and followed her out.

"Excuse me. Do you speak English?" He knew she spoke English—anyone who worked behind the reception desk would speak English—but he wanted to sound like a disoriented tourist.

"Yes, may I help you?"

"I'm looking for a friend of mine, John Lynch, an official from the United States."

"Oh, he left on Monday, three days ago," she said, then caught herself. "I'm not supposed to say anything about our guests."

"I just need to know what room he stayed in." He smiled disarmingly, glancing discreetly at the two-hundred-baht bill he held in his hand.

She hesitated, then took the money and slipped it into a pocket. "The big suite on the top floor."

"How long was he here?"

She looked around to make sure no one was watching. "Saturday and Sunday."

"Did he have any visitors?"

She didn't answer, but she didn't move away either, just looked at him expectantly. He got the message and peeled a couple more bills from the thin stack he pulled from his pocket.

"Two visitors," she said, and then looked down at the bills still in his hand.

The conversation was getting expensive. He decided he may as well get some fun out of it. "Look, would you like to join me for dinner tonight?"

She took in his rugged good looks, the firm set of his jaw, the brown, wavy hair. He gave her his best smile—the practiced one he used to gain the confidence of reluctant sources.

"Maybe."

She was more attractive than he first realized, with a smooth, olive complexion and a petite, curvy figure hidden beneath the conservative hotel uniform. Spending the evening with her would be a pleasure even if he didn't extract any more information.

"It would be a chance to practice your English," he suggested. "I know some great poetry." He took her hand and lifted his chin in a theatrical pose. " 'Shall I compare thee to a summer's day? Thou art more lovely and more temperate.' "

She smiled in amusement. "I would like that," she said. "Shakespeare. I know Shakespeare."

Surprised, he said, "You do?"

"I study Shakespeare at the university."

"Interesting. What's your name?"

"Ceci."

That evening he took Ceci to the Mandarin Oriental Hotel, a Bangkok landmark in the same class as the Siam Intercontinental, thinking it would be a treat for her to be served like a guest in her own hotel. He insisted she order the wagyu beef. It was the king of meat, he told her, tender, succulent, and flavorful. She smiled at his description of how the cattle were raised in a quiet, peaceful environment in Japan, fed a diet of wheat, corn, and hay, and spoiled occasionally with a pail of beer—probably Guinness, he added with a laugh.

He knew his editor wouldn't laugh when he saw the expense report—it was the most expensive beef in the world—but he convinced himself he was on the trail of a big story, big enough to justify the dinner. And he wasn't going to let worries about his expenses spoil the evening with Ceci.

They talked late into the evening. Ceci was born and raised in Bangkok, had never been out of the country. She worked at the hotel while finishing a degree at the university in English literature. Her dream was to work for an international airline, which would give her the opportunity to visit London to see the plays she studied.

After dinner he took her to his hotel room where they spent the rest of the night. He felt a twinge of guilt for taking advantage of a source, but she was a big girl, she knew what she was doing. She didn't ask to be paid for the sex, but he made sure to compensate her well for the information she shared.

She told him that Lynch had secretive meetings with two Americans. One was tall and straight-backed with short gray hair; he wore civilian clothes but exuded an unmistakable military air. The other was a bow-tied diplomat of average height with thinning brown hair. He'd shown his passport when he entered the hotel, but on instructions from Lynch's security detail, the registration desk didn't record his name.

Was there a connection between the pouch inspections and Lynch's visit? Maybe, but the inspection of diplomatic mail seemed to be aimed at the Communist embassies and certainly wasn't significant enough to warrant the interest of the White House. And he'd been able to confirm from other sources that the embassy was telling the truth—no American pouches had been opened.

THE NEXT MORNING HE TOOK A CAB TO THE airport and caught the daily flight to Phnom Penh; he had so much invested in the story he decided to go all in. Since he didn't have a visa, he counted on his press credentials to get him through, but no such luck. He was turned back by Cambodian customs officials, but not before he saw an American diplomat from the same flight pass through. Monahan, he thought his name was. The charge d'affaires. He fit Ceci's description of the diplomat who met with Lynch.

Well, he'd write about the pouch inspections and put in Lynch as a throwaway. Maybe the mention of his visit to Bangkok would flush out more sources.

Dateline: Bangkok, Thailand
Feb. 28, 1970

Cambodia has taken the unusual step of examining all incoming diplomatic pouches. The inspections are apparently to forestall a suspected attempt by Communist-controlled governments to intro- duce large quantities of illegally held Cambodian currency into the country before a long-planned currency exchange to be completed by March 7. While the action is understood to be aimed at the embassies of China, North Vietnam, and the Viet Cong, formally known as the Provisional

Revolutionary Government of South Vietnam, there is some speculation that the United States has been importing riels to support anti-Communist opponents of the Cambodian government.

The U.S. Embassy in Bangkok denied that it was sending Cambodian currency to Cambodia and that any of its pouches were opened. The embassy said the recent visit to Bangkok by National Security Advisor John Lynch was not connected to the inspections. However, one source indicated that the American charge d'affaires in Cambodia had met with Lynch while he was in Bangkok.

According to well-placed sources, the Cambodian government started inspecting diplomatic pouches after receiving reports that an unidentified embassy was expecting large shipments of 500-riel notes, presumably old ones held abroad, in a last-minute effort to exchange them for the new currency. Black-market riels can be purchased in Hong Kong and Singapore and used to finance purchases of food and other supplies for North Vietnamese soldiers. Cambodia has banned the import of riels from outside the country.

Meanwhile, Prince Norodom Sihanouk, Cambodia's chief of state, taking a rest cure on the French Riviera, said today that he plans to visit the Soviet Union and Red China—"these great, friendly countries"—on his way home. In a telegram sent to the Cambodian press agency, the prince said he was leaving a clinic in Grasse, near Nice, in excellent health.

MacNamara could not shake a nagging suspicion that the Cambodian crackdown on illegal currency was directed at the Americans as much as the Communists. There was growing evidence that the Western-leaning Lon Nol was getting aid from someone, and the Americans were the logical source. Sihanouk had to suspect the Americans; he was likely visiting Moscow and Peking to solicit help in keeping Lon Nol in check. But if the Russians and Chinese stepped up their support of Sihanouk, MacNamara knew that would lead to even more American intervention in Cambodia. The United States was facing a loss to the Communists in Vietnam and would not tolerate a Communist government in Cambodia.

Well, he alluded to the Americans as a possible source of the riels, and he mentioned Lynch's visit. That was the best he could do for the time being. He would have to fit the pieces together later. Now it was time to meet Ceci. They were going to a student production of *Macbeth*, which could have been written about modern-day Cambodia.

CHAPTER 11
Korat
MARCH 2, 1970

THE ARMY POST AT KORAT WAS AN ASSEMBLAGE of warehouses and open storage areas, with barracks and mess halls squeezed in, a square-mile supply depot surrounded by a six-foot chain link fence topped with razor wire. Three sides abutted a sparse jungle, the fourth an American air base. On the other side of the air base, a mile down a narrow asphalt road, lay Korat City, one of the larger cities in Thailand but still with dirt streets, open sewers, and intermittent electricity.

Frank quickly adapted to the routine of his new job, supervising personnel and administrative matters for the depot, relying on his small but experienced staff to keep the paperwork flowing. He devoted most afternoons to tennis and lounging around the pool, and evenings to poker amid the amiable companionship of the officers' club. Initially taken aback by the posh ambience of the club and the extravagance of the menu—steak and lobster were a weekly special—he soon acceded to the popular rationale that those who served overseas were entitled to whatever comforts they could muster.

Other than to confirm he delivered the pouch to Phnom Penh, Colonel Neil ignored Frank after he returned from Cambodia. He didn't ask about the laundry, which reinforced Frank's conviction that the visit to the laundry was a pretext, that the real purpose of the trip was to deliver the pouch. On his own initiative, he called Reidy and asked him to ship a new dryer to Utapao. Nobody had asked before, Reidy said, and he was wondering what to do with the dryer gathering dust in the corner of a warehouse.

Otherwise, Frank stuck to his resolution to keep his distance from Reidy, lest he again incur the colonel's wrath. The wisdom of that decision was confirmed one Saturday evening during a rare conversation with Neil after he chanced upon the colonel at the bar of the officers' club.

"I'm glad to see you're sticking around on weekends," Neil said, his speech slightly slurred. "Too many of you young officers head down to Bangkok every chance you get. Creates a morale problem for the enlisted men, the officers out cattin' around while they're stuck on post. And it's not good for you junior officers either—too much of a good thing and all that."

"I agree wholeheartedly, Colonel," Frank said, picking up three beers from the bar and carefully balancing them in his grip as he turned toward two lieutenants waiting at a nearby table. "Our responsibility is to the depot, and we're only asking for trouble if we don't keep our minds on business." The insincerity in his voice was palpable, but the colonel was too far into his cups to notice.

"I'm glad you see it that way, Lieutenant." Neil leaned closer to Frank, his breath stinking of booze. "Take your pal Lieutenant Reidy, for instance. He spends too much time foolin' around in Bangkok and not enough time mindin' the store. He's bad company, if you know what I mean."

"Yes, sir. I don't intend to be down there any time soon."

"That's good, Lieutenant." The colonel patted him on the back, jostling the beers. "You just stick to business and you'll do fine."

But the colonel's warning about young officers fooling around in Bangkok started Frank thinking about Laurel. Despite Neil's suspicions, he hadn't been with a woman since his first night in Bangkok. After living with Joanna for six months, he'd become accustomed to convenient, regular sex. Maybe he could set up a similar arrangement in Korat. He called Mike Reidy later that night.

"Laurel?" Mike asked. "You want me to find a massage girl named Laurel? There's probably a thousand of them by that name. And it wouldn't be her real name anyway."

"But, Mike, you remember her," prodded Frank. "That girl we met at the Rose House Café."

"I've met lots of girls at the Rose House Café."

"Try, will ya?"

"Okay, pal, I'll see what I can do. But be careful. I think you'd be crazy to set up housekeeping with a massage girl from Bangkok."

A FEW DAYS LATER, FRANK SPENT A LONG WEEK-end with Laurel in a run-down, two-story hotel in Korat. Mike had found her in the Rose House Café, sitting in the same spot where Frank first met her. He reported that she didn't seem to remember Frank, but an advance of twenty dollars overcame her reluctance to travel to Korat. Another ten dollars bought the mamasan's consent.

By the time he met Laurel at the Korat bus station, Frank had forgotten Mike's words of caution and attributed her initial lack of recognition to fatigue from the trip and the awkwardness of the situation. And by the time they reached the hotel, she was chatting away as if they were old friends.

Laurel lived up to Frank's expectations, changing into a short, transparent negligee and pulling him into bed with no preliminaries. They made love quickly and hungrily, then a second time in a more unhurried fashion. They lay languidly on the bed the rest of the afternoon and spent the rest of the weekend in the hotel, venturing out only for meals from neighborhood street vendors and hole-in-the wall restaurants.

Frank decided Laurel would do quite nicely as Joanna's replacement. He broached the subject at the end of her visit, and the conversation quickly turned into a negotiation over finances. He was initially put off by her demands—not because they were exorbitant, but because second lieutenants didn't make as much money as she assumed. But, he rationalized, she would incur expenses moving to Korat, and after working out a rough budget in his head, he decided he could afford it.

During the ensuing week, with the help of the mamasan who washed his fatigues, Frank rented a bungalow on the outskirts of Korat, three small but airy rooms overlooking a vegetation-encrusted klong that smelled of sewage. The bungalow was sparsely furnished; he would leave the rest of the job to Laurel. His only contributions were a hot plate and small refrigerator secured from the enlisted mess and a cardboard-framed photograph of himself, which he propped on a bamboo nightstand next to the bed.

An enclosed pit in the yard served as the toilet. The mamasan assured him that Laurel was used to such primitive facilities and would not be inconvenienced in the least. Laurel, however, proved the mamasan wrong. When she arrived with her belongings, she complained about the toilet and the tawdriness of the bungalow and had harsh words for the mamasan who had helped with the arrangements. She was mollified only when Frank gave her carte blanche to complete the furnishings and, at her insistence, advanced a large sum of cash for that purpose. His budget had already gone out the window.

Over the next few weeks, serviceable if less-than-fashionable furniture intermittently appeared, fueled by more and more of Frank's cash. He wondered if he was getting his money's worth, but the hurt look on Laurel's face when he asked about the furniture persuaded him to let it drop.

He was unsettled, however, when Laurel took a job as a hostess in a local teahouse.

"It only restaurant," she insisted. "No boom-boom, no nothing."

"But why bother? I'll take care of you. You don't need to work."

"I want to work." She looked around the bungalow with an expression of exaggerated boredom. "Need something to do."

"Well, what am I supposed to do, wait up for you to come home at night?"

Laurel caressed his cheek and kissed him tenderly on the lips. "You see. No problem."

"Well, I don't like it. What if a GI tries to get after you?"

"No will happen. Mamasan get mad at GI."

Frank relented and adopted a wait-and-see attitude. They would be able to spend weekends together, and spending more time on the post would keep him in the colonel's good graces. Plus, the colonel was right—getting laid so often was beginning to wear on him.

Laurel was true to her word. On the nights he was at the bungalow, she woke him up when she returned from work, full of ardor and affection. Only once did she fail to appear, when Frank returned a day early from a trip to an outlying unit. The next morning Laurel explained that the mamasan at the teahouse had become suddenly ill and required her assistance. When Frank visited the teahouse the mamasan supported the story and expressed her gratitude for Laurel's help. Frank's suspicions eventually evaporated, helped in good part by the new ways Laurel found to entertain him in bed.

One Saturday, he signed out a three-quarter-ton truck from the motor pool and drove Laurel to her parents' village twenty miles north of Korat. They followed the Friendship Highway, an American-built, two-lane road that stretched from Bangkok north to the Laotian border. They turned off and negotiated a narrow, rutted dirt road the last five miles, passing an occasional motorbike but no four-wheeled vehicles.

Laurel's parents lived in a wooden hut with a palm-frond roof, fronting on a large common area shared by a half-dozen families. Her father studiously ignored Frank; he sat on the stoop with his eyes averted. Laurel elicited some interest from her mother with her animated chatter, proudly showing off the American officer she had snared. Her mother eventually acknowledged Frank with a nod in his direction and a flash of betel-nut-blackened teeth.

Frank loaded furniture onto the truck that Laurel retrieved from inside the hut. She explained that her parents wanted her to have the furniture now that she had a place of her own. He suspected she was embellishing the truth, noting her mother's reluctance to part with some of the more serviceable pieces. At one point, she pressed on Laurel a dilapidated stool from the porch in place of a sturdier one from inside, but Laurel would have none of it, insisting that she have the pick of the family possessions. Frank wondered if some of his money might be going to support Laurel's family, which would explain their acquiescence to her depleting their meager possessions.

Concerned about the knot of children watching the proceedings, Laurel stationed Frank next to the truck to keep an eye on the furniture. Her concern was justified, Frank discovered. The spare tire had already been taken.

CHAPTER 12
Bangkok
MARCH 11, 1970

MACNAMARA SMILED SMUGLY. FOR THE FIRST time since he started working on the story, he had confirmation that the Americans were helping General Lon Nol in his efforts to undermine Prince Sihanouk. And it came straight from the horse's mouth—not from the horse the Americans were betting on, but from the one they were helping run out of town. Sihanouk himself suggested Lon Nol was attempting to orchestrate his ouster with American help.

Dateline: Bangkok, Thailand
March 11, 1970

Thousands of young Cambodians today sacked the Viet Cong and North Vietnamese Embassies in Phnom Penh in an outburst of popular indignation against Communist infiltration into Cambodia. From a morning rally at the Independence Monument, the demonstrators marched on the Viet Cong Embassy where they set cars on fire and ransacked the building. After the hour-long attack on the embassy—believed to have been unoccupied at the time—the crowd marched to the North

Vietnamese Embassy, setting several cars on fire there as well.

From Paris, Prince Norodom Sihanouk, the Cambodian chief of state, charged that the sacking of the embassies was part of a plot to "throw our country into the arms of an imperialistic capitalist power," apparently a reference to the United States. Charging that unnamed Cambodian "personalities" had taken advantage of his absence from Phnom Penh to organize the attacks, he announced that he would return to the country to meet with army leaders.

"If they choose to follow these personalities on a course that will make Cambodia a second Laos," Sihanouk said, "let them permit me to resign."

The statement came in the form of a cablegram to the prince's mother, Queen Kossomak. It did not name the "personalities" he implicated, but knowledgeable sources said he was referring to General Lon Nol, the defense minister and premier who is acting chief of state during Prince Sihanouk's extended vacation abroad.

The attacks on the embassies came amid growing concern among Cambodian officials about the presence of North Vietnamese and Viet Cong troops in the country. While Prince Sihanouk has repeatedly protested their presence, the government has generally ignored the incursions as long as they stayed close to the Vietnamese border. General Lon Nol reportedly wants to change that policy and push the Communists out of the country with the help of the Americans.

Most of what he wrote he picked up from government pronouncements and sources he had cultivated among Cambodian diplomats in Bangkok, but he took it a step further by getting Sihanouk on the phone, which turned out to be surprisingly easy. A diplomat provided a phone number in Paris, and Sihanouk answered when he called. It was a huge leg up on other reporters trying to keep up with the story, a feather in his cap.

> In a telephone interview, Prince Sihanouk said that the Communists had a choice between respecting Cambodia's neutrality or seeing pro-American rightists take over his government. "If the Communists will not respect Cambodia's neutrality, then a showdown between the extreme right wing and myself is most probable. A coup d'état is possible, unless I step down before they depose me. Everything is possible. I may be beaten. I do not like civil war. I do not want to see bloodshed among my countrymen."
>
> Sihanouk said he was convinced that right-wing leaders in his government had established contact with the United States, "whether through the embassy, the CIA, or any such organization, I do not know."
>
> "The Americans are inside the castle walls," he charged.

MacNamara loved to write about Sihanouk—he was so quotable. "The Americans are inside the castle walls." Who but Sihanouk would phrase something like that?

And that's what he had to do, he decided—get inside

the castle walls. A lot was happening in Cambodia, and he needed firsthand information to fill out his articles. Maybe Charge d'Affaires Monahan could get him into the country.

He pulled his safari jacket out of the closet; with that and a notebook, he was ready to go. But first, he had to meet Ceci. They were going to a lecture on the poet John Keats at the university. He'd been exposed to more English playwrights and poets in Bangkok than in the States. He enjoyed the respite from the unrelenting foreignness of Southeast Asia, and he enjoyed spending time with Ceci even more.

CHAPTER 13

In Cambodian Waters

MARCH 13, 1970

THE CREWMAN LEANED ON THE RAILING OF THE *Columbia Eagle*, a civilian freighter chartered by the U.S. government, and looked out at the vacant expanse of the sea. His lean, sinewy arms poked out of the rolled-up sleeves of a loose-fitting blue denim shirt like oversized match sticks. Tattoos on his forearm rippled with the movement of muscles and tendons when he raised a hand to tug nervously at his scruffy beard.

Captain William Kocar stood on the bridge and studied the man on the deck below, wondering why he was so visibly out of sorts. Kocar had first noticed his unease in the officers' mess where he worked as a steward. He seemed nervous and jittery and avoided looking the captain in the eye. Kocar initially attributed his demeanor to the stress of a new job in unfamiliar surroundings, but he'd had a couple weeks now to adjust.

The ship was over a hundred miles from the nearest coast, and there wasn't much to bother a seaman in the open ocean. Maybe it was drugs. The captain turned a blind eye to the occasional use of marijuana, but this guy might be overdoing it. Or it could be sex. Homosexuality was as common as dope, and he couldn't do much about that either.

If it wasn't drugs or sex, he didn't know what it could be, out there in the middle of nowhere. No mail, no television, no women, no distractions. Maybe that was it—sheer boredom. They all suffered from it, some worse than others. It was the crewman's first trip; maybe he'd taken on more than he could handle when he signed on in Long Beach.

Or maybe the guy was just an oddball. In his thirty years in the Merchant Marine, Kocar had seen a lot of oddballs. They were all oddballs in one way or another. Who else would put up with a life at sea? Away from home for months on end, nothing to see except the empty ocean, nothing to do to fill the empty time. If the crewman wasn't an oddball yet, he soon would be. The captain shook his head at the absurdity of it and returned to his swivel chair at the center of the bridge.

WHEN CAPTAIN KOCAR STEPPED AWAY FROM THE window, the crewman signaled to an accomplice on the stern, then turned and walked quickly into the superstructure of the ship, climbing two decks to the officers' quarters. When Kocar left the bridge a few minutes later and entered the passageway to his cabin, the crewman was waiting, lurking in the shadows. He quietly stepped up behind the captain and pressed a pistol to his back.

"Step inside, Captain," he whispered. "Don't turn around and don't make a sound. If you do, it's the last sound you'll ever make."

"What do you want?" Kocar demanded, staring at the gray metal cabin door inches from his face. He couldn't see his assailant, but he knew who he was. He was an oddball, all right, and a dangerous one.

"Never mind what I want," the crewman said, pressing the pistol deeper into Kocar's back. "Just do what I say." He opened the cabin door and pushed the captain into the room.

"You didn't take to being a mess steward, I presume." Kocar turned to face him. "If it's a promotion you want, there are more regular ways to go about it. Channels to go through and all that. And I must say, I don't know what you can expect after only a few weeks on the job."

"The job's fine, Captain," the man said with a sneer. "You've been a good employer. But now I'm working for somebody else, and you're the one taking orders."

He motioned for the captain to sit at the small desk in the corner.

"I want you to call the bridge, Captain. Tell the first mate to order an abandon ship drill. Tell him to assume there's a bomb on board." The crewman smiled menacingly, showing a row of broken teeth. "And if he believes it may be more than a drill, that's okay too."

The crewman spread a sheet of paper on the desk, careful to keep the pistol leveled at the captain's head. Two columns of names were scrawled on the page. "The ones on the left, twenty-four of 'em, they go, Captain. The ones on the right, fourteen plus you, stay on the ship. Tell the first mate to come get the names, and warn him not to screw it up."

Kocar reluctantly picked up the phone and rang the bridge. "Mr. Foley," he said when the first mate picked up, "I want you to sound the abandon ship alarm. Turn the ship into the swells and bring the engines to a full stop so the boats can be lowered."

Kocar stared blankly at the crewman as he listened to Foley's response. His voice rose an octave when he spoke again. "It doesn't matter, Foley, if it's a drill or not. I want the men off the side as if there's a bomb on board, and I don't want any backtalk."

His voice softened. "But, Foley, not everybody goes. Come to my cabin and I'll give you a list of those who do. I want you to personally make sure the men on the list— and only the men on the list—get into the boats. Got that? You're to take personal charge."

Kocar listened as Foley spoke, then scanned the two columns of names. "That's right, Foley. I'm keeping a skeleton crew on board. Everybody else goes."

The captain replaced the receiver. "Well, that's what you wanted?" He looked calmly at the crewman, then at the gun pointed at his face. He felt no fear. In his years at sea he'd been confronted with more alarming situations, like a typhoon or two.

"That'll do, Captain. You just keep following orders and nobody will get hurt."

A moment later there was a knock on the door. The crewman motioned for Kocar to open it, concealing himself in a corner.

First Mate Foley stood in the passageway. "The list, Captain?"

Kocar tore the paper in half and handed the longer list to Foley. "These men go, Foley. Nobody else. Load them into the lifeboats and tell them to pull away from the ship as quickly as they can." Kocar looked at a chart hanging on the cabin wall. "Give them a course heading for Sattahip, Thailand."

Foley studied the list a moment, then looked up. "Yes, sir, I understand. I'll take care of it." He hesitated. "You mentioned a bomb, sir. Is that the situation?"

"Between you and me, Foley, yes, it may be. But you and the others staying on board needn't worry. Just follow orders and we'll be okay."

Kocar closed the door and looked at the crewman. "Now, what's this all about?"

"Politics, Captain. You're carrying a load of bombs to be used in the Vietnam War. My people think the war's wrong. So we're doing something about it."

"And what exactly are you doing?"

"We're taking your ship to Cambodia, to Sihanouk-ville."

"What good will that do? They're neutral. They'll just give it back."

"I don't think so, Captain. I think they'll keep it. Maybe sink it. But one way or the other, I don't think the bombs you're carrying will ever get to Vietnam."

The abandon ship alarm sounded in the passageway. The crewman walked to the porthole and watched as two boats were lowered to the water. The engine on one of the boats wouldn't start; two men worked on it while others waited anxiously in the boats or milled about on the deck above.

"Ring the bridge again, Captain," the crewman ordered, annoyed at the slow progress. "Tell them to quit stalling. They can rig a towline between the boats and shove off with one engine."

Kocar relayed the instructions to the bridge. Shortly, amid a cacophony of shouts between the deck and the boats, a line was tossed from one boat to the other.

Foley's voice rose above the din. "Okay, men," he shouted, addressing the throng gathered at the railing, "into the boats. Let's go. Get a move on!"

The last of the departing crew struggled down the ladder, and the boats pulled sluggishly away. Satisfied, the crewman nodded at the captain.

"Okay, Captain, now it's our turn. We're going up to the bridge." The crewman followed the captain into the hallway, prodding him with the gun. They climbed a ladder to the next deck and entered the bridge, startling Foley and four others huddled over the chart table, engrossed in worried conversation.

"Gentlemen," Kocar announced, "this man has a gun at my back, and he says there's a bomb on board. He also says that we're going to Cambodia, not Thailand." He waited for the words sink in. "We're being hijacked."

The crewman nudged the captain toward the others, then stepped back and covered them with the pistol, a .32-caliber semiautomatic. It was a reliable weapon, the captain knew, if somewhat underpowered, but its short effective range would be more than adequate in the close quarters of the bridge.

The men stood quietly as the crewman addressed them. "You need to keep three things in mind." He spoke quietly, confident that he had the upper hand. "First, the captain's right. There's a bomb on board, and if you don't do what I say, I'll blow up the ship. Second, even if you were to jump me or kill me, you won't find the bomb. It's ticking away, and it will continue to tick away until I defuse it or it goes off. And third, I'm not alone."

The captain knew they could overpower him, but not before he got off a few shots. The magazine held eight bullets, enough that a couple of them would be killed or wounded, and then they'd have to find and disarm the bomb. He dismissed the idea.

"And there's one more thing," the crewman said. "I'm committed. This ship is carrying napalm bombs intended for Vietnam. I believe it's wrong to kill the Vietnamese, and I'm willing to die for what I believe in." He looked at each man in turn. "And I'm willing to take you with me."

The crewman ordered everyone off the bridge except Kocar and Foley. He made himself comfortable in the captain's chair and waved the gun toward the central console. "Gentlemen, let's be on our way."

Kocar stepped to the intercom and rang the engine room. "Mr. Eggers, we're going to change course to Cambodia. The bridge has been relieved. We're taking orders from armed men and have to do what they say. You're to follow orders, no heroics."

The captain stepped to the engine order telegraph and rang up ahead full, then addressed the first mate. "Heading two seven five degrees, Mr. Foley."

The captain stepped to the window and looked out at the lifeboats, now standing a hundred yards off the ship. He didn't like leaving them, but the sea was calm and they were in a busy shipping lane; a passing ship would pick them up soon enough. If not, they could make it to the Thai coast, even with only one engine. He was more worried about the men remaining on board. He intended to fully cooperate with the hijackers, but even then there was no telling what they might do.

CHAPTER 14
Washington, D.C.
MARCH 14, 1970

JOHN LYNCH SAT AT THE HUGE CONFERENCE table in the Situation Room in the basement of the White House. Two admirals and an assistant secretary of state sat with him, reviewing cables. Aides hung fresh maps at one end of the room, a steward busied himself filling coffee mugs at the other. CIA Director Fish stepped into the room and surveyed the men seated at the table, hoping to get a fix on the crisis before she jumped into the middle of it.

A voice crackled from a loudspeaker fastened to the ceiling. "Sitch Room, this is CINCPAC. Can you read me?"

Lynch pushed a button on the receiver resting on the table. "We read you loud and clear, CINCPAC. Now get the admiral on the line."

A new voice came out of the speaker. "Gentlemen, this is Admiral Kenneth P. Norton."

"Lynch here, Admiral. Two of yours are in the room—Admirals Jan Brooks and Bob Harrison—along with Tom Henderson from State and the CIA director. What's the situation?"

"The *Columbia Eagle* just crossed into Cambodian waters. A Coast Guard cutter—the *Mellon*—has been trailing her for the last twelve hours. I've ordered the *Mellon* to escort her back to international waters by any means available."

"Do you think that's wise, Admiral?" Henderson asked. "It's a very sensitive situation in Cambodia right now. We don't want anything to set them off. We can't afford an international incident."

"Well, unfortunately, it's already an international incident," Norton replied. "An ammunition ship was hijacked to a country that we're not particularly good friends with. That ammunition could end up with the Communists. I think we have every right to go after her, even if it means violating their territorial waters."

Lynch knew from past dealings with the admiral that he was a haughty know-it-all, not one to easily take advice from his juniors—and he thought everyone was his junior. Still, he was CINCPAC—Commander in Chief, Pacific—not a man whose opinion could be ignored.

"Admiral Norton," Fish asked, "would your thinking be any different if I told you we may be close to bringing Cambodia over to our side?"

Lynch gave her a dismissive look and interrupted before the admiral could respond. "Admiral, if you're going to take her by force, why didn't you do it before she got to Cambodia?"

Admiral Norton was silent for a moment. "Well, the opportunity didn't present itself."

"What you mean is, there's no way to guarantee she won't be blown up, isn't that right?"

"That's the situation, yes."

"And now if she's blown up, it'll be in Cambodia."

Lynch looked at Henderson and Fish, who shook their

heads in unison. "Admiral, the consensus here is that you should stay out of Cambodian waters." He maintained eye contact with the others to make sure they stayed in agreement. "Let the ship go in and let's see if we can't handle it through diplomatic channels."

"Very well." Admiral Norton sounded displeased; he didn't like to be second-guessed, especially by civilians. "I'll rescind the orders."

CHAPTER 15

Sattahip

MARCH 16, 1970

MACNAMARA SAT AT THE BAR IN GRACIE'S PLACE, a café on the beach in Sattahip, a small town on the Gulf of Siam a hundred miles southeast of Bangkok. This is what it's supposed to be like, he thought, reveling in his good fortune. The young reporter, aged beyond his years by sleepless nights and long, arduous months in faraway places, writing copy in a bar in some exotic locale—and writing about an international incident, no less.

He had a scoop, of sorts, having had the foresight to figure out where the crewmen forced off the *Columbia Eagle* would come ashore. As far as he could tell, he was the only reporter in town. And even though he didn't have the story firsthand, he had it secondhand, which was better than anyone else. Even his editor was impressed—he finally gave him a byline.

Dateline: Sattahip, Thailand
March 16, 1970
By Robert A. MacNamara
Exclusive to The Herald

The seizure of the American munitions ship *Columbia Eagle* in the Gulf of Siam three days ago is reported to have been the act of two "hippies."

This report came from Arthur Bleier and Paul Engh, crew members of the *Rappahannock*, an American freighter that rescued 24 castaways from the *Columbia Eagle* in the Gulf on Saturday night. Bleier and Engh said the *Columbia Eagle* crewmen told them the captain of the *Columbia Eagle* issued an order to abandon ship while being threatened with a gun by a "hippie" of American nationality assigned as a steward in the officers' quarters. The steward, described as a bearded, long-haired hippie in his twenties, was suspected by other crew members of being a user of narcotics.

Twenty-four of the *Columbia Eagle*'s crew, some believing that a drill was underway, were hustled into two lifeboats. The ship, with 14 crew members and the captain remaining on board, steamed off at full speed toward Cambodia.

The rescued crew members were not permitted to come ashore in Sattahip pending the completion of immigration formalities complicated by the unexpected nature of their arrival.

The *Columbia Eagle*, a commercial ship chartered by the U.S. government, loaded a cargo of 500- and 700-pound napalm bombs at Long Beach, California. The ship was bound for Bangkok. Much of the United States' bombing of South Vietnam is carried out from U.S. air bases in Thailand.

David E. Monahan, the American charge d'affaires in Cambodia, said today that the *Columbia Eagle* was anchored near a small island five miles west of the Cambodian port of Sihanoukville.

"I know very little at this time," he said. "I only know that the ship was hijacked by two sailors and entered Cambodian waters late yesterday evening."

In Washington, Defense Department sources said that the *Mellon*, a U.S. Coast Guard cutter cruising in the area on duties related to the war in Vietnam, had picked up a radio message that the freighter's bridge had been relieved. It appeared that the gravity of the situation was not fully appreciated in Washington until the ship had already entered Cambodian waters. The State Department cabled instructions to Charge d'Affaires Monahan to request the assistance of the government in Phnom Penh to obtain the return of the ship, including permission for the *Mellon* to escort it back to international waters.

MacNamara was intrigued by his brief telephone conversation with Monahan. The diplomat didn't hide the fact that he had no idea what was going on. He said he intended to go to Sihanoukville to look into the matter and would know more then.

And that, MacNamara decided, was what he had to do—get himself to Sihanoukville, two hundred miles farther down the coast. Instead of relying on third- and fourth-hand information from an unreliable cortege of informants in Bangkok, he could get secondhand information from a fresh cortege of unreliable informants in Cambodia.

CHAPTER 16

Korat

MARCH 17, 1970

FRANK WORRIED THE COLONEL WOULD NOTICE his frequent absences from the post. Neil was vocal about his disdain for junior officers who neglected their duties to enjoy the local hospitality. "It's the draft," Neil groused in the officers' club after tipping a few beers. "It's the draft that forces such ill-suited men into the service."

But the colonel *did* call him on the carpet over the missing tire. The motor pool sergeant reported the loss despite Frank's suggestion that he would have a better chance of getting the new mechanic he needed if he overlooked the matter.

"And don't get after Sergeant Stout for turning you in," Neil warned after dressing him down. "He did right. If we had more men like him, the army would run a lot better."

"You don't have to worry about that, Colonel," Frank said, trying to sound contrite. "I was only away from the vehicle a few minutes. I didn't think anybody would have time to screw with it. But I was wrong, and it won't happen again."

"It'd better not, Lieutenant."

Frank turned toward the door, but the colonel stopped

him. "By the way, I've noticed you're spending a lot of time off post lately."

Uh oh, Frank thought. Here it comes.

"Maybe this tire thing is just one more sign of your increasing inattention to matters here at the depot. I don't know what you do in town, Lieutenant, but I can guess—and spending more time with the local women than you do here in the office doesn't reflect favorably on your performance."

The colonel was building up to something more consequential than the loss of a tire, Frank realized. He wasn't worried about his efficiency report—he wouldn't be making the army a career—but Neil could make it difficult for him to see Laurel. He enjoyed their time together more than ever as she became more and more inventive in bed. He was getting his money's worth, and he didn't want the colonel upsetting the arrangement.

"Sir, I've never missed work," Frank insisted, "but you're right. I intend to spend more time on post attending to my duties." Laurel was working anyway; he would have to make do with less frequent visits to the bungalow.

"Not a problem, Lieutenant," Neil said, mellowing. He stepped around the desk to lay a paternal hand on Frank's shoulder. "I was young once too, you know. As long as you get the job done, I have no complaints."

Frank was still suspicious. He'd become attuned to the fluctuations in the colonel's demeanor. Neil could be pleasant when he wanted something; otherwise, junior officers were just a bother, to be ignored or reprimanded.

"By the way," Neil said, moving to the safe and removing another canvas pouch, "I'd like you to make another trip to Phnom Penh."

"I didn't tell you about the last time," Frank objected. "I had some trouble at the airport. I barely got through."

"I know about that, but don't worry. You won't have any problems this time."

Frank was boxed in. The colonel's message was clear—if he wanted to continue seeing Laurel, he had better cooperate. Frank meekly extended his arm and allowed the colonel to fasten the chain to his wrist.

"Is somebody going to meet me this time?"

"The same fellow, Monahan, the head of mission. I've laid on a special flight from Utapao for tomorrow morning. He'll meet you at the Phnom Penh airport when you arrive."

FRANK WENT DIRECTLY TO THE KORAT AIRSTRIP from the colonel's office, pausing only to call the laundry and alert Sergeant Canedo that he was on his way. It was St. Patrick's Day. He should be hanging out with Mike Reidy in Bangkok searching for an Irish pub, not stuck at some backwoods laundry where a cold beer would be hard to come by and Guinness was out of the question.

He caught the last flight of the day to Utapao and squeezed into a narrow space between the cockpit and a pile of bulky mail sacks. He couldn't see out, but he didn't miss the view—he was too busy worrying about the reception he'd get in Phnom Penh in the morning. His interrogators would be none too happy to see him again.

Sergeant Canedo met him with the laundry truck. "Glad to see you, Lieutenant," Canedo said with genuine warmth. "You did so well with that dryer, there's a few more things I'm hoping you can requisition for us."

Frank laughed. "Sorry, Sarge. I'm not here on

business—at least, not laundry business. I just need a place to stay tonight, and from the mess I saw last time, I figured you guys wouldn't notice an extra lodger."

"Hey, we even cleaned up after you called, Lieutenant," Canedo protested. "You won't recognize the place."

"You didn't dump all the dope, I hope."

Canedo eyed him warily. "Uh, we may be able to scare something up, if you want."

"I haven't had a toke since stateside. I wouldn't mind a drag or two. Up here, away from the brass, I don't think the army would mind."

"You're on," Canedo said, delighted the lieutenant would be such good company. "That'll give us a chance to tell you about the new vehicle we need. This one here is about worn out."

The truck was a standard army three-quarter ton, four-wheeled pickup with a canvas roof over the rear. The six-cylinder engine was designed in the 1930s and installed on a 1951 Dodge chassis. It was out-of-date when new and had taken a beating on Thailand's rough roads. Frank made a mental note—he could buy more goodwill with Canedo if he could get Reidy to ship him a replacement.

If Canedo and his crew had cleaned up the laundry, it wasn't apparent to Frank. A gleaming new dryer stood in a corner, but the rest of the place was still a mess. Parts of dismantled washers and dryers mixed with pieces of uniforms and personal gear were spread over the floor. In the backyard, the same Thai woman stooped over the fire, cooking fish with rice and vegetables smothered in a smelly, reddish-brown fish sauce. She grinned at Frank, displaying a bottom row of blackened teeth, betel nut juice dribbling down her chin.

"Care to join us for dinner, Lieutenant?" Canedo asked politely.

Frank looked at the unappetizing slop sizzling in the frying pan. "I've already eaten, thanks. I'll just have a beer for now. Or," he hinted, "maybe something stronger."

Ramos and Greenwald wandered into the yard and scooped up platefuls of food. Squatting near the fire, they ate in silence, occasionally grunting their satisfaction for the benefit of the mamasan. They glanced curiously at Frank from time to time, unaccustomed to being in the company of an officer.

"What's wrong with the truck?" Frank asked Ramos, making conversation while Canedo was inside rolling a joint. "Sergeant Canedo says you guys need a new one."

"Yeah, we messed it up on that trip into Cambodia a few months back," Ramos said. "The connecting rods are shot. They get worse every day."

"What were you guys doing in Cambodia?" Frank was surprised they crossed the border. "You do laundry for the other side too?"

Ramos was about to answer when Sergeant Canedo stepped into the yard and shot him a warning glance. "Ramos means the time we were up near the border delivering stuff to the orphanage," Canedo said. "Worn-out sheets and stuff. Civic action and all that. Win their hearts and minds."

Ramos nodded eagerly in agreement, but Frank could tell they were hiding something. He took a drag on the joint Canedo offered. "Sergeant, if you don't want to tell me what you were doing in Cambodia, that's fine, but maybe I can't find you a replacement vehicle."

Canedo knew he should keep his mouth shut, but

he was already counting on a new truck. "Well, I guess Ramos let the cat out of the bag." He looked at Ramos reproachfully. "It was for Colonel Neil. We carried some stuff in for him. Screwed up the truck on the way back."

"What'd you carry in?"

"Oh, nothing much. Just some things." Canedo treaded carefully. He didn't know how far he could trust the lieutenant, and he didn't want to get on the colonel's bad side.

"Come on, Sergeant," Frank pressed. "What kind of 'things'?"

"Supplies, mostly."

"What kind of supplies?"

Reluctantly, he said, "A few rifles and some ammo. The colonel told us to keep it quiet."

"Who'd you take it to?"

Canedo guffawed, passing the joint to Greenwald. "Cochise, he looked like to me. Some Cambodian guy. But the colonel treated him like he was a big deal. Said he was a general."

Frank wondered what Neil was up to, taking laundrymen into Cambodia with weapons and ammunition, sending him to Phnom Penh with mysterious pouches. Neil was obviously more than he appeared to be, more than the commanding officer of a backwater supply depot. Frank made a mental note to keep a watchful eye on Neil. Maybe he could come up with some leverage to protect his relationship with Laurel.

THE TRIP TO PHNOM PENH WAS A REPETITION OF the first. Frank was greeted by the same committee of soldiers and customs officials who ushered him into the room where he had been interrogated before. And, to his dismay, there was no sign of the charge d'affaires.

Well, screw him, Frank decided. If Neil's buddy didn't care enough about the pouch to meet him at the airport, that was his tough luck. The Cambodians could go ahead and cut it off, he didn't care. It was considerably lighter than the last one—there couldn't be much in it anyway.

Then Monahan pushed his way into the room. He exuded authority—a tanned diplomat with gray-flecked hair wearing tortoise-shell glasses and a cream-colored linen suit—but the Cambodians were intransigent. No matter how vehemently Monahan protested, they wouldn't allow the pouch into the country without inspecting it first.

"Okay," Monahan said, relenting and addressing Frank for the first time. "Looks like you have to take the pouch back to Thailand, Lieutenant. We don't open our diplomatic mail for anybody. Standard policy."

"Fine with me," Frank said sullenly. "I don't feel too welcome here."

Monahan escorted Frank back to the C-130 sitting on the tarmac, its engines idling. He was about to board when Monahan handed him a thick envelope. "Take this to Neil," he directed. "He's expecting it. It's important."

Frank reluctantly took the envelope and stuffed it into his fatigues. He had a depressing feeling he was never expected to deliver the pouch, that Neil knew he would be turned back at the airport. He wasn't there to deliver the pouch; he was there to pick up the envelope. Neil couldn't care less that the Cambodians might have roughed him up. Well, he'd go along with the charade. Maybe it would be enough to keep the colonel from putting the kibosh on his extracurricular activities with Laurel.

The colonel's driver picked him up at the Korat airstrip and delivered him directly to the 501st headquarters. As Frank expected, Neil was unconcerned that the mail didn't get through. His attention was riveted on the envelope Frank pulled from his shirt.

The colonel took the envelope and held it reverently in his outstretched hands. "Don't sweat the pouch, Lieutenant. This envelope is more important. You'll never know how or why, but I hope it's some consolation that you've played a critical role in your country's efforts to win the war over here. The contents of this envelope may well lead to a lasting friendship with the new government of Cambodia."

CHAPTER 17
Bangkok
MARCH 19, 1970

REIDY AND MACNAMARA SAT ON THE PATIO OF the Mandarin Oriental Hotel, listlessly picking at their dinners. It was the beginning of the hot season, and the heat and humidity dampened their appetites.

Mike chuckled.

"What's so funny?" Bob asked

"You should have heard Frank Schaniel," Mike said with a laugh. "He was so pissed he could hardly see straight."

"Oh, yeah?" Bob was only half listening. He was mentally composing his next article and not making much progress.

"Seems Colonel Neil sent him into Cambodia on a wild goose chase, supposedly to deliver some diplomatic mail, but Neil forgot to tell him there was a coup going on."

MacNamara's ears perked up. "Schaniel was in Cambodia? Yesterday? The day of the coup? Christ, I've been trying to get in there for a month. How'd he do it?"

"The Air Force flew him in. It was the second time, actually. To deliver some diplomatic mail to the embassy and, this time, to pick something up for the colonel."

"Pick up what?"

"Someone from the American Embassy gave him a big envelope." Mike laughed again. "Frank didn't hear about the coup until after he got back. Let me tell ya, he was mad as hell."

"So how was Neil supposed to know there was going to be a coup?"

Reidy turned serious. "You know, that's the funny thing. He apparently knew it was going to happen. Frank said Neil made a big deal about how whatever was in the envelope would help forge a relationship with the 'new' government in Cambodia."

"That's curious. There's still a lot of talk about the Americans helping this Lon Nol, the new guy in Cambodia. You know anything about that?"

"No. I told you before, if any supplies were going to Cambodia, I'd know about it. Especially if weapons . . ." Mike's voice trailed off.

"What's wrong, Mike? You think of something?" Bob leaned forward in anticipation.

"There's one more thing Frank said, something he heard from some army guys in Utapao. It happened a couple months ago. Seems Colonel Neil delivered some M16s—not many, maybe a few dozen—to someone in Cambodia. Could've been Lon Nol, for all I know."

MacNamara was skeptical. A few dozen rifles weren't enough to mount a coup. "Schaniel say anything else?"

"No, not that I remember. I probably shouldn't have told you even that much."

MacNamara was frustrated. A lot was happening in Cambodia, and he couldn't get his arms around it. The Columbia Eagle hijacking and now the overthrow of the Cambodian government. In a few hours he had to file his "definitive" report on the coup. The problem was he didn't have much to put in it, only self-serving pronouncements from Lon Nol in Phnom Penh and Prince Sihanouk in Moscow.

Reidy was sympathetic, but he was too wrapped up in his own concerns to worry about MacNamara's. He told Bob that he'd managed to stem the thefts from his warehouses, but the magnitude of the losses was becoming apparent. "When Colonel Neil finds out how much is missing, he'll go berserk."

"Don't worry," consoled Bob. "The most they can do is ship you home and throw you out of the army. That wouldn't be so bad, would it?"

"Maybe not for someone like Frank Schaniel, but I need the army. It's the only way I'm going to get my citizenship papers."

When Mike was growing up in Ireland, his father kept bread on the table by wrestling cases of soda six days a week from a horse-drawn cart. Mike gave him a hand from time to time, enough to know that he wanted something more out of life. He wasn't likely to find it in Ireland, he knew. He'd have to emigrate like the other young people looking for something better.

The way out was a scholarship to the University of San Francisco arranged by Barry Martinson, a kindhearted but gullible Jesuit missionary from his village. Reidy convinced the good father that his most fervent desire was to become a missionary himself and that only the lack of a Jesuit education held him back. If truth were told, he wasn't even much of a Catholic—to his mother's chagrin—but he rationalized that a ticket to the United States and a free college education justified the deceit.

"There's no way I'm going back to Ireland," he told Bob. "They're too poor over there. And," he added with a mischievous grin, "the lassies don't believe in premarital sex."

MacNamara laughed and got up from the table. "I've gotta go, Mike. Ceci and I are going to another play tonight."

"Mac, you're not getting serious about that gal, are you?"

"There's no 'getting serious' over here, Mike. You know that. One day you're in love, the next day you're headed home."

"Just be careful. The wily ways of women and all that."

"You don't have to worry about me. And be sure to let me know if you come up with any tidbits the folks back home would like to hear. I'm spending so much time with Ceci I'm off my game, not developing stories like I should. My editor's starting to ask questions."

"Okay, I'll keep you in mind," Mike said. Then, as an afterthought, "Say, Mac, you're not going to print this stuff about the warehouses, right?"

"You know I won't, Mike. You're a friend, not a source. How could I turn on a guy who knows more Irish songs than I do? And I already did an article about American goods ending up on the black market in Cambodia. I think the *Herald*'s subscribers are tired of reading about people stealing the stuff they paid for with their hard-earned tax dollars."

MacNamara turned serious. "Anyway, I'm more interested in the American connection to Lon Nol. I know there's something there. I can feel it in my bones.

This stuff about Colonel Neil has given me more to think about."

MacNamara returned to his room and inserted a sheet of paper into the typewriter.

Dateline: Bangkok, Thailand
March 19, 1970
By Robert A. MacNamara
Exclusive to The Herald

Prince Norodom Sihanouk, chief of state of Cambodia, was overthrown yesterday while out of the country, the Phnom Penh radio announced. Except for the broadcast, the Southeast Asian country was cut off from the world. The nation's two commercial airports were closed to traffic shortly after noon.

Lt. Gen. Lon Nol, the right-leaning premier and defense minister, has apparently seized power. The announcement came after a week of anti-Communist rioting, now believed to have been instigated by Lon Nol, in which the North Vietnam and Viet Cong embassies were sacked.

These events move Cambodia closer to open hostility with the Vietnamese Communists, who are operating in large numbers on the Cambodian side of the long border with South Vietnam. Prince Sihanouk, a neutralist whose policy swung right and left in an effort to strike a balance between the warring governments, has shown a pronounced shift to the right in the last year, apparently in an effort to placate Lon Nol. He became increasingly harsher in his pronouncements against the

Communists and cut back on his tendency to balance anti-Communist statements with strident attacks on "American imperialism."

Increasing pressure by the North Vietnamese and Viet Cong, largely because of their need for sanctuary in territory safe from American firepower, heightened the political struggle in Cambodia by causing discontent with Prince Sihanouk's policies within the military. In Washington, some officials believe the new leadership in Cambodia will lead to a more sustained effort against Communist forces operating in the border regions, thus enhancing the American military position in South Vietnam.

There is no discernable evidence that Americans were involved in the coup, with embassy officials here denying any such development. George Hinman, the Senate majority leader and Prince Sihanouk's friend, said he deplored Sihanouk's ouster, adding, "I give you my word that we are not involved in this."

John Wertz, chairman of the Senate Intelligence Committee, echoed Hinman: "The government of the United States supports democracy everywhere and had nothing to do with the recent events in Cambodia."

In his communiqué, General Lon Nol assured foreign governments that the ouster of Prince Sihanouk meant no change in the country's policy of "independence, sovereignty, peace, strict neutrality, and territorial integrity."

Well, that was it. Sihanouk was out, Lon Nol was in, and the Americans said they had nothing to do with it. Were they telling the truth? Or were they trying to save Lon Nol the embarrassment of their involvement becoming public? Or another unsettling possibility—was it such a secret that even Senators Hinman and Wertz didn't know, a classic case of one branch of the government not keeping the other informed? Or worse yet—a CIA operation that *nobody* else knew about? Not Congress, not the Pentagon, not even the president? The CIA was known for its freewheeling ways with little respect for the constraints Congress tried to impose. If it had a hand in the coup, it could mean the American army in Vietnam had an ally in Lon Nol and didn't realize it. The consequences could be disastrous—the American military could be quick to attack anybody they perceived was not firmly on their side.

He resolved to redouble his efforts to get into Cambodia. He would cover two birds with one stone—the *Columbia Eagle* and the coup—and while in Cambodia, he would sniff around for Americans hiding in the weeds.

CHAPTER 18
Washington, D.C.
MARCH 19, 1970

A PERTURBED JOHN LYNCH SLIPPED INTO A CHAIR in the Situation Room. The same two admirals—Brooks and Harrison—were seated at the conference table. Sharee Fish huddled with State's Tom Henderson over a map in a corner.

"I want to know why we have to be here again, that's what I want to know," Lynch growled, directing his annoyance at Henderson. "Seems to me there's not much of a crisis left. The ship's in Cambodian waters and either they'll release it or they won't. If they don't release it, we'll blow the goddamn thing up, just like Admiral Norton wanted, and that'll be the end of it."

Henderson winced. "I don't think it's quite that simple, John. The Cambodians want to give the ship back. The question is, how can they do it without embarrassing their new government?"

"Who gives a shit if they're embarrassed?"

"I do, John, and so do you. We allowed a munitions ship to be hijacked to Sihanoukville at the worst possible time. Monahan met with Lon Nol earlier today, and, to put it mildly, Lon Nol is pissed. In the middle of his coup d'état, the *Columbia Eagle* shows up. While Lon Nol is telling the world that Cambodia will remain neutral,

Sihanouk and his pals point to the ship as evidence the United States is helping him out."

Lynch turned to Fish for confirmation, but she avoided his gaze. He gave her a look of ill-disguised contempt and got up to leave. "Well, give me a buzz when you have something," he said in disgust. "I'll worry about it then."

After Lynch stalked from the room, Henderson pulled Fish aside. "I sure hope you can handle this, Madame Director," he said. "You know where the word 'lynching' comes from, don't you? A few hundred years ago the mayor of Galway was a guy named Lynch, and he hanged his own son."

Fish was familiar with the story. She'd first heard it from John Lynch himself, who used it from time to time to keep people in line. The mayor's son murdered another suitor for his betrothed, a crime often overlooked in those days, a killing of passion rather than malice. But the mayor's son was sentenced to death, and when no one else would carry out the sentence, the mayor did it himself.

"This Lynch won't hesitate to hang *us* if the shit hits the fan," Henderson warned.

CHAPTER 19

Sihanoukville

MARCH 22, 1970

MACNAMARA HOUNDED THE CAMBODIAN embassy in Bangkok—leaning on Monahan for help, promising a favorable article in return—until they issued him a visa. Now that he had made it into Cambodia, he wondered if it was worth the effort. He stood in the lobby of the Sihanoukville post office and reread the story he had just cabled to San Francisco. They called it a "non-story" in the trade, something to fill the space when there was nothing much to report. He wondered if there would ever be more to report, or if the Cambodian government would simply leave the *Columbia Eagle* swinging at anchor while Sihanoukville continued to vegetate under the hot tropical sun.

Dateline: Sihanoukville, Cambodia
March 22, 1970
By Robert A. MacNamara
Exclusive to The Herald

From the dusty hills of this somnolent port city, the hijacked American freighter *Columbia Eagle* can be seen, squat and ugly, on the harbor's horizon.

A one-street town of 16,000 people, Sihanoukville sprawls along the rugged coastline and
just barely keeps back the stifling jungle growth.
A few two-story shops, owned by Chinese or Vietnamese merchants, dominate the village, selling
wines from Communist China, toys from Hong
Kong, and radios from Japan.

Town policemen bicycle through the streets,
stopping occasionally for crushed ice and lemon
sauce or picking up free cigarettes from shop owners who hope to one day get a favor in return.
Down at the pier, which angles into the harbor
waters, two ships are tied up, one from Spain and
the other from France. About 15 ships a month
visit this port, Cambodia's only harbor. Americans
in Saigon believe great amounts of supplies come
through the port for the North Vietnamese and
Viet Cong, but with no cranes and only a collection
of older American and Czech trucks, it would be a
slow business.

Sihanoukville emerges from its stupor only on
weekends when scores of French, German, Russian, and, occasionally, Chinese diplomats and
their staffs arrive from Phnom Penh for a couple
days at the beach.

The hijacked *Columbia Eagle* continues to rest
at anchor in the harbor. William Kocar, the ship's
captain, is being held incommunicado by Cambodian
authorities. David E. Monahan, charge d'affaires at
the U.S. Embassy in Phnom Penh, said his attempts
to see Captain Kocar have, so far, been fruitless.
An embassy source indicated that one cause for

the delay was the Cambodian government's concern with its own problems resulting from the coup this week that ousted Prince Norodom Sihanouk as chief of state.

MacNamara left the post office and strolled along the harbor, wondering if he could safely return to Bangkok. He should probably stay in town, he decided, at least until Monahan left. It would be a couple more days at most, and he didn't want to miss any developments in the *Columbia Eagle* situation. He was willing to bet nothing much would happen, but it was such an effort to get there, he was reluctant to leave on the off chance something would.

He stopped along the quay and looked out at the quiet waters of the small harbor. He couldn't see the *Columbia Eagle*, tucked away in a remote backwater of the bay, but he felt its presence. The ship was a bomb waiting to explode, in more ways than one.

He walked into Tom O'Neil's—the only bar in Cambodia pretending to be an Irish pub, a lonely shamrock hanging over the entrance—hoping to find Monahan. Sure enough, the diplomat sat at his regular table, eating lunch and nursing a local Anghor beer, engrossed in conversation with an American MacNamara didn't recognize. At first, he thought it might be Captain Kocar, and his heart skipped a beat at the thought of an interview. But the man was too young to be Kocar, and he looked more like a soldier than a sea captain, sitting erect in the chair, his gray hair cropped short, wearing starched dungarees and a clean blue chambray shirt.

His interest piqued, MacNamara took a seat at the bar where he could watch Monahan and his companion without being obvious about it. He surveyed the selection of beers on display, all but Anghor purporting to be imported from Europe, but no Guinness or Harp among them. He knew they were counterfeit anyway, locally brewed, mostly the same beer with different labels. He passed on the Zwisler Ale and Adelman Lager and ordered a bottle of BigDick Miller Stout. Contrary to the name, he knew it would be weak and unremarkable, but at least it would be cold, and he had tired of the harsh taste of Anghor.

"I DON'T BELIEVE IT," MONAHAN SAID TO NEIL. "I just don't believe you would take it on yourself to do something like this."

Neil smiled confidently. "Don't worry, Monahan. Things will blow over in a couple days. Then we'll quietly unload the ship and deliver the stuff to Lon Nol as planned. He'll be happy. I'll be happy. You'll be happy."

"You don't understand, Colonel." Monahan took a sip of his beer. "Lon Nol doesn't want that ship unloaded. His opponents are claiming his coup was backed by the U.S., and that ship gives them fuel for the fire. It's an embarrassment to him. He doesn't want it unloaded—he wants it gone."

"How will anyone ever know?"

"They'll know, believe me. The Russians have people here. The Chinese have people here. The North Vietnamese have people here. You can bet there are a lot of eyes on that ship. There's no way it can be unloaded without people knowing about it, no matter how long you wait for things to cool down. And what about your two hijackers—how are you going to keep them under wraps?"

"Maybe we shouldn't even try to keep it secret," Neil replied, unperturbed. "Lon Nol was going to get the stuff anyway. All this did was advance the delivery. Now that he's in charge, who cares if the world finds out about it?"

Monahan looked at Neil aghast. "We have to keep it secret, Colonel, because General Lon Nol wants to keep it secret." He spoke slowly and patiently, like a school-teacher explaining a problem to a fifth-grader, and a somewhat dull one at that. He wondered if the booze had finally taken its toll, if that explained why Neil wasn't performing up to his résumé. "His hold on the country is tenuous. It wouldn't take much for Sihanouk to oust Lon Nol before he gets a firm grip on things if they find out he had American help."

The charge d'affaires leaned closer, his face inches from Neil's. "And if that were to happen, Colonel, every-thing you've worked for goes up in smoke."

Neil sighed in resignation and leaned back in his chair. "Well, I still think it was a good idea." He sounded like the petulant schoolboy Monahan mentally pictured.

"Do this, Colonel," Monahan said, issuing orders with newfound authority, confident that the CIA had gone too far this time and he had the upper hand for once. "Get out of here, okay? Before anybody figures out who you are. There's an American reporter sitting at the bar right now. He's going to ask me about you. I'll tell him you're with State. But get out of here before he can do any digging." He paused. "And take your two hippie friends with you, Colonel. Leave the ship to me. I'll handle it."

Just as Neil grudgingly pushed himself away from the table, a bullet cracked the window that had framed his head an instant before. A second bullet shattered Monahan's skull above the left eye. The eye remained open as his head crashed into a plate of greasy fish paste fried with banana leaves and vegetables and stared sightlessly past the chopsticks lying on the table. Blood ran down his nose and dripped into the steamed rice.

MacNamara dropped to the floor at the sound of the gunfire. The restaurant was quiet for a heartbeat, then erupted with screams and a flurry of activity as customers and staff rushed for the door, overturning tables and chairs in their haste to escape. MacNamara cautiously raised his head, only to look into Monahan's vacant eye and gag at the sight of his head half-blown away. He took a breath to collect himself, then stood and brushed off his clothes. He looked around for Monahan's companion, but he was nowhere to be seen.

He needed a drink—a strong drink, not this fake German beer—but it would have to wait. First, he had to write the story.

Dateline: Sihanoukville, Cambodia
March 23, 1970
By Robert A. MacNamara
Exclusive to The Herald

American Charge d'Affaires David E. Monahan was shot to death yesterday by an unidentified gunman in this Cambodian port city. Monahan, the chief of the U.S. mission in Phnom Penh, was here to investigate the hijacking of the *Columbia Eagle* 10 days ago by two dissident crew members. He was having lunch at a dockside restaurant with an American companion when he was shot once in the head.

Police have not yet arrested any suspects. Witnesses said the gunman, reported to be of Chinese extraction, disappeared into the streets along the waterfront after firing two quick rounds. There is some speculation that the intended victim was the other American, who has not been identified.

Meanwhile, North Vietnam and the Viet Cong advised Cambodia that they are recalling their diplomats from the country. Their embassies were sacked during well-organized demonstrations staged two weeks ago to protest the presence of tens of thousands of North Vietnamese and Viet Cong soldiers on this side of Cambodia's border with South Vietnam. Premier Lon Nol, who brought about last week's ouster of Prince Norodom Sihanouk as chief of state, is thought to have been behind the demonstrations.

In a telephone interview, Lon Nol said he regretted the closing of the North Vietnamese and Viet Cong Embassies, which would disrupt his attempts to negotiate with the two Communist regimes for the withdrawal of their troops. Nevertheless, he said his government would try, by all peaceful means, to ensure the evacuation of Vietnamese troops from Cambodian territory. He said he did not want military aid from the United States or any other friendly nation, only their support for Cambodia's desire to be a truly neutral state, a Switzerland or Sweden of Southeast Asia.

Lon Nol said he deplored the murder of Monahan and speculated the incident was related to the hijacking of the *Columbia Eagle*. He has not decided on the disposition of the ship, he said, and hinted that the arrival of an American munitions ship in the midst of the country's internal crisis had acutely embarrassed the government. Prince Sihanouk and his Communist backers charged that the ship is evidence the United States is helping the anti-Sihanouk forces.

The acting head of the U.S. mission in Cambodia, Richard A. Harmetz, called on the Foreign Ministry early today to present his credentials and was told that a decision regarding the *Columbia Eagle* would be made soon.

Meanwhile, Cambodia's new government has closed this port to ships bearing munitions for Vietnamese Communists, cutting off an avenue of supply for their war in South Vietnam.

MacNamara cabled the article from the post office and returned to his hotel room with a bottle of Johnnie Walker scavenged from the market near the port, a rare find in the impoverished, war-stricken country. He was sick of Sihanoukville, and he intended to drink enough to forget where he was, to escape, at least temporarily, from the corrupt government officials constantly pressing him for bribes, from the hot, humid, miserable weather, and from the specter of death that permeated the town. He couldn't wait to get back to Bangkok, back to Ceci.

Sihanoukville was a major disappointment. Sure, he had witnessed the murder of an American diplomat—another journalistic coup—but the *Columbia Eagle* hadn't budged, and he hadn't developed any fresh insights into Lon Nol's coup d'état. Worse, he had the feeling the real story had slipped through his fingers—the American lunching with Monahan, who had disappeared as completely as the gunman.

Worse yet, he couldn't shake the image of Monahan's bloodied head resting in a plate of fish and rice, one eye staring at him from across the room.

CHAPTER 20
Sihanoukville
MARCH 28, 1970

MACNAMARA WAS RELIEVED THAT HIS TIME IN Cambodia was coming to an end. He'd stayed longer than necessary, certainly longer than the coup, the *Columbia Eagle*, and Monahan's murder warranted. He hadn't come up with much on any of them, and still didn't know if they fit together. It was a jigsaw puzzle with many pieces still missing.

He smiled. At least he understood the scene on the *Columbia Eagle* he'd just witnessed. World-shaking events played out against a backdrop of intrigue, culminating not in drama or pathos, but in strained humor, reflecting the tension between the American and Communist governments.

Dateline: Sihanoukville, Cambodia
March 28, 1970
By Robert A. MacNamara
Exclusive to The Herald

The hijacked freighter *Columbia Eagle*, her cargo of 1,753 long tons of napalm, and her crew of 14 were returned to United States' control today, and she sailed quickly out of Cambodian waters.

The ship was returned to her captain's authority in a brief exchange of formalities as she stood where she had since March 16, about five miles offshore from this Cambodian port city.

Corvette Captain Ang Kim Ly, Cambodia's deputy chief of naval staff, said, "In the name of my government, I give this ship back to her owners."

When the sentence was translated from French by Richard A. Harmetz, the acting head of the American mission in Cambodia, the ship's captain, William Kocar, replied curtly, "Thanks," and with that the ceremony ended. Kocar said the ship would sail for Bangkok, her original destination.

A small group of newsmen were then escorted into one of the vessel's five holds, a move to demonstrate that none of the cargo had been unloaded. This was to dispel suspicions, assiduously nurtured by Communist propaganda, that the *Columbia Eagle* was part of an American plot to furnish arms for the overthrow of Prince Norodom Sihanouk. In the hold that was inspected, the cargo, consisting entirely of 500- and 700-pound napalm bombs, appeared intact.

The only skepticism was expressed by Louis Ferrarov of *Tass*, the Soviet press agency, who looked at the crates of silvery napalm bombs and said, "They're empty."

Michael Foley, the *Columbia Eagle*'s first mate, replied, "Oh, no, they're full of happy little Czechoslovaks," a reference to the recent uprising in Czechoslovakia in defiance of the Soviet Union.

MacNamara's smile faded. He was as skeptical about the ship's cargo as the *Tass* reporter. Napalm bombs in one hold didn't guarantee the other four held the same thing. Napalm bombs would be of no use to Lon Nol's military—they didn't have an air force—but other armaments would, and cargo in one hold didn't prove the others hadn't been emptied of small arms, artillery, and ammunition. Still, he thought they were probably intact because any effort to unload them would have been noticed.

After the turnover of the ship, MacNamara caught a water taxi back to shore and walked up the street to the compound rented by the Americans, hoping to interview Richard Harmetz. He hadn't expected Harmetz would have any fresh insights into the *Columbia Eagle* or Monahan's murder—or that he would share them if he did—but he'd hoped he might offer a quote or two to help fill out the article.

It hadn't rained in weeks, but the humidity was through the roof and the air was hot and muggy. His shirt clung to his back, and perspiration spread under his armpits. The locals were used to the heat, and the food stalls lining the street were busy even in midday. He surveyed the offerings as he passed—papayas and yams, pork and chicken grilling on hibachis, rice steaming in pots, mixed green vegetables sizzling in frying pans. People stood around the stalls, eating off palm leaves with chop sticks, washing the food down with iced coffee.

A couple blocks from the harbor he came to the residence maintained by the American government for visiting diplomats and other government officials, the town lacking a hotel with the level of comfort and security the Americans required. The small house was enclosed by a six-foot concrete wall, casually guarded by a local resident in a dirty T-shirt who sat, unarmed, on a folding aluminum chair. He waved MacNamara through the unlocked gate.

MacNamara's knock was answered by a skinny, unkempt man with long hair and a thin, straggly beard. MacNamara asked for Harmetz, but the man said he hadn't returned yet from the ceremony on the *Columbia Eagle*. MacNamara assumed the man was a government operative of some sort—part of Harmetz's security detail, perhaps, although he didn't look the part—but, unbidden, the man introduced himself as Bay Cobb, one of the *Columbia Eagle* hijackers. He invited MacNamara into a small side room furnished with a broken-down sofa and single chair; two mattresses and loose bedding were pushed into a corner. Larry Clark, the other hijacker, was sitting on the sofa, languidly leafing through an old magazine.

They had been held incommunicado since the *Columbia Eagle* arrived in Sihanoukville and were eager to talk. MacNamara could hardly believe his luck.

Earlier today, this correspondent interviewed, quite by chance, the two young American seamen who hijacked the munitions ship—Bay Cobb, mess steward, and Larry Clark, engine room wiper. He was seeking the acting American charge d'affaires in the walled house rented by the Americans; instead, Cobb, sporting shoulder-length hair and a wispy beard, answered the door and invited the visitor into his quarters.

Cobb, 25, from New Orleans, Louisiana, and
Clark, 20, from South Mission Beach, California,
were eager to tell their story. Both denied charges
they were "pill-popping, marijuana-smoking hippies," as another crewman had described them.
Cobb said the two had taken only amphetamine
tablets to stay awake during the few days they
held the captain and bridge at gunpoint while
they sailed 700 miles across the Gulf of Siam to
Sihanoukville.

Cobb said they hijacked the ship because they
were against the war in Vietnam. He acknowledged
they had threatened to murder the captain and
crew and were guilty of mutiny and piracy, but he
considered this "on a smaller scale" compared to
the "outright murder of delivering napalm bombs."
He added that it was a coincidence that Prince
Sihanouk was deposed at the same time. He said
he appreciated the hijacking had embarrassed the
new Cambodian government, but added, "If the
Cambodians want the world to believe they follow
a policy of neutrality, they shouldn't release the
ship."

Both looked pained when told that the Communists were saying it was a plot by the Central
Intelligence Agency. "It's a Weather Underground
plot," Cobb said proudly. "A Weather Underground
plot more than anything," Clark added. He said
they were not Weather Underground members, but
"we support groups that hold similar ideas and
have common enemies."

Cobb said they were still under detention by

the Cambodian authorities but had been turned over to the temporary custody of the American mission. They had been assured, however, that the Americans would not be allowed to extradite them. They expected to be released shortly and had no plans to leave the country.

Meanwhile, the Cambodians report no progress in their investigation of the murder of American Charge d'Affaires David E. Monahan in a café here six days ago. At the time he was killed, he was having lunch with an unidentified American who has since disappeared. Some sources here conjecture the unidentified American was connected to the *Columbia Eagle* and was the intended victim, targeted to prevent the offloading of its cargo, but the rumor cannot be confirmed.

MacNamara reflected on his meeting with the hijackers as he walked the story to the post office. The interview was another feather in his cap; even his editor would be impressed, maybe enough to upgrade his "Exclusive to the Herald" byline to "Senior Correspondent." But meeting the hijackers had left him oddly deflated. He had convinced himself the hijacking was part of a secret American plot to support Lon Nol, but Cobb and Clark were so hapless he found it hard to believe they could be part of anything so sophisticated. They seemed clueless about the ramifications of what they had done, Clark so disconnected that the most important thing to him was that MacNamara look up his brother with the 558th Supply and Service Company when he got back to Thailand.

CHAPTER 21
Washington, D.C.
APRIL 4, 1970

"IF YOU DON'T KNOW, HOW THE HELL AM I SUP-posed to know?" The president glared at Sharee Fish, who was sitting uncomfortably in a straight-backed chair on the other side of the desk. "What you're telling me is, if we give this guy Mon Lol—"

"Lon Nol," corrected John Lynch, sitting next to the CIA director, glancing up without expression from the yellow pad on his lap.

"Lon Mol, Lon Nol, what's the difference?" the president snapped. "You're saying if we give this guy a bunch of weapons, who knows what he'll do with them, that he might even use them against us, but we should give him the stuff anyway?"

"That's about it, Mr. President," Fish replied. "He's more anti-Communist than Sihanouk, even though he's still parroting the 'neutral Cambodia' line."

"Well, we all know what *that* means," the president added bitterly. "'Neutral' to those guys means they'll chase the Viet Cong around if that's convenient, but they'd just as soon chase our boys, and if that gets too rough, they'll go after somebody else."

The president turned to the briefing papers on his desk and thumbed through the casualty reports—two hundred Americans died in Vietnam in the last month. He turned to a series of articles clipped from the *San Francisco Herald* that confirmed what the CIA had been telling him: ever-increasing numbers of North Vietnamese troops were sneaking over the border from Cambodia to attack American troops in Vietnam.

Lynch recognized the president didn't have a handle on the situation and was struggling to make a decision. He knew from his long association with the president that it was time to step in.

"Our man in Thailand thinks this Lon Nol will be a pretty solid ally," Lynch said, motioning to the report lying open on the president's desk. "He's had extensive contact with him. Says he's convinced Lon Nol is pro-American. Sees it as a golden opportunity."

"Well, how can he be certain of that? He's just taking Lon Nol's word for it? That and a dime will get you a cup of coffee."

"The analysis of the situation and the recommendation to back Lon Nol came from our mission in Cambodia," Fish said. "It was prepared by my people with Monahan's input, shortly before he was killed, hand-carried out by an army lieutenant. Our man in Thailand has added his endorsement, and he seems to know what he's talking about."

"I wish I could bank on that," the president said. "If I had a nickel for every goddamn bureaucrat who said he knew what he was talking about but didn't know his ass from a hole in the ground, I'd be rich."

"You're right, Mr. President," Fish continued. "No matter what our people tell us, there's no way to know for certain what Lon Nol will do. He says he wants the weapons to chase the Viet Cong back into Vietnam, but it's entirely possible he'll harass the ARVN in the border areas as well. But we can be fairly certain that if we *don't* give him the weapons, he'll get them somewhere else— he's practically advertising for arms—and then we won't have any leverage over what he does."

"Well, I've heard that line before too," responded the president, mellowing slightly, absently smoothing his tie. "Another crappy little country playing us off against the Russians or the Chinese or someone else. 'If you don't help us, we'll go to somebody else, and then you'll be sorry.' Well, I say fuck 'em."

The president's intransigence unsettled Fish, but Lynch was used to the charade. The president was about to grant the director's request, but if things went sour, he wanted to be able to say his hand was forced. Lynch's job was to orchestrate the decision.

"Mr. President, there's something else," Lynch said, deftly stepping into his role. "Sihanouk has established his government in exile in Peking, and he still has a lot of support in Cambodia. His mother is some sort of queen and carries a lot of weight. If we don't get some help to Lon Nol, he may not be strong enough to keep Sihanouk from coming back, and there won't be any question of whose side *he'll* be on—he blames us for his ouster."

"That will worsen an already precarious situation in Vietnam," added Fish, building on Lynch's argument. "With a hostile country on our flank, the North Vietnamese would be free to run their troops and material into South Vietnam from Cambodia, completely unmolested. So far, what little cooperation we've gotten from the Cambodians has been helpful."

The president stared at the report in front of him. "Congress will scream if we give them military hardware," he grumbled. "They'll accuse us of widening the war. Especially Bill Waite, the bastard, and Brian Forbes. They'll say all we're doing is killing more American boys, that the weapons will be used against us. And hell, they may be right. That part of the world is so volatile you don't know whose side someone is on from one day to the next!"

"You have the authority," Lynch assured the president, carefully measuring the conviction in his voice. "If Congress says you can't do it, that's one thing. But they haven't—at least, not explicitly—and you have the authority to take whatever steps are necessary to protect American troops in Vietnam and shorten the war."

"What about the press? I see the daily papers. I know they're nosing around." He picked up the latest *Herald* article and skimmed it again. "This crappy little rag from San Francisco seems to be ahead of the pack."

"Press or no press," Fish said, "we have little choice."

"Well, go ahead then," sighed the president. "Go ahead, but do it quietly. Muzzle this *Herald* reporter, for one thing. He's the only one who seems to have an inkling of what you're up to. I don't want Congress to get wind of it until it's too late to do anything about it."

The president looked at Fish. "And I don't want to know all the particulars. You've been sneaking around long enough without involving me. There's no reason I need to know the details now. Just don't give this Lon Nol anything big—a few machine guns or something. If something goes haywire, I want to be able to put the kibosh on it before it blows up. And put somebody in charge who knows what the hell they're doing!"

"We have just the man," Fish said, rising to leave. "Our man in Thailand. John has met him and agrees. You won't have any problems, Mr. President."

"You're goddamn right I won't." The president pointed a finger at Lynch. "Because John here is going to make *sure* there aren't any problems."

PART TWO
The Cambodian Incursion

CHAPTER 22
Korat
APRIL 5, 1970

FRANK WORRIED THAT COLONEL NEIL WOULDN'T let him have time off to meet Joanna, who would be in Bangkok on a stopover between flights. He wasn't keen on her visit, not now when things were going so well with Laurel, but he had to admit he missed her more than he thought he would. His pulse quickened at the thought of spending a couple days with her. Maybe he could sell Neil on the idea that visiting Bangkok was part of his duties, that the depot adjutant should show the flag at some of the depot facilities in the city.

He walked into the colonel's office with a perfunctory knock. "Sir, I think it's about time I made an unannounced visit to some of the outlying units. Not an inspection, really, but to check the morning reports, duty rosters, mail rooms, that sort of thing—like I did at the laundry in Utapao."

Neil eyed Frank suspiciously. "Lieutenant, I thought you were going to spend more time around the post?"

"Well, I have been, sir," Frank replied defensively. "And this'll be the same thing. I won't be working in Korat, but I'll be spending more than full time on depot business."

"This isn't some ploy to get together with Lieutenant Reidy, is it?"

"No, sir!" Frank shook his head emphatically. "I didn't plan to visit his unit at all."

Neil was quiet a moment, then a malicious grin spread across his face. "Well, maybe an inspection trip wouldn't be such a bad idea," he said. "In fact, it's not a bad idea at all. You should go and inspect some of the units, Lieutenant."

"Yes, sir." Frank realized Neil had something up his sleeve, but he had to take the risk. "I'll put together an itinerary and leave tomorrow."

"You do that, Lieutenant," Neil said, his smile disappearing. "And be sure to include Reidy's unit on that itinerary after all."

Too late, Frank smelled the trap.

"I want you to tear his records apart," Neil continued, rising from his desk and giving Frank a menacing look. "I want you to report to me every discrepancy, every inadequacy, every deviation from those impossible regulations that you AG assholes put together."

Neil pointed a threatening finger at Frank. "And don't try to pull the wool over my eyes, Lieutenant. If you try to cover up anything—and I mean anything—I'll string your ass up alongside Reidy's."

JOANNA HAD BETTER BE WORTH IT, FRANK thought, as he stuffed civilian clothes into his duffel bag the next morning. She'd better have the same thing on her mind that he had on his. Even then, the price might be too high. He would have to come up with a report on Reidy's unit that would pass muster with the colonel but keep Mike out of serious trouble. It would be a fine line, and he wasn't sure he could manage it. Still, he couldn't pass up the chance to see Joanna.

Frank hired a civilian car and driver for the hundred-mile trip, stopping by the bungalow to leave a note for Laurel explaining his sudden departure. An emergency required his presence at the depot facilities in Bangkok, he wrote, adding that he would be back in a few days. He smiled. It might take her a few days to find someone to translate the note.

He sat in the back seat of the Toyota, staring out the window at the passing scenery, his mind on Joanna. He pictured her greeting him in her tight Pan Am skirt and blazer, the uniform accentuating her pert breasts, slim waist, and sensual hips. He felt a pull at his groin and glanced self-consciously at the driver, but he was concentrating on the traffic, weaving in and out of the vehicles that clogged the two-lane road. Like all Thai drivers, he squeezed to one side of his seat to make room for Buddha, leaving half a buttock hanging in the space between the seat and the door.

By the time Frank arrived at the Siam Intercontinental, he could hardly contain his enthusiasm. He waited impatiently for Joanna in the bar, drinking a beer and looking out on the gardens of the Sra Paduma Royal Palace. The morning had melted into early afternoon by the time she walked through the door, as beautiful as he remembered.

Frank took her into his arms. "Joanna, Joanna, Joanna," he whispered as he buried his face in her silky, perfumed hair. "It's so good to see you. I missed you so much."

Joanna held him at arm's length and studied his face.

"You really miss me?" she asked doubtfully. "I think maybe you find local girl to keep you company."

Her accent stirred forgotten memories. "Joanna, nobody could take your place."

"That's true," she said with a laugh. "But maybe you're just one horny boy." She gave him a big kiss and snuggled affectionately in his embrace.

They sat at the bar, sipping drinks and sharing news of mutual friends and the details of their lives in the months they'd been apart. San Francisco was the same as ever, Joanna reported. Efforts to end the war were intensifying, protests continued unabated, and the papers saw no end in sight. Ming had stopped by to see her when he was home on leave from Vietnam.

Eventually tiring of the conversation, Frank led Joanna upstairs to their room, followed by a porter who stacked her luggage inside the door and gave Frank a knowing grin as he pocketed his tip and left. Frank wrapped his arms around Joanna's waist and let his hands slide down her back, cupping her soft buttocks and pulling her tightly against his groin.

"Frank," Joanna said, tensing and breaking the embrace. "I must go first, deliver a package to my cousin on ship." Reaching into her purse, she pulled out a thick manila envelope sealed with strips of orange duct tape.

"What do you mean?" Frank's voice was thick with anticipation. "What cousin? Can't you do that later?"

Frank took the envelope from her hand and let it drop to the floor, pulling her back into his arms. She resisted at first, then melted in his embrace.

"I guess my cousin can wait," she said, pushing Frank onto the bed.

He watched with growing agitation as she unbuttoned her blouse and unhooked her bra, then unfastened her skirt and let it drop to the floor. She knelt in front of him and unzipped his pants. His pecker popped out stiff as a board. She smiled.

That must be it!

She crawled on top of him and planted her lips on his, reaching between her legs to adjust her panties to accommodate his erection.

It was over quickly—Joanna was in a hurry. "Frank, I must go now," she said, getting up from the bed and pulling on her clothes. "But I will not be long. Only a couple hours. My cousin is a crewman on the *Columbia Eagle*, just arrived from Cambodia. The ship that was hijacked. Wait for me. When I come back, there will be plenty of time, okay?"

JUST AS WELL, FRANK THOUGHT AS HE RODE IN A taxi to Reidy's warehouse. He would have just enough time to take care of business, leaving the rest of the weekend for Joanna. Assuming Mike would cooperate and confess to a few minor errors in his record-keeping, Frank could condense what should be a two-day inspection into a few hours. He hoped it would be enough to satisfy the colonel.

Reidy met him at the gate. "Remember last time?" he asked, as he led Frank to his office.

"Too well," Frank replied, recalling the damp evening they'd spent surveilling the depot. "I'd just as soon forget it," he added, settling into a decrepit wicker chair Mike foraged from a corner of the messy room.

"Fine with me." Mike sat on the edge of the desk and

fiddled nervously with a paperweight. "In fact, the thefts or whatever have finally stopped." He scratched his curly hair, which he still wore longer than army regulations allowed. "Funny thing, though—those trucks we saw weren't here the next morning."

Frank shrugged noncommittally, but Mike was not to be put off. "In fact, they weren't even expected. What do you make of that?"

"I make nothing of that, Mike," Frank snapped, "nothing at all. And Neil wouldn't like it if I tried to make something of it. What he would like is for me to screw you over on this inspection, and maybe that's not such a bad idea. If you keep bothering me about those trucks, I'll make sure he finds out how screwed up things really are down here."

"Okay, okay," Mike said, raising his hands in resignation. "I didn't mean to set you off. Just thought it odd, is all. Thought you might be curious."

"Well, I'm not. Now, let's get started."

Frank turned to the filing cabinets lining the wall. In short order, following Mike's directions, he noted that two enlisted men recently reassigned from the warehouse were still carried on the morning report and that the duty roster was out-of-date. Frank made a list of these and other trivial irregularities and stuffed it into his pocket.

"And, Mike, I mean it," he warned as he made his way to the door. "I don't want to hear about your imagined conspiracies any more than Neil does."

JOANNA WAS NOT AT THE HOTEL WHEN FRANK returned. He napped for an hour, but she was still not back by the time he woke. With the coming darkness, he was concerned enough to call Reidy and ask him to pick him up in the depot jeep.

"So, where'd she go?" Mike asked as they pulled away from the curb. He deftly nudged the jeep into the traffic on Pot Buri Road.

"She went to deliver something to her cousin, on a ship somewhere in the harbor." Frank slumped dejectedly in the passenger seat.

"What ship?"

"The one that was hijacked off Cambodia a few weeks ago. The *Columbia Eagle*."

"What was she delivering?"

"I don't know," Frank replied irritably. "An envelope. I didn't ask her what was in it. Letters from family, I guess. Personal stuff."

Frank's concern turned to alarm when, hours later, after driving through a jungle of wharves and warehouses and questioning anyone they could collar who spoke English, they found the ship tied to a dock in a remote, desolate bay. The foreboding, sinister profile of the vessel looming against the darkening sky heightened his unease. The aging steamer's once-white hull was streaked with rust, the paint cracked and chipped. The only sounds to break the ominous silence were creaking timbers and wakes of passing boats slapping against the hull.

The two lieutenants cautiously climbed the gangway to the quarterdeck. A tall, muscular seaman stepped out of the shadows and barred their way. Frank started to explain why they were there, but the seaman cut him off. He didn't care about the reason for their visit, he told them, only that it be brief. A ship's officer materialized out of the gloom, dressed in a dark pea coat and peaked cap, and introduced himself as First Mate Michael Foley.

"You're looking for a woman?" Foley inquired through a thin smile. "There's no woman here. As you can see, this is no place for a woman." He swept his hand across the deck, which was covered with disorderly piles of rigging and equipment. Frank had to agree that Joanna would have been out of place. Lacking an alternative, however, he persisted.

"Your crew, were any of them expecting a visitor?"

"No, no," Foley replied. "They wouldn't expect a visitor because that wouldn't be possible. Not after our recent trouble in Cambodia."

"May I speak with them?"

Foley's smile disappeared. "That's not possible either," he said. "As you can see, we are about to depart." He gestured again to the deck behind him, where a singular lack of activity belied his words.

"She's a friend of mine," insisted Frank, his voice rising with frustration. "She came here to see her cousin."

"How could that be?" Foley asked, as if the answer were obvious. "The crew are all Americans." Foley abruptly turned and retreated into the darkness.

"Wait!" cried Frank, starting after him. "Why do you think she isn't an American?"

The seaman blocked his way, cutting short his protestations with a not-so-gentle push toward the gangway. Frank and Mike reluctantly returned to the dock and stood uncertainly in the shadows. As they mulled over their next step, an army jeep pulled up to the gangway. Colonel Neil was driving. The captain Frank had encountered on his first visit to the docks—Captain Broderick from the 558th Supply and Service Company—sat beside him. Frank started toward them, but Mike held him back.

"Don't," Mike whispered. "If Neil finds us together down here, he'll have our necks!"

Frank looked at Reidy in disgust. "Mike, this is no time to worry about your goddamn job," he said, attempting to shake off his grip. "Joanna is missing, and maybe Neil can help."

"I don't like it." Mike tightened his hold on Frank's arm. "What's Neil doing here? Joanna's probably back at the hotel by now anyway."

They watched in silence as Neil and Broderick climbed the gangway. The crewman greeted them with a salute, and First Mate Foley stepped up with a welcoming smile. With a sinking heart, Frank realized that Mike was wrong, that Joanna wasn't back at the hotel, that the unexpected appearance of Colonel Neil confirmed her disappearance.

Mike put Frank's concern into words. "Looks like Neil's in cahoots with these guys. If they had anything to do with Joanna's disappearance, he's bound to take their side in any argument you may want to start."

They crept closer to the ship and crouched behind Neil's jeep. The insignia of the 558th Supply and Service Company was painted on the bumper. They strained to hear what Neil and Foley were discussing but could catch only meaningless snippets of conversation. After a few minutes Neil reappeared at the top of the gangway and turned to shake Foley's hand. In his other hand he held a manila envelope sealed with orange duct tape.

"Let's get out of here," Frank hissed, grabbing Mike by the arm and hustling him deeper into the shadows. "He's got Joanna's envelope!"

CHAPTER 23
Bangkok
APRIL 7, 1970

MIKE REIDY STARED AT THE LIFELESS BODY LYING on the concrete slab in the Bangkok morgue. Frank stood near the door, dreading the words he knew he would hear.

"Recognize her?" the American military policeman asked matter-of-factly, holding up the corner of the dingy white sheet that covered her body. Lieutenant Sexton was heavy-set and dripping sweat, another officer who wouldn't have made the grade in the infantry.

"It's her—Joanna Tsai," Mike replied, a catch in his voice. Her body had been immersed overnight in one of the klongs that drained sewage from the city. Her face was bloated and discolored, and a large bruise disfigured her forehead. On her finger was the opal ring Frank had purchased in Bangkok and sent to her for her twenty-fourth birthday.

Frank moved to see for himself, but Mike held up a hand to stop him.

"You don't want to look, Frank. Best to remember her as she was."

"How'd it happen?" Frank asked, standing back. He didn't want to believe the body on the slab was the same woman he'd made love to the day before, but Mike knew her well enough—there could be no mistake.

"Apparently drowned," Sexton replied. "Stumbled, hit her head, fell in. They smelled alcohol when they pulled her out this morning, strong enough to pick up through the stench of the sewage."

Sexton worked the ring off Joanna's finger and handed it to Frank, then led them through the dank caverns of the morgue to a makeshift office used by the Americans. He lowered his untidy bulk into a chair behind a desk strewn with old magazines and piles of disorganized forms and reports.

"Look, Lieutenant Sexton, I want an autopsy," Frank said, blinking away tears. He sat on a rusted, paint-flecked folding chair in front of the lieutenant's desk, gripping Joanna's ring tightly in his fist, his anguish mixed with guilt. He shouldn't have been so cavalier about their relationship. He shouldn't have thought he could shake it off like a tryst with a streetwalker in North Beach. He should have told her how much she meant to him. Now it was too late.

He accepted a cigarette from the lieutenant and puffed on it nervously.

"No way," Sexton said, shaking his head. "Can't be done. The Thais won't do it, and we don't have jurisdiction."

"But I think she was murdered, by some guys from a ship—"

Sexton held up his hand. "I don't even want to hear it, Lieutenant. All I want to know is next of kin." He rustled through the papers on the desk looking for the appropriate form. "We have a small unit here, and the whole country to cover. Other than you supply guys, all the army sent to Thailand is the police, so we get stuck doing everything you don't do."

"Look, you've gotta investigate," Frank insisted. "It may have been more than a simple murder. It may have been—"

Sexton interrupted again. "I'd like to help, Lieutenant. I really would. But my hands are tied. The Thais would think we were meddling. Anyway, we don't have any Inspector Clouseaus over here, just a bunch of overworked, dumbass gumshoes."

Frank wasn't ready to give up. "Okay, I hear you, Lieutenant. She's dead. In the grand scheme of things, it doesn't matter how she died. I know that. There's no bringing her back. But she deserves more than another cursory report buried with the others on your desk."

"Look, I'll tell you what," Sexton said, relenting in the face of Frank's persistence. "I'll at least keep tabs on it, push the Thais a bit. Who knows, maybe they'll do an autopsy after all. If anything comes of it, I'll give you a call."

"WHY TELL ME?" MIKE ASKED, SITTING WITH Frank in the lounge of the Siam Intercontinental, a martini on the table in front of him. "Tell it to the police. I have my own troubles."

"Mike, there's nobody else I can turn to. The Thai police won't investigate. The MPs can't do anything—you heard what Lieutenant Sexton said. It's up to us."

"What's up to us?" Mike asked irritably. "I'm sorry she's dead. I really am. She was my friend too, remember. But there's nothing to be gained by getting involved. And even if we came up with something, it's too late. You saw yourself—the ship's gone."

Frank had cajoled Reidy into another visit to the

harbor after they left the morgue. The *Columbia Eagle* had slipped its berth earlier that morning.

"Lieutenant Sexton said she wasn't found anywhere near the ship," Frank argued. "Or on the way to the ship. And how could she have been drunk? She was sober when she left here, and she was planning to come right back. And that bruise you described—I bet she was hit over the head and thrown into the canal."

"Okay, okay, I hear you," Mike said. "But it's no business of ours, at least not of mine. And there's nothing we can do about it anyway."

"But there is." Frank leaned across the table and gripped Mike's arm. "The 558th may be the key. If we can find that Captain Broderick, maybe we can find some answers."

"Frank, there's no fucking way I'm going out to the 558th. They're a hundred miles from here, in Kanchanaburi. Go yourself if you want, but leave me out of it."

Mike started to get up, but Frank pulled him back into the chair. "If you don't go with me, Mike," he said, a determined look on his face, "my report to Neil on the status of your unit's records may not reflect favorably upon you."

"You wouldn't do that, Frank!"

"I would," Frank said, the hint of a smile tempering his grim expression.

CHAPTER 24

Kanchanaburi

APRIL 8, 1970

THE NEXT MORNING, THEY DROVE WEST FROM Bangkok on the winding highway the Japanese had followed in their conquest of Siam during the Second World War. The 558th Supply and Service Company was stationed on the River Kwai, not far from where British prisoners built the bridge made famous by Columbia Pictures.

"They're here to support the Thai Black Panther Division," Mike explained. "It's getting ready to go to Vietnam. With the Thais joining the Koreans and the Anzacs, the war will look more like a global effort. And the president's apparently willing to pay whatever it takes to make that happen."

The war was a quagmire from which America was unable to extricate itself. It'd been five years since the first American ground forces landed in Da Nang, and hundreds of thousands of soldiers and marines were still in Vietnam, sinking deeper into the muck. Americans at home had been lied to so often about the war they no longer believed their government's optimistic pronouncements. They scoffed when Secretary of State Hall told Congress there was "light at the end of the tunnel."

The phrase became the subject of endless derision in the press, a handy reference to the growing gap between what the government said and the deteriorating situation in Vietnam.

The last president was forced from office for widening the war in the misguided hope it could be won, and the current president was upping the ante in the hope the North Vietnamese would settle. If he could talk other countries into sending troops to help with the fight, maybe the North Vietnamese would realize they had nowhere to go but the conference table, that they were up against the entire non-Communist world. And why not let foreign soldiers do some of the dying instead of young American boys?

Rice paddies stretched endlessly on both sides of the road. Oxen prodded by wizened peasants with bent backs plodded through the slush. Green mountains loomed in the distance, shadowed by dark, ominous clouds, pregnant with the afternoon's downpour.

"So, what's an American quartermaster company doing with the Black Panther Division?" Frank asked. He recalled reports of the division being readied for Vietnam but hadn't realized the extent of American involvement.

"Well, the deal is if we train and equip a first-class division, the Thais will send it to Vietnam. When it returns, they think it'll be seasoned enough to repulse whatever Communist hordes are threatening their own borders. The Special Forces are doing the training."

"And the 558th?"

"They're doing the equipping. In fact, the weapons and other stuff are coming from our depot. They started requisitioning in grand style a couple months ago. Huge amounts of stuff. No time for the paperwork to show up from Washington, but Colonel Neil gave the go-ahead."

The rice paddies terminated at the outskirts of Kanchanaburi, a busy commercial hub on the river. They drove slowly into the center of town, followed by curious stares of shoppers crowding the street. The town was barren of the raucous nightclubs and steamy massage parlors that usually marked the presence of American troops.

"The Special Forces and the 558th must keep to themselves," Frank remarked. "From the looks we're getting, I'd guess these people don't see many Americans."

They parked the jeep and inquired about the 558th with a combination of gestures and broken English at a restaurant on the main street. The waitress shrugged and pointed to a guard shack at the bridge that crossed the river. They walked over, trailed by an entourage of excited children.

"Where are the Americans?" Frank asked the Thai soldier manning the post.

"No Americans here," the soldier replied brusquely, waving them off. "All in Bangkok."

"No," Frank said with a shake of his head. "American soldiers training, uh, working with Thai army. Black Panther Division."

The soldier shook his head. "No Americans here." He abruptly turned his back and resumed his surveillance of the midday traffic, terminating the conversation.

Could Mike be wrong? Frank wondered. Was there really a Black Panther Division getting ready for Vietnam? Maybe it hadn't been formed yet. Or maybe it was fictitious, a false story planted by the administration to fabricate broader participation in the war. But even if the Thai division didn't exist, the 558th certainly did—he had seen the vehicles himself.

The jeep was surrounded by a bevy of curious children when they returned, but nothing had been disturbed. The spare tire was still attached—Mike had chained it to the frame. Frank felt a tug on his sleeve and looked down at a wide-eyed boy about ten years old dressed in scruffy clothes.

"GI, you have money?" the boy asked. "You give me money?"

That's more like it, Frank thought irritably. At least someone has seen an American before. To the street urchins, American soldiers were a source of sustenance, and they could be insistent.

"No money," Frank replied, pulling free of the boy's grip.

"You look for GIs? Maybe I tell you. You give me money."

"Hey, get lost, would you? We don't need your help."

"I know where GIs are. I tell you. You give me money."

"The soldier at the bridge said there aren't any GIs here. And I can see that for myself. So leave me alone, okay?"

"GIs here," the boy persisted. "I tell you."

"Okay, where are they?" Frank relented. Maybe it would be easier to get rid of the kid if he let him have his say. He handed the boy a ten-baht coin. The boy looked at the coin with an exaggerated expression of disappointment, then stuffed it into his pocket and held out his hand for more.

"Where are you from?" Frank asked, his curiosity

piqued. The boy spoke better English than one would expect in a backwater town, and he was obviously accustomed to shaking down American soldiers. "You're not from around here, are you?

"Bangkok," the boy replied proudly, pushing out his chest. "I from Bangkok."

Frank handed him another coin. "Okay, now tell me about GIs."

The boy pointed up the road that followed the river. "You go that way. GIs up there."

"How far?"

"Maybe little way."

"How many are there?"

The boy shook his head. "Don't know. Never see GIs."

"Well, if you've never seen them, how do you know they're there?"

"GIs there," the boy insisted, pointing up the river.

Frank turned to Mike, who had been enjoying the charade. "Well, Mike, what do you say? Shall we go find out for ourselves?"

"Well, we've come this far, may as well finish the job. I'm not coming out here again, that's for sure."

A half hour later they stood on a rise overlooking a military encampment beside the river. A few Thai soldiers sat listlessly among neat rows of tents. Frank retrieved a pair of binoculars from the jeep and studied the camp.

"Well, I don't see anything out of the ordinary. A fairly small unit. A Thai flag flying at the gate. No Americans. Hey, wait . . ."

He tightened his grip on the binoculars and adjusted the focus.

"Over there, Mike," he said, pointing to the far end of the camp. "By those vehicles. There's some Americans, I think. One, two, I see three Caucasians. Working on a truck. It looks like a motor pool."

"American trucks?" Mike asked.

"Can't tell. They're military trucks, American-made, but that doesn't mean anything. We've given a lot of stuff to the Thai army over the years." He focused on the vehicles. "Can't make out a unit designation. Hey, wait a minute, see that five-ton at the far end of the motor pool? There's an American star on the hood."

Mike took the binoculars and scanned the motor pool, then shifted his attention to a flurry of activity near the main gate. Four Thai soldiers were piling into a jeep.

"I don't like the smell of this," he said, watching the soldiers. "They're in a mighty big hurry for some reason—and maybe it's us. What say we make tracks?"

"I think you're right. Nothing else to see here anyway."

They climbed into the jeep and turned back toward the town.

"Strange," Mike said as they drove down the road. "If that's the Black Panther Division, it sure doesn't amount to much. And three Americans are hardly enough to call a company."

"Let's talk to that kid again," Frank suggested. "Maybe he knows more than he told us."

They found the boy sitting in the dirt near the spot where they had left him, munching on a plate of pork and rice. The coins had been quickly spent. The boy stood and looked at them expectantly as they approached.

"Okay? You give me more baht?"

"Yeah, maybe," Frank said, clinking some coins together in his pocket. "But first, maybe you tell us more. How many Americans are up there?"

"Don't know," he answered. "No see GIs."

"Don't they come into town?"

The boy shook his head. "At night, GIs drive through. No stop. No come during day."

"They just drive through at night?"

The boy nodded. "After dark. Many trucks. Very many."

"Where do they go?"

"That way," he said, pointing toward Bangkok. "Come back sometimes long time and go back up river."

Frank and Mike exchanged puzzled looks.

"How come nobody else told us about them?"

The boy looked around nervously. "Monks say they are spirits. Not to look at them. Not to see them."

"Spirits, huh? Well, how come you're not afraid of them?"

The boy straightened to his full height, the top of his head barely reaching Frank's chest. "Me from Bangkok. I know they GIs, not spirits. Monks try to fool us."

Frank reached into his pocket and pulled out two bills. "Here, kid. Buy an ice cream or something."

Frank looked up as a jeepload of Thai soldiers careened into the town from the direction of the river. "They the ones we saw back at the camp?"

"Don't know," Mike replied. "But whoever they are, they're in a mighty hurry."

The jeep screeched to a stop two blocks up the street, and the soldiers spread out among the restaurants and shops. One of them spotted Frank and Mike and let out a shout.

"I think we better get out of here," Mike said. "They don't appear to be too friendly."

They jumped into the jeep and headed out of the town. Keeping one eye on the rearview mirror, Reidy worked his way through the pedestrians and vehicles that clogged the road. The Thai soldiers climbed into their jeep and trailed after them, a hundred yards back, having as much trouble as they were threading through the traffic.

"They must be the same guys," Frank said. "I don't know what their problem is, but I guess we'd better not stick around to find out." He unhooked the canvas top and wrestled it into a niche behind the rear seat to get a better look.

"No question," Mike agreed. "If we pissed them off, let them write a letter."

"That camp must be some big secret or something," Frank said. "Doesn't make sense though. There doesn't seem to be much going on there. Maybe that's the secret— the Black Panthers and the Americans aren't there, and we're not supposed to know that."

The traffic thinned near the edge of town. Reidy turned onto the two-lane asphalt road that led to Bangkok and picked up speed. The Thais pulled out a quarter mile behind them. Reidy pressed his foot to the gas to maintain the lead.

"You know, Mike," Frank said, turning to study the jeep, "I think there's an American in the back seat."

"Yeah, I see him," Mike said, looking in the rearview

mirror. "He's got a cap pulled low over his head, but he's pretty big for a Thai."

"We going to be able to lose 'em?"

"I hope so."

Suddenly the windshield exploded, immediately followed by the unmistakable crack of a gunshot.

"Jesus Christ Almighty," Mike screamed. "They're shooting at us!"

Frank was just as shaken. Brushing bits of shattered glass from his fatigues, he crouched lower in the seat and looked back at the jeep chasing them. "And they're gaining on us, Mike. Can you make this thing go any faster?"

"Frank, what's going on?" Mike shouted, pressing the gas pedal to the floor, the engine whining in protest. "Maybe it was just a warning shot. Maybe we should pull over. If they mean to kill us, we're sitting ducks on this road."

Kanchanaburi was far behind them now, the road bordered by empty fields and rice paddies. There was nowhere to turn off, nowhere to hide.

"We're not pulling over." Another round whistled over their heads. "If they're shooting at us now, they're not likely to stop if we pull over."

"Well, what do we do?" Mike was panicked.

"You still have that .45 in back?"

"Are you crazy?" Mike looked at Frank in disbelief. "If we shoot back, we'll really be in for it."

Frank ignored Mike's protests and climbed awkwardly into the back seat, retrieving the .45 from the bottom of the tool compartment. He didn't see how returning fire could make matters worse; with the next round they could be dead anyway. He found himself methodically working the problem—maybe some of that army training had taken root after all.

Mike reached back with one hand and grabbed Frank's sleeve. "Frank, don't do it," he begged. "This is crazy. It's suicide."

The jeep started to drift off the road. Mike jerked his arm back and gripped the wheel with both hands.

Frank turned his attention to the jeep closing in on them. Mike didn't have much to worry about, he knew. There was little chance he would hit the jeep. The only time he'd fired a .45 was in ROTC summer camp, and he'd missed the stationary target fifteen yards away. Not just the black circle in the middle—the entire target. But maybe he could scare them off, or at least slow them down.

Settling as comfortably as he could in the back seat, Frank twisted around and rested an arm on the folded canvas top, propping the pistol on his wrist. He was surprised by how calm he felt. Admin officers weren't supposed to be cut out for this sort of thing. A couple months ago he was a pudgy college kid with horn-rimmed glasses who could barely run a lap. Now he was in a firefight and felt right at home.

He sighted down the barrel and squeezed the trigger. The concussion whipped his arm back. There was no effect on the jeep behind them.

He could see the American clearly now, his cap pulled off and blond hair blowing in the wind. He was shouting encouragement to a Thai soldier who was sighting down the barrel of an M1 carbine balanced on the windscreen.

Frank stared back at the soldier along the barrel of his .45. He squeezed the trigger a second time and watched as the round lifted off the top of the driver's head, blood and brains spewing like a volcano over the American sitting in back. The jeep left the highway in a slow spin, lazily twisting through the air and exploding in a sheet of flames, throwing bodies haphazardly into the rice paddy beside the road.

CHAPTER 25
Bangkok
APRIL 8, 1970

WHEN FRANK RETURNED TO THE HOTEL A MESsage from Lieutenant Sexton was waiting. Frank assumed the MP had been alerted to the shooting on the highway. Frank was still shaken by the encounter but decided to face the inevitable questioning sooner rather than later. He sat on the edge of the bed and forced his finger to dial the lieutenant's number.

"I did some more checking on Joanna Tsai," Sexton said, "and I got them to do an autopsy after all. Thought you'd be interested in the report."

Frank breathed a sigh of relief. Sexton either didn't know about the shooting or didn't know he was involved. He fought the urge to blurt out what had happened.

"What's it say, Lieutenant?" He bit his lower lip to maintain control, focusing on a mental image of a smiling Joanna sitting at their kitchen table in San Francisco.

"Well, for one thing, she didn't drown. She was dead before she hit the water."

The comforting image of Joanna dissolved into a kaleidoscope of recent events—the visit to the morgue, Joanna's battered body lying on the cold slab beneath a white sheet, a jeep careening off the road and exploding in a spray of hot metal and broken bodies. He sensed he was at a turning point, that nothing would ever be the same. You don't see the corpse of a woman you loved—yes, he admitted it—and kill a jeepload of soldiers and easily get over it. And now that he knew Joanna was murdered, he didn't want to get over it—he wanted to find out who did it, and why. He was grief-stricken and angry, but he was also at ease with his new mission. Vengeance: his new North Star.

"And there's more," continued Sexton, oblivious to Frank's inner turmoil. "Somebody went to considerable lengths to make it look like she drowned. Forced water into her lungs, alcohol into her stomach. They didn't want an investigation. They tried hard to make it look like an accident."

Frank shifted his focus to Joanna's luggage, still stacked by the door, and tried to concentrate on what Sexton was saying.

"Look, Lieutenant Schaniel," continued the MP, "I know this is tough on you, but it all seems a bit strange. You have any more ideas about what could have happened to her?"

"No, none, Lieutenant," Frank replied. "What about the ship?"

"Well, nothing there. It left yesterday, supposedly for Macao. The manifest was scrap iron. Nothing significant."

"Thanks, Lieutenant." Frank was still struggling to keep his emotions in check, and he needed time to think things through. "I appreciate what you've done, and I appreciate your letting me know."

"Sure thing," Sexton said. "It doesn't look like we'll be able to find out anything more, but I'll keep you posted."

Frank walked to the window and looked out at the

manicured lawns of the palace gardens flanked by neat rows of tropical flowers. It reminded him of Golden Gate Park, and his thoughts drifted to the day he visited the park with Joanna and Ming Chu, shortly before Ming and Mike Reidy left for Southeast Asia. They walked arm in arm along the path that wound through the panhandle, the trees winter bare, the grass worn and tired. Twigs and a blanket of dry leaves crackled underfoot. A rock band played loud music from the back of a flatbed truck. Hundreds of hippies swarmed around the makeshift bandstand, dancing and clapping their hands to the beat. Joanna was crying.

"Joanna, don't sweat it," Frank said. "It's no big deal. Honest. We'll be back before you know it."

"I know," she sobbed, wiping tears from her cheek. "I know I shouldn't worry, but I can't help it."

"What's really bothering you is there are lots of beautiful women over there whose mission in life is to snag an American," Frank said, trying to get a smile out of her. "Well, let me reassure you—Ming doesn't intend to fool around."

Joanna and Ming laughed. "What about you, Frank?" Joanna asked. "You fool around? Find a pretty Asian girl? Huh? You bring back Thai wife?"

"Well, you never know, Joanna. Better keep those cards and letters coming. Plenty of chocolate chip cookies, too."

Joanna turned serious. "Frank, you be okay, I know. I mean, there's no war in Thailand, right? But Ming will be in Vietnam. That's different."

She looked sadly at their diminutive companion and squeezed his arm tightly to her side.

"I'll be better off than Frank, actually," Ming said. "Saigon. Comfortable hotel. Clean sheets. Hot and cold running water. It's still one of the more continental cities in Southeast Asia, war or no war. Heavy French influence on the architecture, cuisine, everything. You better feel sorry for Frank, not me."

Ming was another young man who would never have joined the military if it wasn't for the draft, but unlike Frank, he resolved to make the most of a bad situation. He went on active duty after law school and studied Vietnamese at the Defense Language Institute in Texas. Rapid promotions rewarded demanding assignments, and he quickly shot to the top echelons of the Intelligence Corps, promoted to major before his twenty-sixth birthday.

"Well, you write me too, Ming," insisted Joanna. "You write me when you get there. You tell me that true, then I believe you."

The scene faded into the palace gardens, but the memory left Frank oddly disturbed, as if there was something more he should remember, something connected to Joanna's death. Joanna had a premonition that something bad would happen, but there was more to it than that, something he couldn't quite put his finger on. His mind was too muddled from the events of the last two days to sort it out. He determined to give it more attention later, when he was rested and his mind was clear—but it stayed in the back of his mind, unexamined, until it was too late.

CHAPTER 26
Washington, D.C.
APRIL 9, 1970

THE NEWS OF JOANNA TSAI'S DEATH REACHED John Lynch early on a dreary Washington morning as he thumbed through the overnight reports in preparation for his daily briefing of the president. He was interrupted by a messenger who handed him a terse note from the CIA director: "Package delivered. Courier terminated by parties unknown."

What now? he wondered. He stared gloomily into the small fire crackling on the hearth, seized by a sense of foreboding. Such a crappy little operation—he knew it would be trouble. The little ones always were. How the fuck did he get talked into this one?

He didn't know Joanna Tsai. He'd met her only once, when she picked up the envelope. She was just another spy who died in the line of duty. Her death was regrettable, but it was one of the risks of her line of work. What bothered him was that the CIA didn't know why she died or who was responsible. He wondered if he should be worried, if there were people out there who knew about their Cambodia plans and might try to interfere.

Should he tell the president? Tsai's death was insignificant compared to the weighty matters on the president's desk, and he probably wouldn't remember authorizing the operation anyway. And didn't he say he didn't want to be bothered with the particulars? No, he wouldn't tell him. There was nothing the president could do about it; it would only serve to upset him for no good reason. Lynch would keep it to himself for the time being. He'd keep it in the box where the president and the CIA director had put him.

CHAPTER 27

Bangkok

APRIL 10, 1970

CAMBODIA WAS ON THE FENCE. IT COULD GO either way, and Bob MacNamara was having a difficult time tracking the ebb and flow, the many moving parts. Lon Nol's coup was a *fait accompli*, yet he still hadn't been able to consolidate power. He appeared to have gained the backing of the military, but would that be enough? Many government officials were still loyal to Prince Sihanouk and his mother, Queen Kossomak, and he had the Chinese on his side. He continued to take potshots at Lon Nol from Peking, reminding the world that the coup was "absolutely illegal."

At first, the Cambodian people reacted with equanimity to the evolving situation, one government no more likely to affect their lives than another. Then Sihanouk announced the formation of a "national liberation army" to free Cambodia from the grip of the "new dictator" and the "American imperialists" who were shoring him up, and Sihanouk's partisans took to the streets to demonstrate their support. Now the citizens were getting jittery, and Lon Nol's grip on the country seemed increasingly tenuous.

Through it all ran the thread of American involvement. The United States was quick to recognize Lon Nol's

new government, conveniently ignoring the fact that Sihanouk had been democratically elected. American policy
was to support democracies throughout the world, but
MacNamara knew American policy could be quickly
discarded when it conflicted with short-term interests.
There were already indications of increasing cooperation between Lon Nol's troops and American-supported
ARVN forces operating along the Vietnamese border.

So how to put it all together? Tentatively placing his
fingers on the typewriter keys, he tried to ignore the mental clock ticking in his head. Maybe it didn't matter what
he wrote. Chuck Fox and that Eileen McClellan would
cut it to tatters anyway. He wrote thoughtful, informa-
tive articles, and they sliced and diced them into pieces
simple enough for the readers of the *Herald* to digest. Fox
left him with a byline but no longer treated his reports as
"exclusive." He'd soured on MacNamara's ability to dig
up fresh information.

Dateline: Bangkok, Thailand
April 9, 1970
By Robert A. MacNamara

While off in Moscow and Peking, looking for help
to get North Vietnamese troops out of his country without a military showdown, Prince Norodom
Sihanouk found himself thrown out of power. His
successor, Lt. Gen. Lon Nol, assumed the prince's
goals of neutrality and independence. He suspended
civil rights, obtained an expression of recognition
from the United States, and lent a willing hand to
eager South Vietnamese troops who want to fire

artillery into the ranks of the North Vietnamese and Viet Cong in Cambodia.

Prince Sihanouk is still not discounted as a force in Cambodian politics, but none of the Americans closest to the situation share Nebraska Sen. George Hinman's view that Sihanouk's downfall is a terrible disaster. There is fear that the coup might provoke Hanoi into further encroachments into Cambodian territory, but there is also hope that with a more determined anti-Communist regime in Phnom Penh, the ground forces of Cambodia and South Vietnam, supported by American air power, could effectively deprive Hanoi of its Cambodian sanctuary.

The new government's willingness to cooperate with South Vietnamese troops was recently demonstrated in the area known as Parrot's Beak, which juts into South Vietnam. Cambodian troops tried to drive a Viet Cong battalion back across the border into South Vietnam and called in South Vietnamese artillery fire to help. American officials said it was the first time Cambodian and South Vietnamese forces worked openly together against the Viet Cong.

At the same time, other events in the country demonstrated continuing support for Prince Sihanouk. In a town 70 miles north of Phnom Penh, his supporters staged a mass demonstration during which two members of the National Assembly were knifed to death. These actions and the earlier closing of the North Vietnamese and Viet Cong Embassies left no doubt that the North

Vietnamese and the Viet Cong are not prepared to accept the change in Cambodia's leadership without a struggle.

Because of the enduring support for Prince Sihanouk and the intransigence of North Vietnam and the Viet Cong, General Lon Nol appears unable to consolidate power. His ability to retain control of the country without the active intervention of the United States is an open question.

MacNamara read the last paragraph with a jaundiced eye. He had speculated about American involvement so much that his editor wondered if it was anything more than the musings of a reporter with nothing else to write. He had to admit it was mostly conjecture. He kept expecting to come up with corroboration, but nothing seemed to develop. Still, he knew it was true; he could feel it in his bones. He would just have to keep digging until he could prove it.

CHAPTER 28
Korat
APRIL 11, 1970

COLONEL NEIL ACCEPTED FRANK'S REPORT WITH little interest. Frank glossed over his visit to Reidy's unit. It should have been obvious the inspection was superficial, but the colonel didn't seem to notice.

"Thanks, Lieutenant," Neil said with a curt but cordial dismissal. "Good job."

Frank was more uneasy than relieved. He had expected the colonel to bring up his visit to the *Columbia Eagle*. Surely Neil would have recognized him from the description the crewmen would have been given him. Frank was resigned to a confrontation—would have welcomed it, prepared to demand an explanation for Joanna's death. But the colonel didn't broach the subject, and Frank was suddenly reluctant to bring it up himself. The time wasn't right. He was still unsettled by the memory of Joanna's lifeless body in the morgue and the shooting on the highway. He wasn't sure how much Neil knew, and he wanted to do some more investigating before precipitating a confrontation the colonel seemed willing to postpone.

That evening, Frank quietly let himself into the headquarters building, feeling like a trespasser in his own office. He pulled Neil's personnel file from the filing cabinet and quickly thumbed through the pages. Michael Ira Neil.

Oxford. Lawyer. Training commands. Staff positions. Advanced schooling, even taught at West Point. Combat assignment in Vietnam. It was a typical army career, nothing out of the ordinary except for his educational accomplishments. Perhaps faster-than-usual advancement—he was a Rhodes Scholar, after all—and no blemishes.

Broderick's file was no more revealing. His career paralleled the early years of Neil's. He was currently assigned as a liaison officer with the 558th Supply and Service Company, although the file didn't indicate with whom he was supposed to be liaising.

Frank was about to close Broderick's file when an entry caught his eye. Broderick had been assigned to the 558th on the same day Neil became commanding officer of the 501st, and, he discovered as he rapidly compared entries, there was no record of either officer's previous assignment. No mention of a duty station, only an innocuous notation, "Langley," in each file. Other than that, a big fat blank.

Frank's pulse quickened when he noted another peculiar entry. Both officers held top secret/crypto security clearances, the highest security classification in the military. It was unusual for officers assigned to supply activities to hold such a clearance; in fact, it was unusual for officers anywhere to hold such a clearance.

The only "Langley" he knew was the CIA headquarters in Virginia, but that didn't make sense. Army officers, especially those assigned to quartermaster duties, wouldn't normally have anything to do with the CIA. The Army and the CIA would step on each other's toes before they would cooperate, case in point being the early years in Vietnam when they tripped over each other's operations. In one instance the CIA recruited an entire village to spy on North Vietnamese troops in the area, only for the Army to come in on a search-and-destroy mission and burn the village to the ground.

With no love lost between the Army and the CIA, it was improbable that Neil and Broderick would be connected to the CIA, and if they were, they would want to keep it secret. The notation "Langley" was a dead giveaway. No, it had to be something else, a code for a secret operation or assignment. More intriguing was that Neil and Broderick were in it together, and now they were in Thailand together.

A footstep outside interrupted Frank's thoughts, and he quickly replaced the folders and concealed himself behind a desk. He held his breath as Neil entered the office and walked to the cabinet where Frank had been standing. The colonel rummaged through the drawers, then departed with a thin stack of files under his arm.

Frank waited to be sure the colonel was gone, then looked through the file cabinet to see what had been taken. Neil's file was still there, but Broderick's was missing— and so was his. He looked grimly at the door through which the colonel had disappeared and wondered what Neil would be up to next, how Neil would screw him over, for surely that was what he intended to do.

Later that night in the officers' club, Colonel Neil was uncharacteristically gregarious. He bought a round of drinks for Frank and the other officers who lined the bar and regaled them with stories of his service in Vietnam. He'd been a battalion commander with the Big Red One in operations in the Ah Shah Valley. To him it was a great adventure on the path to glory and promotion. Frank suspected the colonel's troops saw it differently, resentful they had to risk their lives to further the colonel's career.

"I can't wait to get back," Neil said. "The war's going to be over before long, mark my words, and I want another piece of the action before it's too late." He looked at the men standing at the bar with ill-disguised contempt. "That's where any self-respecting officer should be. This quartermaster stuff is bullshit."

Embarrassed, the officers looked away or found something to study in their drinks. Neil realized he'd gone too far. "Of course, you fellas are performing an important and necessary job here," he added. "You can be proud of supporting the left flank, the Air Force and all that. And I'm proud to be here, really, proud to be a part of it."

Frank nursed his beer, reflecting on Neil's remarks. Were they directed at him? To remind him that he was just a desk jockey, that he'd better keep his fingers out of the real military stuff? Or was he reading too much into it, his thoughts warped by suspicions fueled by conjecture and innuendo? Maybe Neil was no more than the retreaded infantry officer he appeared to be, his remarks the lament of an aging soldier worried his career would be over before he was promoted to general. But then he remembered Neil walking down the gangplank of the *Columbia Eagle* with Joanna's envelope tucked under his arm. There had to be more to Neil than met the eye.

Frank slept fitfully on the wooden floor of his hooch, his .45 at his side, worried that Neil might come after him during the night. What happened, he wondered, to the young lieutenant who arrived in Thailand two months earlier, looking forward to a carefree year among the pagodas and temples and beautiful women of the enchanting Orient. Joanna was murdered, that's what happened. He felt her absence like a knife in his gut, a pain that wouldn't go away.

He wondered how Laurel was faring and felt a nagging guilt that he had abandoned her to spend time with Joanna. He hadn't seen her since he left for Bangkok. Was she anxious about his absence, concerned that he had not returned? Probably not, he decided. It seemed like an eternity, but it had been only a few days. And, truthfully, he doubted she missed him. She accommodated his needs—she gave him his money's worth—but deep down he knew she was only going through the motions. It was a business arrangement, and she held up her end of the bargain. If he wasn't at the bungalow looking for sex, what did she care? It was paid time off.

The cool, damp air penetrated the thin slats of the floor, and he rolled onto his side and pulled the blanket up to his chin. The night was dark and still, except for crickets chirping in the bushes. The bunk looked more and more inviting from his makeshift bed on the floor.

Neil was right—he would never have cut it as a combat soldier. He remembered gleefully announcing to his brother Joe that he had orders to Thailand. Let others suffer the rigors of Vietnam; for him, it would be the uneventful safety of a supply depot in the backwaters of the war. He wondered what Joe would think if he could see him now, huddled fearfully on the floor of his hooch, envious of the soldiers in Vietnam who at least knew who their enemy was.

The squeak of rusty hinges on the screen door interrupted his thoughts. Two shadowy figures slipped into the tent and tiptoed to the bunk. One held a pistol. He heard their muffled exclamations when they found only a bundle of clothing nestled in the bed.

Frank raised himself on one elbow and aimed his .45 where he judged the knee of the nearest intruder to be. He hoped he wasn't overreacting, but it *was* the middle of the night, and one of them *did* have a gun. He recalled from his limited military training that the best defense was a good offense, and the only offense he had was the gun in his hand.

The blast of the .45 produced a cry of pain, and the two assailants scrambled out the door.

"Rats," explained Frank to the bleary-eyed officers who stumbled over to investigate. "I thought I got one, but I guess not." They seemed satisfied that Frank was participating in a favorite local sport—exterminating rodents—but groused that he was doing it later than protocol allowed.

Frank followed the officers out of the hooch, pausing only to stuff an extra clip of bullets into his pocket, and walked quickly to the headquarters building. He let himself in and flipped on the lights, this time making no effort to conceal his movements. So what if Neil found him in the office? He'd just as soon deal with him now as let the authorities do it later. Neil was responsible for Joanna's murder—the two intruders in his hooch confirmed his suspicions.

He broke the latch to Neil's office and walked directly to the safe. He'd committed the combination to memory his first week on the job when he surreptitiously watched over Neil's shoulder as he opened it. Joanna's envelope was inside, one end neatly slit open. He slipped a packet of documents from the envelope and, without pausing to study them, made copies on the Xerox machine in the corner. He returned the papers to the safe and stuffed the copies into his shirt. It was deathly quiet as he stepped out of Neil's office and, suddenly more cautious, re-fastened the latch to conceal his entry.

Frank signed a jeep out of the motor pool after wasting several agonizing minutes trying to convince the motor pool sergeant that he was authorized to do so. Exasperated, he lost his temper. "Sergeant Stout, I'm not taking any more crap from you. Now give me the goddamn keys. If you want to turn me into Colonel Neil like last time— you fucking ratfink—fine by me."

Sergeant Stout stared at him, shocked into silence. Second lieutenants didn't address senior NCOs like that.

"I mean it, Charles. Give me the jeep. I don't have time to fuck with you anymore."

Sergeant Stout handed over the keys without another word, and Frank took off at a fast clip, not taking the time to pull up the canvas roof. He drove along the inside perimeter of the post with the headlights dimmed, avoiding areas where troops were billeted. He bullied his way past the military policeman at the gate and drove into Korat, following a circuitous route to the bungalow he shared with Laurel.

Parking two blocks away, he watched from the shadows until he was sure he had not been followed. The city was asleep. A dog nosed through a pile of garbage spilled in the street. A single streetlamp dimly lit a nearby intersection; otherwise, the street was dark and quiet.

Frank carefully worked his way toward the bungalow, hugging the storefronts to keep from being seen. Slipping around a corner, he stopped short at the sight of a jeep parked in front of the bungalow, an American soldier armed with an M16 standing next to it. Frank crouched in a doorway and watched helplessly as two soldiers dragged Laurel from the bungalow and roughly wrestled her into the back of the jeep. The sentry climbed in beside her, and they sped off, the street silent again except for the echo of Laurel's terrified whimpers.

Frank heard a footstep behind him. Tensing, he turned to stare into the muzzle of an M16 inches from his face held by a beefy soldier with a 558th patch on his sleeve. The soldier gestured for Frank to stand up, but instead Frank drove his shoulder into the man's abdomen, pushing him into the wall and knocking the breath from his lungs. He ripped the rifle from the soldier's grip and smashed the butt against the side of his head. He raised the weapon to strike again, but the soldier slipped to the ground, unconscious. Frank dropped the rifle and sprinted back to his jeep.

He needed help. He couldn't fight this thing alone. He didn't even know what he was fighting, what he was caught up in. He thought of Ming Chu. Maybe Ming could help. Ming would be as upset as he was about Joanna's death, and Ming was high up in army headquarters in Saigon. Saigon was far removed from Thailand, but where else could he turn? Ming was smart, he worked in intelligence, he had contacts—maybe Ming could figure out what was going on.

CHAPTER 29

Saigon

APRIL 12, 1970

LATE THE NEXT MORNING FRANK STRAPPED HIM-
self into a seat on a Boeing 707 chartered from Westover
Airlines by the Military Airlift Command, manifested
from Bangkok to San Francisco with a stop in Saigon. His
uniform was in disarray, caked with mud and stiff with
dried sweat, and his thoughts were still muddled from the
night's dizzying events.

After witnessing Laurel's abduction and knocking his
assailant unconscious, he sped through the night down
the winding highway to Bangkok, heavy showers obscur-
ing the roadway and soaking his clothing. Wind struggled
to wrest the wheel from his grip and drove tears of fear
and anguish from his eyes. At dawn, exhausted, he had
pounded on Reidy's door.

Frank filled him in as best he could. Mike was
unsettled by Frank's tale, but far from convinced that it
amounted to all that Frank made of it. Still, he allowed
himself to be talked into securing a seat for Frank on the
flight to San Francisco. Frank convinced him that, orders
or no orders, he had to get out of the country.

"Frank, you prick, you know I can get you on the
plane," Mike said. "I'm a supply guy, and I'm owed a
lot of favors in this town. But I'm still going out on a

goddamn limb. You'd better make sure this doesn't come back on me."

"No sweat," Frank said with false assurance. He didn't know if he could keep Mike out of trouble, but he was determined to get on that flight no matter the consequences. "It'll work out. You'll see. I'll cable you from San Francisco."

But when the flight left Saigon after a short refueling stop, Frank was no longer on board.

MAJOR MING CHU DROVE FRANK INTO SAIGON from Ton Son Nhut Air Base. The boulevard was clogged with traffic and lined with decrepit mansions and apartment buildings barricaded behind sandbagged emplacements and barbed wire. Ming pointed out the presidential palace where President Thieu met with his advisors. He was probably there now, wringing his hands over the disappointing progress of the war and scheming how to wrest more equipment and supplies—and money—from the Americans.

They pulled up to the Continental Hotel, a majestic but tired edifice with a two-story colonnaded façade that beckoned them into the cool, dark interior, a respite from the hubbub of the busy city streets. The hotel was built in the 1880s by a wealthy French plantation owner and was now managed by an Italian, Vincenzo Bartolotta, whose father bought the hotel in 1930. Located in the heart of the city across from the National Assembly, it had long been the home of foreign correspondents in Saigon. During the Second World War, the weekly magazine *Time* set up shop on the first floor, *Newsweek* on the second. Now, during the Vietnam War, it was the hangout of television and newspaper reporters from the States, a safe haven from which to cover the war without having to go out and see it.

The terrace bar overlooking the garden remained a center of intrigue, where reporters met each afternoon to share rumors and gossip and to joke about the banal pronouncements of the military spokesmen. That very day the press officer described the ambush of a "search and destroy" patrol in the Central Highlands—fourteen Americans were killed—as a successful effort to ferret out a Viet Cong headquarters.

After Ming left for MACV with the papers from Neil's safe, Frank showered and slipped into the clean fatigues Ming had brought for him, then repaired to the bar and ordered a cold beer. A slim man in his late thirties with long, prematurely grey hair slipped onto the barstool beside him. He was dressed in a cream-colored suit and paisley tie, a fresh carnation pinned to his lapel.

"Lieutenant Schaniel? I'm Vincenzo Bartolotta, the hotel manager. Ming asked me to look after you."

"Wow, special treatment?" Frank turned to shake the man's hand. "How do you know Ming?"

"We go way back. Renewed our friendship when he was assigned to Saigon last year."

"You knew him in the States?"

"No, but I know his 'origin' story." Bartolotta laughed. "I've heard it enough times. Born in the Klamath Valley, the youngest of eight children. His Chinese immigrant parents the first to grow potatoes in Oregon. The farm so remote he lived with a family in town to attend high school."

Frank joined in the laughter. "Yeah, we've all heard it—a number of times."

"You know, Frank, he credits you with breaking him out of his shell. He was a smart kid, no question, but growing up, he never had a chance to develop much in the way of social skills. His family was too insular and the farm too isolated for much interaction with the wider world."

"Yeah, I'm surprised we became friends, we're so different. He's a pleasant, affable guy—everybody loves him—and I'm a bit rough around the edges, I admit. Some of his friends don't understand why he bothers with me."

"Well, Ming says it worked both ways. You got him to open up, and he helped tone down your boorishness."

Frank laughed again. "That's a good way to put it, I guess."

Bartolotta got up from the bar. "Frank, I help Ming out from time to time, so if there's anything you need while you're here, let me know. We'll take care of it."

Frank looked at him curiously. "Vincenzo, for you to be in business in Saigon, you must be helpful to a lot of people."

"One has to do what one has to do," Bartolotta said with a weary smile. "Just like you're doing now."

"What do you know about that?"

"Ming clues me in from time to time. As I said, I sometimes help Ming out."

After Bartolotta left, Frank's thoughts turned to the life he'd shared with Joanna in San Francisco. They were inseparable whenever she was in town—other than the one drunken interlude with Eileen McClellan—and Ming was often in their company. They doted on him, making good-humored fun of his natural reserve, and he flourished in their attention. It was a happy time, and Frank

wished it had never ended. The fucking army. The fucking war.

Ming walked into the bar, interrupting Frank's
thoughts. His fatigues were clean and pressed, his face as
smooth and unlined as when they were students.

"Well, Lieutenant Schaniel," Ming said with mock
gravity as he sat on the barstool vacated by Bartolotta
and beckoned the waiter. "You have caused quite a stir
at MACV."

"The papers?"

"Yes, the papers. We're not sure what they are yet.
They're in code. We have some good men working on it,
but so far they haven't been able to make any sense of
them."

"What would Joanna have to do with that?"

"Well, we're not sure about that either. We'd like to
know where she got them. Do you know where she was
before coming to Bangkok?"

"No idea. We hardly had time to say hello." Frank
flashed back to a naked Joanna undulating on top of him
at the Siam Intercontinental. "But you know as well as I
do she flew all over the world."

"Well, my men are looking into it. In the meantime,
how about dinner?"

They took a taxi to Tudo Street, the favorite haunt
of American GIs off duty in Saigon. The street was lined
with dance clubs and massage parlors hung with huge
neon signs and blinking lights. Loud, raucous music
blared from the doorways. Young Vietnamese men in
Western dress tried to entice passing GIs into their estab-
lishments while others loitered on motor scooters parked
along the curb.

"Makes you wonder why our guys are doing the fighting and these guys are out having a good time," Ming said. "They may be loyal to the South Vietnamese government, may be Viet Cong sympathizers, may even be Communist agents, you never know. The government's talking about dropping the draft age from twenty-one to eighteen—that would clear them out soon enough."

Ming paid the cab driver and led Frank to a Chinese restaurant in a back alley. "I can't stand Vietnamese food," he explained, "and the grub in the mess hall is worse. This war can be tough on the stomach."

The restaurant's wine selection was limited to Mateus, a sweet Portuguese rosé, served warm and in mismatched glasses. "Well, here's to the war," Ming said, raising a repurposed jelly jar. "Enjoy it while we can."

"How about you, Ming?" Frank asked, sipping his wine. "You heard from Joanna?"

"No, not since I left San Francisco in October. I called when I passed through the city last month, but she wasn't home."

"Funny," Frank said. "She's been pretty good about keeping in touch. I would have thought she would have written to you. Actually, I thought she mentioned she saw you in San Francisco."

"She wouldn't have known how to get hold of me," Ming said. "Say, Frank, are you sure that was Joanna you saw in the morgue? The body was a bit disfigured, we understand. We talked to the MPs, and they aren't all that sure."

Frank looked up in sudden anger. "Christ, Ming, they didn't even try to be sure." Ming signaled for him to lower his voice, but Frank ignored him. "They didn't go for fingerprints or dental charts or anything. That fat-assed MP lieutenant couldn't wait to close the file. He was pissed that I insisted she was an American, like the extra paperwork would kill him or something. He only gave it a go after I pressed him."

Frank took a deep breath. "But yeah, I'm sure it was her. Reidy identified her, and she was wearing my ring. It was Joanna." He brushed aside the memory of Joanna's corpse beneath the soiled sheet in the morgue. He only wanted to remember the good times they shared in San Francisco and that last afternoon in Bangkok.

"It's okay, Frank, it's okay," Ming said, laying a comforting hand on his arm. "My staff will get to the bottom of it. Now fill me in. Tell me everything you know, so I can get them pointed in the right direction."

CHAPTER 30
Saigon
APRIL 13, 1970

THE NEXT AFTERNOON, MING ESCORTED FRANK into MACV headquarters, known as Pentagon East, the heart of the war effort in Vietnam. Surrounded by barbed wire, sandbag bunkers, and bored sentries manning .50-caliber machine guns, the compound sprawled over ten acres next to the Tan Son Nhut Air Base.

They entered a formidable concrete structure—a huge mortar-proof blockhouse—and made their way through a labyrinth of hallways to the tactical operations center, a two-story windowless enclosure dominated by a huge map of Southeast Asia. Lights flickered on the map, controlled by technicians huddled over a row of IBM computers, each the size of a refrigerator. Fluorescent lights cast an eerie, artificial pall over the room, making the technicians look like lifeless, sallow-faced extensions of the machines, the drone of computers and dull hum of air conditioning masking their voices.

Ming led Frank to a large conference room separated from the operations center by a floor-to-ceiling glass wall. A long, rectangular table surrounded by padded leather chairs filled the interior. A bank of telephones rested on a shelf on one wall, and charts and maps were propped haphazardly against another.

General Edward Dewey Chapin, commander of the American forces in Vietnam, sat by himself in a chair pulled away from one end of the table, as if the separation would insulate him from the unsavory matters to be discussed. He thumbed through a sheaf of papers on his lap, seemingly oblivious to Ming and Frank entering the room. Ming introduced the other officers at the table: Major General Terry O'Malley, Chapin's intelligence chief and Ming's superior; Colonel Bob Vaage, from operations; and Captain Jeff Diltz, from Ming's section.

"I'll get right to the point," General O'Malley said, taking charge of the meeting with the tacit acquiescence of General Chapin. "It's been a long night for our intelligence people. In the few hours since you arrived from Bangkok"—he nodded at Frank—"we've done three things."

He raised an index finger to start the count, pausing dramatically to underscore the importance of the information he was about to impart. Frank grimaced at the man's officiousness. In his short six months in the army, he'd encountered a number of career officers like O'Malley, and he hadn't taken to any of them, an insurmountable gap between the citizen-soldier and the true believer.

"First, we've deciphered those papers you brought, Lieutenant. Not that it was that difficult." He glanced at General Chapin to make sure the remark was appreciated, but Chapin didn't look up from the papers he was reading. "The code is a new one and from an unidentified source, but it was still no match for our computers."

"Second," he said, holding up another finger, "we checked out Colonel Neil. Army personnel tells us he spent last year on special assignment to the CIA. But"—he paused with two fingers waving in the air—"the CIA boys say they've never heard of him."

He's more than officious, Frank decided—he's pompous and self-important as well. An older version of Captain Broderick. Probably spells his name with one R—*Terence*—like Broderick and his U. An example of what happens when an officer of limited talent manages to reach the top echelons of the military. The Peter Principle, hard at work.

O'Malley raised a third finger. "And we checked out Joanna Tsai—she was a Chicom spy." He spat the last statement in Frank's direction, then waited for a reaction.

Blood drained from Frank's face, and beads of perspiration popped out on his upper lip. He turned to Ming for reassurance, but Ming remained expressionless, his gaze fixed on the table.

Frank knew Ming couldn't believe Joanna was a spy any more than he did, but he understood Ming's reticence to reveal his feelings, especially to these guys. O'Malley wasn't about to brook any disagreement anyway. Well, he'd follow Ming's lead. He'd keep his own counsel until he heard the rest of what the general had to say.

"A spy," repeated O'Malley. "She's been helping Neil rob us blind. They're arming the entire goddamn Cambodian army behind our backs."

Ming raised his head and looked at Frank with a pained expression. "Frank, this is as hard for me to accept as it is for you, but there's no Black Panther Division getting ready for Vietnam, and the 558th Supply and Service Company isn't working with the Thai army. Those supplies Lieutenant Reidy has been handing over, he's been handing over to the Cambodians. To General Lon Nol."

"And that was the small stuff," O'Malley interjected. "Those papers you brought confirm the *Columbia Eagle* was chock-full of small arms, not just the napalm bombs listed on her manifest. Rifles, machine guns, mortars, grenades—an entire arsenal. The Pentagon was as surprised as we were. Seems somebody has been fiddling with the requisitions for their own unauthorized purposes. Worse, there's another ship on the way."

"Our best guess," continued Ming, "is that your 558th has been trucking the material from Reidy's warehouses in Bangkok into Cambodia."

General Chapin stirred in the corner, and the others fell silent.

"There are six of us in this room," Chapin said in a low voice, his eyes still fixed on the papers he was holding. "And only six of us are to know about this. Ever." He raised his eyes and looked around the table. "All I need is for a story to break that an army officer—a colonel to boot—has gone over to the other side." His voice rose in anger. "We'll take care of this Colonel Neil, but when we're finished"—his eyes narrowed—"this whole thing is never to have happened."

Chapin stood and leaned over the table, his palms pressed flat on the surface. Frank had seen plenty of photos of the general—he was a ubiquitous presence in the newspapers and frequently on the covers of the weekly news magazines—but in person he loomed larger than life. He stood a good six foot four, and with his short, gray hair and tanned, chiseled face, he looked like he was born to lead an army, an older version of Colonel Neil.

"O'Malley, you go to Washington," Chapin ordered.

"Stop by CINCPAC in Hawaii on the way. Make sure they understand the importance—the absolute necessity—of an immediate Cambodia incursion. We've been talking about it long enough. Convince them now's the time. We need to find and destroy the North Vietnamese headquarters, and at the same time we can put the skids to Colonel Neil's little operation before his weapons end up with the Communists."

He turned to Frank. "Lieutenant, you and Major Chu get on the horn to that Lieutenant Reidy. Tell him to watch for the next ship and let us know when it shows up. Tell him that's an order directly from me. But for Christ's sake, don't tell him any more than you have to, and impress on him the importance of keeping it to himself."

Frank smiled to himself at the thought of Mike's reaction. He would not be happy about his new assignment.

"Then, Lieutenant," Chapin continued, "I want you to go back to Thailand and keep an eye on Neil. Don't let him out of your sight. When he moves to take charge of the next shipment, I want you on his ass."

He nodded at Captain Diltz, who held up a shiny metal disc for Frank's inspection. "Put this on one of Neil's vehicles," Chapin ordered. "We can track it by air. And once we have that bastard where we want him, we'll bomb the shit out of him and his traitorous soldiers."

Chapin turned to Vaage. "Colonel, prepare for an incursion into Cambodia. We've gone through the drill enough times, it should be old hat. Send Brandon Crocker's First Cav into the Parrot's Beak region. I want him ready to go in two weeks."

Finally, he nodded at Ming. "Major, I'm giving you operational control of Alpha Company of the First of the Seventh, one of Crocker's companies up at Quan Loi. After the bombers are finished with Neil, you take them in and clean up the pieces. Bring back every American body. They are to have died heroes here in Vietnam. Nobody is ever to know any different, or we—meaning the United States of America—will be in a heap of trouble."

General Chapin straightened and looked resolutely at the officers seated at the table, then turned and strode from the room.

A heap of trouble? Frank knew Chapin was a Missouri boy, but you'd think it would have been squeezed out of him by now. Anyway, the country was already in a heap of trouble with all the war protests going on—a fuckup in Cambodia wasn't likely to make much difference. But Chapin's the commanding general—he must know what he's talking about.

"Ming, I didn't want to bring it up in there," Frank said as they threaded their way out of the building. "But how am I supposed to go back to the 50lst? Neil will kill me, literally." The shock of learning that Joanna was a Communist spy was overcome by concern about what General Chapin wanted him to do.

"We've thought of that," Ming said. "As we see it, he'll know by now you're in Saigon, and he'll at least guess you visited MACV. But he'll be afraid to touch you. He'll figure we haven't had time to put the pieces together, and that once we do, there won't be enough time to stop him. He won't want anything to happen that might precipitate a quicker reaction—like bumping you off."

"Yeah, but by the same token, he may figure he can do me in because it's too late for you to intervene."

"Well, Frank," Ming said with a wry smile, "that's the risk you'll have to take."

"Thanks, pal. That gives me a lot of confidence."

CHAPTER 31
Bangkok
APRIL 17, 1970

THE SITUATION IN CAMBODIA WAS BECOMING desperate. North Vietnamese troops, in ever-increasing numbers, continued to use Cambodian territory to stage forays into South Vietnam. The Cambodian army wasn't able to cope. Lon Nol was frantic, escalating his pleas for military aid. If he didn't get help from the West, he intimated, he would have no choice but to make a deal with the Communists.

MacNamara wondered what the U.S. would do. The president would be inclined to give the Cambodians whatever they wanted, he knew, adding another ally to the fight against the Communists. But Senators Waite and Forbes introduced an amendment to the military appropriations bill prohibiting not only the deployment of American troops into Cambodia but the expenditure of funds to finance any other country's troops. The president was between a rock and a hard place.

Well, it would make interesting copy. Of course, Chuck Fox wouldn't think so. He never saw a story he didn't think he could improve. He'd probably hand it to that Eileen McClellan with instructions to delete the speculation and chop it down to a hundred words.

Dateline: Bangkok, Thailand
April 17, 1970
By Robert A. MacNamara

Two weeks ago, Secretary of State William Noel
Hall reaffirmed that the United States "had nothing
to do, directly or indirectly," with the overthrow of
Prince Norodom Sihanouk as chief of state of Cambodia, and that the administration did not expect
a request from the new government for military
aid. But following recent fighting in the border
region, new Premier Lon Nol issued an urgent
appeal for military hardware from any country
that would provide it. He reiterated that Cambodia
is determined to remain neutral, but the continued
presence of North Vietnamese and Viet Cong troops
in its border areas is considered a grave threat to
the country's security.

A Cambodian government spokesman hinted at
a shift in Cambodia's policy of opposing coordinated
military action between Cambodian and South Vietnamese troops against Communist forces along the
border. An indication of the government's renewed
interest in cooperation with South Vietnam and the
United States is the recent fighting in the Parrot's
Beak region. Cambodian troops reportedly killed
300 Viet Cong soldiers after ambushing them in a
renewed effort to push Viet Cong out of the area
and to recapture border posts.

By telephone from Phnom Penh, acting Charge
d'Affaires Richard A. Harmetz disclosed that the
United States had received a request for arms and

military supplies. He stated that the administration is examining the list submitted by Cambodia.
In Washington, Senate Majority Leader George
Hinman reacted to the news by urging the administration to reject the arms request. Sen. John
Wertz, chairman of the Senate Intelligence Committee, threatened to convene a hearing on the
issue.

The president is under pressure from Congress
and the State Department not to extend such aid
for fear of widening the war in Southeast Asia. But
his military advisers are apparently telling him
that without such aid, Cambodia will become an
undisturbed sanctuary from which North Vietnamese and Viet Cong troops can continue their forays
against South Vietnamese and American troops in
Vietnam.

MacNamara recognized that if the president granted
Lon Nol's request for military hardware it would be perfect cover for what he suspected the administration was
already up to. Once the Americans publicly supplied
weapons to the Cambodians, no one would be able to
prove they'd been doing it all along. On the other hand,
the administration was so accustomed to doing things on
the quiet, they might miss the opportunity to go legit.
Legitimacy would bring publicity, and the president
would be reluctant to incur the wrath of Congress.

CHAPTER 32
Washington, D.C.
APRIL 17, 1970

THE PRESIDENT SLUMPED IN HIS CHAIR AND stared at the cherry blossoms blooming outside the Oval Office. He rested his elbows on the arms of the chair and supported his chin with the steepled tips of his fingers. John Lynch and Sharee Fish sat across the desk from him, waiting patiently for him to make up his mind.

The president was wrestling with a difficult, politically fraught decision. Lon Nol was begging for military aid and promised to use it to support the administration's efforts in Vietnam, but Congress adamantly opposed any aid that might widen the war. Congress wanted Cambodia to remain neutral but left it to Lon Nol to look somewhere else for the weapons he would need to confront the Communist troops in his country.

The president swung his chair around and looked at Lynch and Fish. "Well, all things considered, I think we gotta help this guy," he said. "Our intelligence confirms the situation's as desperate as he describes it, right? And he could be a solid ally if we help prop him up."

"He doesn't want to be an ally," interjected Fish. "He wants to be neutral. He says he needs the arms to enforce his new 'active neutralism' policy. He wants to push all non-Cambodians out of the country."

"Yeah, but that's okay. I get it. I can appreciate the guy just wants to be left alone. And the people he would be pushing out aren't us, are they? They're NVA and Viet Cong, right?"

"That's right, Mr. President. But there's no guarantee he won't go after our troops as well."

"But we're not in Cambodia, are we? And if we were to mount an operation there, it would be temporary, just to give him a hand with the North Vietnamese. I don't see how he could object to that."

"What about Congress?" Lynch asked.

"Yeah, that's a problem," the president said wearily. "Those guys want me to end the war but don't give me the means to do it. Instead, they tie my hands. This is a perfect example. We could help Lon Nol push the Communists out of Cambodia and zap them when they step into South Vietnam. Perfect. What's wrong with that?"

Lynch snorted. "Sounds good in theory, Mr. President, but I suspect it wouldn't be quite that easy."

The president sighed. "I suppose you're right, John. If only the world were so simple."

Lynch looked at Fish. "How about your covert operations? Any help there?"

"Well, apparently not enough to satisfy Lon Nol. We delivered a convoy of materiel a week or so ago—an entire shipload of small arms—in addition to the stuff we've managed to divert over the past few months. Mostly weapons earmarked for the imaginary Black Panther Division."

Lynch turned to the president. "Lon Nol may be a greedy bastard, Mr. President, but at least he hasn't let on that he's already received American arms. That would put the nail in the coffin as far as Congress is concerned."

"Thank God for small favors," the president said wearily.

"We have another ship scheduled to arrive in Bangkok in two weeks," continued Fish. "We hadn't intended to give the cargo to Lon Nol, but I suppose we could. It won't be enough to satisfy him, but it should help."

"Well, let's do this," the president said, sitting up straight and fixing his gaze on the CIA director. "Sharee, step up your covert operations. Get Lon Nol as much as you can while still keeping it quiet. At the same time, we'll publicly give him some aid. Not enough to piss off Congress, but enough to tell the world we're willing to help, even if he's not solidly in our camp."

"Good idea, Mr. President," Fish replied, brushing an imaginary thread from her coat. "We could give Lon Nol that Soviet stuff we captured in Vietnam. There's not much, maybe a few thousand rifles, but it would be good cover for the big stuff."

Lynch nodded. "That should work. Congress could hardly complain if we're not giving him American weapons, and that'll give us an excuse to get a few planes into Phnom Penh with more than a few rifles."

The president looked at his watch, signaling the end of the meeting. "Okay, let's do it. Keep me posted."

Lynch was relieved. The secret stuff was wearing on him. Once they gave Lon Nol some weapons and told the press about it, they'd have their foot in the door to give him more, and the new shipments would swamp the stuff they'd already delivered. No one would ever be able to prove what they'd been up to behind Congress's back.

"One more thing," added the president, stopping them at the door. "What about that *San Francisco Herald* reporter? He's still sniffing around your secret operation, isn't he? Why haven't we done something about him?"

"Well, it's not so simple anymore, Mr. President," Lynch replied. "We've had some success in muzzling the press in the past, but now they have their hackles up about the war. I say we just leave him alone. He's still a country mile from figuring out what we've been up to, and who reads the *Herald* anyway?"

The president chuckled and dismissed them with a wave of his hand. "Okay, John, do what you think best. But be careful. Even a blind squirrel can sometimes find an acorn."

Lynch looked at Fish to include her in the president's warning. "We'll be careful, Mr. President," he said. "We'll make sure that reporter never puts the pieces together."

CHAPTER 33
Bangkok
APRIL 21, 1970

MACNAMARA SUSPECTED THE PRESIDENT'S OFFER of token military aid to Cambodia was nothing more than a smokescreen, a cover to sneak in more substantial stuff. But he couldn't prove it, so he would write what he had. He would continue digging, looking for connections between Washington and Lon Nol and the war in Vietnam. For now, the best he could do was drop a hint here and there and hope Chuck Fox would let him get away with it.

Dateline: Bangkok, Thailand
April 21, 1970
By Robert A. MacNamara

U.S. officials here disclosed that the administration has agreed to supply several thousand rifles to Cambodia but cautioned against "inflated expectations" of further American military aid. The decision was transmitted in a cable to U.S. Charge d'Affaires Richard A. Harmetz in Phnom Penh. Harmetz was told to inform the Cambodian government that no ammunition is available for the rifles and to suggest querying Indonesia on the possibility of supplying ammunition.

The rifles are automatic weapons of Soviet design captured from Communist forces in South Vietnam. The officials indicated that the United States does not wish to start a large aid program but feels compelled to show the new regime that it has friends.

Meanwhile, separate sources reported that three cargo planes landed at Phnom Penh airport with a shipment of American-made weapons. The U.S. Embassy in Phnom Penh denied the reports.

Officially, the United States has agreed to provide only the rifles mentioned in the cable to Harmetz. Diplomatic sources speculate that the United States does not wish to respond to Lon Nol's appeal in a more substantial way at this time, but that the shipment marks the start of an unofficial program to help the government until an official and public effort can be arranged.

The article was one of the shortest pieces he'd filed from Thailand. There was little chance Fox would put it on the front page, and there wasn't enough in it to spark the interest of the anti-war movement. He was supposed to be "objective"—the mantra of good journalism—but he couldn't help but take sides. Too many people were getting killed in Vietnam for him to look the other way.

Ceci shared his skepticism about the war. She laughed at the "domino theory"—the idea that if Vietnam fell to the Communists, Cambodia and Thailand would soon follow. "We Thais have governed ourselves for thousands of years," she said, "even when the Japanese came during the Second World War. We've had everything from monarchies to dictatorships and now a military regime—but we would never allow the Communists to take over. It's not in our national character."

"You may be right, but if Laos and Cambodia go Communist, Thailand will be hard-pressed to resist the red hordes."

"We would do whatever it takes, like what Shakespeare's King Henry said: 'Once more unto the breach, dear friends, once more; or close the wall up with our English dead.'"

He was again surprised at the breadth of her knowledge of British playwrights. How did he find the one girl in Thailand who knew as much about English literature as he did?

"That's what America does," he said. "Once we get into a war, there's no getting out, no matter how badly it goes, no matter how misguided the effort. Our boys just keep piling up on the walls."

"Why don't you Americans listen to your Martin Luther King?" She pulled a book from her bag and opened to a bookmarked page, as if she'd anticipated the discussion. "'Somehow this madness must cease. We must stop now. I speak as a child of God and brother to the suffering poor of Vietnam. I speak for those whose land is being laid waste, whose homes are being destroyed, whose culture is being subverted. I speak for the poor of America who are paying the double price of smashed hopes at home.'"

"Unfortunately, once we get involved, there's no turning back. It's in our genes. It's our national character, as you put it. 'Theirs not to reason why, theirs but to do and die.'"

"That's Tennyson," Ceci said, delighted to have recognized the poem. "'The Charge of the Light Brigade.' But that was a hundred years ago. It's the same in Vietnam now?"

"America in Vietnam is a combination of the Light Brigade and King Henry—valorous charges against a determined enemy, but leaving its dead piled in the jungles and rice paddies with no victory in sight."

MacNamara couldn't stop the war, but he could do his small part to undermine it. He resolved to redouble his efforts to get to the bottom of whatever the United States was up to in Cambodia. He owed that much to the young Americans who hadn't been able to dodge the draft as he had, many of whom would never come home.

CHAPTER 34
Korat
APRIL 21, 1970

FRANK RETURNED TO KORAT AS IF NOTHING
had happened. Colonel Neil expressed sympathy for his
father—MACV had fabricated emergency leave orders to
cover his hurried departure—but otherwise didn't question his absence. He even bought Frank a beer in the
officers' club, making small talk about Billy Casper winning the Masters Tournament.

Frank had to remind himself of Neil's treachery. It
was hard to believe he was the traitorous mastermind that
MACV made him out to be, but Frank had confidence in
MACV's assessment, and Joanna's envelope in Neil's safe
was damning corroboration. Even if Neil wasn't a traitor,
he had to be responsible for her death.

Frank kept busy the next few days with routine office
duties, desultorily working through the pile of papers that
had accumulated on his desk. He sucked in his breath
when he came across the death certificate of Sergeant
First Class Michael Anthony Clark of the 558th Supply
and Service Company, who died in a traffic accident near
Kanchanaburi. Frank figured he was one of Neil's men,
part of the plot to divert arms to the Cambodians, and
the attempt on Frank's life was meant to keep their illicit

activities secret. He was sorry the sergeant was dead, but he wasn't to blame—Neil was responsible, he was sure of it.

He penned the obligatory letter for Colonel Neil's signature expressing condolences over Sergeant Clark's death. He wrote the usual half-truths—exemplary soldier, died doing his duty—addressed to a Larry Clark, his brother and next of kin, at a post office box they shared in Langley, Virginia. Sergeant Clark left no wife, no children, no trace other than a post office box near the headquarters of the Central Intelligence Agency. Langley. Was that his connection to Colonel Neil?

Frank kept close tabs on the colonel, occasionally shadowing him to make sure he didn't slip away from the post, but Neil seemed determined to be easy prey. He conspicuously attended to his regular duties and whiled away his off hours drinking at the officers' club. All very normal.

In the evenings, after Frank was satisfied the colonel was securely ensconced at the bar, he would check out a jeep—Sergeant Stout no longer argued—and search for Laurel in the city. The bungalow was completely empty, as if she had never lived there. The furniture, bedding, and Laurel's clothing had disappeared, along with everything else she had accumulated with Frank's money. The landlady shrugged noncommittally when he questioned her about Laurel's disappearance.

"Who took the furniture?" he asked

"Men," she replied.

"What men?"

"Men," she said.

Frank knew what she was thinking. Laurel wasn't

her concern. The rent was paid. Laurel could live there or not, she didn't care. She'd collected six months' rent in advance and would keep her part of the bargain, leaving the bungalow vacant for the remainder of the term. Beyond that, she owed Laurel nothing. When she rejected the hundred-baht bill Frank offered to prod her memory, he knew she was telling the truth—she really didn't know what had become of Laurel.

The mamasan at the teahouse was no more helpful. She wouldn't even acknowledge that Laurel had worked there, feigning ignorance when Frank produced a photograph for her inspection. One of the girls remembered Frank, though, and pulled him aside. Laurel had not been to work for a couple weeks, she whispered, and had not left word as to her whereabouts.

The following Saturday Frank drove to Laurel's village, but her parents gave him the cold shoulder, staring blankly into the distance, pretending not to know who he was. When unfriendly-looking men from the village started trailing after him, he gave up and returned to Korat.

After days of fruitless searching, visiting bars and massage parlors and showing Laurel's photograph around, Frank's concern bordered on desperation. He didn't want to believe that anything serious could have happened to her. She didn't know anything about his activities. Would they harm her just because she knew him?

Frank decided it was time to confront Colonel Neil, to force him to disclose what had become of Laurel and who had killed Joanna. He waited for the staff to leave in the evening, then barged into the colonel's office. Neil was gone. The door to the safe was ajar, revealing a gaping, empty hole.

The phone in the outer office rang. It was Reidy. The ship had arrived, he reported. The *Columbia Eagle* again, steaming that very moment up the Chao Phraya River to tie up at the same wharf as before. And, Mike added, he found Laurel. She was back at the Rose House Café.

Frank slammed the phone down in frustration. Neil intended to meet the ship, he was sure of it. He couldn't let him get away. Chapin had ordered him to stay on his tail, and that's what he intended to do. He rushed out of the office to search for Neil, first in the officers' club, then the officers' quarters. He hurried through the depot's warehouses and open storage areas, ignoring the surprised looks of the soldiers he brushed aside, unconcerned that he might run into Neil and have to explain his behavior. The sooner they met, the better.

When Frank reached the motor pool, he discovered that Neil's jeep was missing. He'd left three hours earlier, Sergeant Stout told him, apparently headed for Bangkok. Frank checked out a jeep and chased after him, pausing only to retrieve the metal disc Captain Diltz had given him.

CHAPTER 35

Air Force One

APRIL 28, 1970

JOHN LYNCH AND SHAREE FISH SAT NEXT TO each other on the Boeing 727, designated Air Force One when the president was on board, on their way to Vietnam.

"I can't help but feel uneasy," Lynch said. "I don't know what to make of it."

The day before, they had learned of General Chapin's inquiry about Colonel Neil. The routine request for information had passed over the CIA director's desk by chance, a week after it had been received by the agency. Fish immediately alerted Lynch.

"Don't worry," Fish assured him. "I have my man well placed in the general's headquarters. If there were any reason for concern, Major Chu would have given me a heads-up."

"Well, it's time to meet with Chapin on this Cambodia thing anyway," Lynch said.

They carried with them the president's final approval for the Cambodian incursion. Lynch knew only too well why they were personally delivering orders Chapin had already received by cable—his job was to remind the general that it was the president and the president alone who called the shots.

They were relaxing on the sofa in the president's stateroom, sipping cocktails. Lynch got up to retrieve a bottle of gin from the bar and leaned over to refill Fish's glass. The top two buttons of her silk Hermès blouse were undone, and he could see the rise of her generous breasts. She was wearing one of her signature Ralph Lauren blazers over a hip-hugging wool skirt that was hiked up to mid-thigh. A large circular pendant with a sunburst design hung in her freckled cleavage, a nod to the influence of the flower children on contemporary fashion. She wore her hair long and black—black with the help of her hairdresser, he suspected—like Joan Baez. She was no spring chicken, but she was well put together and retained the vestiges of her youthful beauty.

"Well, Sharee, we have a few hours to kill before we land," he said, looking at her with a glint in his eye.

"You have something in mind, John?"

He sat down beside her and ran a hand up her inner thigh.

"I was thinking we could relive old times."

Sharee sucked in her breath. "John, don't go any higher unless you mean it."

"That's exactly what I mean," he said in a husky voice. He leaned over and planted a sloppy kiss on her lips. She wrapped her arms around his neck and buried her tongue deep in his mouth, then pushed his head down to her bosom. Lynch nuzzled her breasts for a moment, then broke the embrace and looked over at the president's bed. "Do you think he'd mind?"

"What he doesn't know can't hurt him," Fish said, breathing heavily.

Lynch laughed. "I hope that rule applies to this Cambodia thing, or we really *are* fucked."

Lynch rose, straightened his clothes, and rang for the steward. "Richie," he said, when Flight Sergeant Savitch entered the room. "Director Fish and I are going to be working on a highly classified matter for the next couple hours. Could you bring us a chilled bottle of champagne, and maybe some caviar?"

Sergeant Savitch nodded without expression, but Lynch picked up an invisible wink. "Not a problem, Mr. Lynch. I'll have it here in a minute, then make sure no one disturbs you so you can get your work done."

Sergeant Savitch returned five minutes later with a bottle of Dom Pérignon nesting in a bucket of ice. In the other hand he balanced a tray of Russian caviar, toast, and small dishes of chopped eggs and onions.

Lynch eyed the tray appreciatively. "Thanks, Richie. That's all we'll need for now."

Lynch smothered caviar on a piece of toast and handed it to Fish. "Eat fast, my dear. Time to get our work done."

CHAPTER 36
Bangkok
APRIL 29, 1970

MIKE DROVE FRANK TO THE ROSE HOUSE CAFÉ. IT was early evening, and the lights of the city began to flicker on as swarms of people took to the streets to do their shopping, the relentless heat of the day having dissipated into a muggy blanket of humidity.

"I don't think you should see her," Mike warned. "She was scared. Wouldn't talk to me. Asked me to leave her alone."

"How'd you find her?"

Mike looked at him sheepishly. "I hadn't been to the Rose House Café for some time," he said, embarrassed to admit he'd been out looking for fresh companionship. "Just stopped by to see if they had any new girls, and there she was."

"What'd she say about me?"

"Nothing, really. Only that she didn't want to see you again. She asked me not to tell you where she was."

Laurel smiled engagingly when she saw him walk through the door, in the dim light mistaking him for just another GI out for a good time. The smile disappeared when she recognized him.

"Go away," she hissed, glancing nervously at the

mamasan standing behind the counter. "I no can talk
to you."

Frank ignored her protests and approached the mamasan. He handed her an American ten-dollar bill, twice the
normal charge, and nodded toward Laurel. The mamasan
smiled broadly and motioned for Laurel to accompany
him to the back. Reluctantly, Laurel led him to a cubicle
and began to spread out towels and prepare the bath as
she would for any customer.

Frank took her by the shoulders and turned her to
face him.

"Laurel, did they hurt you?" he asked. He still struggled with guilt, knowing he was responsible for whatever
had happened to her. He couldn't shake the memory of
the scene at the bungalow, when she was wrestled into the
back of the jeep, weeping in the darkness.

Laurel avoided his gaze.

"Laurel, tell me," Frank pleaded, shaking her gently.
"Tell me what happened."

Laurel sobbed and pressed a clenched fist to her
mouth. "Yes, they hurt me," she blurted. "They drag me
out, take me away."

"Did they beat you?"

Laurel nodded. "Push me. Shout. Always shout at me."

"You mean they threatened you?"

"Say if I go back bungalow, they hurt you. Tell me no
see you. I no want them hurt you."

She looked up at him with tears in her eyes. He felt a
twinge of skepticism, wondering if the tears were sincere
or if she was trying to bolster her story.

"Who were they? Who told you not to call me?"

"I no see them before. Soldiers. American soldiers. They say you bad."

"Why? Did they say why I was bad?"

"They ask me where you are, where you been, who your friends. How I know? I say. They ask me over and over. Always questions. She scream at me."

"She? A woman questioned you?"

Laurel nodded. "She bad. She yell in my face."

"Where did they take you?"

"Here. Bangkok. Tell me never go back Korat."

"Where were they from? What unit? Were there any patches on their sleeves?"

Laurel shrugged. "Don't know. Officer in charge."

Frank suspected he knew who it was. "Neil? Did they call him Colonel Neil?"

"Yes, Neil. And Joanna."

Frank was stunned. Joanna? It couldn't have been Joanna. Joanna was dead.

"Laurel, this is very important. What did this Joanna look like?"

"Tall woman. White skin. Maybe Malay, maybe Chinese."

The description could fit Joanna, but that was impossible. Reidy had identified her body, and she was wearing his opal ring. Joanna wasn't alive—Neil was just trying to cast doubt on her death or deflect suspicion that he was involved. Frank wasn't fully convinced that Joanna was a spy, but—spy or no spy—she was dead, and Neil was responsible.

Frank's feelings of affection for Laurel slipped away, like water draining from the tub. Maybe it was the shock of hearing Joanna's name, rekindling the sorrow that had consumed him since her death. Maybe it was the realization that Laurel didn't have the slightest affection for him, didn't care whether she ever saw him again, whether he lived or died. She was a massage girl, and he was a customer.

"Laurel, did they give you baht?"

"No money. Say they hurt you. I scared for you." Her eyes filled with tears again.

"No money at all?" When Laurel turned away, he had his answer. They didn't hurt her. They simply paid her more money than he had. She would have told them anything for the right price. He'd always known, deep down, that money was the glue that kept her with him, but he preferred to pretend there was more to their relationship than that.

Frank left Laurel sobbing in the cubicle, his concern for her having evaporated. To her he was just a bank account. He hadn't expected much—it was a business proposition for him as well—but even if she had no feelings for him, she could at least have been straight with him, told him the truth, not made him drag it out of her. He'd paid for that much at least.

LATER THAT NIGHT FRANK AND MIKE REIDY CAU-tiously approached the *Columbia Eagle*, picking a circuitous route through a jumble of crates piled on the wharf. They crouched behind a stack of tires and studied the ship, which was lit by harsh spotlights hanging from the mast. No effort was made to keep the ship from being noticed.

Long, canvas-wrapped snouts protruded from a shapeless mass of cargo stacked on the deck. Crewmen swarmed over the deck, shouting instructions to the crane operator loading pallets of equipment onto two dozen military trucks waiting on the wharf.

"That's all guns," Mike whispered. "I'll bet those barrels are 105 howitzers. The long narrow boxes on that pallet near the stern are M60 machine guns. There's mortars, shells, the works. Frank, there's a whole arsenal on that ship, enough to equip a small army."

"And going to the 558th," Frank added, nodding at the nearest truck. The distinctive insignia of the 558th Supply and Service Company was painted on the bumper.

Mike pulled at Frank's sleeve and pointed to the quarterdeck. Colonel Neil stood at the top of the gangway, engrossed in conversation with First Mate Foley. Neil's gestures indicated he was in charge of the operation and wasn't satisfied with its progress.

"Mike, you better let the guys in Saigon know what's going on," Frank said. "Use the commo center at the air base. Get hold of Ming at MACV. If they give you any guff, use General Chapin's name. Ask for him if you have to, or a General O'Malley."

"No way, Frank!" Mike was incredulous. "You do it if you want. I'm not going to the air base, and I'm not calling Chapin. You think I'm crazy? I'm just a shit-ass second lieutenant—he's a four-star general!"

"Mike, there's no time to argue. You have to do it. The order to watch for the ship came from Saigon, didn't it? You did that, didn't you?"

"Yeah, but I didn't like that either. Look, what am I supposed to say? 'Hi, General, you don't know me, but this is Lieutenant Reidy over here in Thailand, and somebody's unloading a ship?' Frank, that's a one-way ticket out of the army."

"Lieutenant, just do it," Frank insisted. "Ming knows you. And I'll guarantee you this—if you don't do it, you *will* be out of the army and that citizenship thing will be off the table."

"If it's so important, why don't you do it?"

"Because I've got to keep an eye on Neil. Those are *my* orders. Now get going, and come back for me as soon as you can. We've got other things to take care of."

Reidy reluctantly left to send the message, and Frank settled behind the pile of tires to continue his surveillance, waiting for the last of the weapons and equipment to be loaded onto the trucks, each a standard army five-ton freighter with a fourteen-foot bed that could carry 10,000 pounds of cargo. They were pretty much indestructible, well suited for the roads into Cambodia. Frank guessed they were housed in the motor pool that he and Reidy had discovered on the River Kwai.

Shortly before dawn, the crane swung the last load off the ship. The bright lights were extinguished, and diesel engines roared to life, heralding the new morning beginning to pierce the eastern sky.

Nervously fingering the small disc in his pocket, Frank searched the wharf for Reidy, hoping for backup, but there was no sign of him. Unwilling to miss what could be his last opportunity, he crept down the wharf and climbed into the back of a truck. He burrowed among the crates and attached the magnetic disc to the metal frame, then jumped silently to the pavement and slipped into the shadows to await Reidy's return.

CHAPTER 37

Utapao

APRIL 30, 1970

DAWN WAS BREAKING THROUGH THE OVERCAST as Frank and Mike drove into Bangkok's Don Muang Airport. They skirted the civilian terminal and drove across the tarmac to the U.S. Air Force compound. A bleary-eyed duty sergeant answered Frank's impatient knock on the door of the dispatch shed.

"No, no planes to Utapao until this afternoon," the sergeant replied to Frank's query. "Even then, there may not be room if you aren't already on the manifest. Pretty crowded these days."

"We can't wait that long. We have to get to Utapao this morning."

"Sorry, Lieutenant. Nothing I can do for you."

The sergeant started to close the door, but Frank blocked it with his boot.

"Do you have any planes on the ground that won't be used today?"

The sergeant sniggered. "I suppose so, Lieutenant, but I doubt they'll give you one for a shuttle to Utapao. It takes a lot more rank than you have to rate a trip like that."

Frank looked at the airman's name tag. Oberle. A goddamn German. Lives by the rules.

"Where's the officer in charge?"

"Shit, Lieutenant, what's the hurry? It's not even six o'clock. The captain's still sleeping, would be my guess."

Frank shoved Sergeant Oberle aside and walked into the room. He picked up the telephone and rang the military operator. "Put me through to MACV in Saigon," he demanded. "This is a top-priority call."

The sergeant watched him skeptically. He straightened up and paid attention, though, when Frank spoke again.

"Hello? MACV? Get me General Chapin. That's right, General Edward Chapin. Tell him Lieutenant Schaniel is on the line from Thailand."

Thirty seconds later, Frank smiled in satisfaction. "General? I'm here in Bangkok. Look, something's come up. I need a plane. I can't explain now, but I need you to tell this Air Force sergeant here to break one free for me."

Sergeant Oberle took the receiver and held it gingerly to his ear. He listened a moment, then placed it deferentially back on the hook. He looked at Frank with newfound respect.

"Satisfied?" Frank asked. "I think you better roust your captain, and tell him to get his ass over here."

AS THE PLANE DIPPED IN FOR A LANDING AT THE Utapao airstrip, Frank nudged Mike awake and pointed to the laundry truck parked beside the tarmac. He congratulated himself for having requisitioned a new one. They would need a reliable vehicle before the day was out.

Sergeant Canedo and his men had loaded helmets, flak jackets, M16s, and ammunition into the back of the truck, along with four jerrycans of extra fuel and tuna sandwiches for lunch.

"Good job, Sergeant," Frank said, inspecting the equipment. "Looks like you got everything we need."

"Everything you ordered, Lieutenant. But what's it for?"

"Hopefully, for nothing. We'll only need it if we get into a jam."

"We? What do you mean 'we'? Where are we going?"

Ramos and Greenwald were standing off to the side. Frank motioned them closer. "Something real important has come up." He looked around to make sure they were alone. "Lieutenant Reidy and I are on special orders from Saigon. It's top secret, and we need some help."

Ramos was leery. "What do we have to do, Lieutenant?"

"We're going into Cambodia to bring back an army officer." He tried to frame it so it didn't sound so screwy. "Like a rescue."

"Why don't the Special Forces or somebody do that?" Greenwald asked, reluctant to get involved. "All we know how to do is laundry. That last trip was bad enough."

"There's no time to explain." Frank looked at each man in turn, trying to impress upon them the gravity of the situation without letting them know how desperate he was for their help. "I need you on this, but it could get rough. I can't deny that. You don't have to go if you don't want to."

They were quiet for a moment, mulling it over. Canedo spoke first. "Well, I'm going. I'm afraid you'll fuck up the new truck on your own." Ramos and Greenwald nodded in begrudging agreement. Canedo was their NCO; they went where he went.

"Okay, let's get going," Frank said, concealing his relief. "Sergeant Canedo, you drive. I'll ride shotgun. Lieutenant Reidy will sit with Greenwald and Ramos in the back."

THE SENTRY AT THE GATE CONFIRMED THE 558th convoy had passed less than two hours earlier, headed in the direction of the Cambodian border. "More trucks than I've ever seen in these parts, Lieutenant. And loaded for bear. Sandbagged machine guns on the cabs and the whole works."

They turned down the highway, following the convoy, driving for hours before topping a bluff within sight of the river that marked the boundary between Thailand and Cambodia. Below them the last of the 558th trucks were struggling over a narrow plank bridge, each stopping briefly at a military checkpoint on the far side.

"Okay, let's go," ordered Frank. "Head for the bridge."

"How we going to get across, Lieutenant?" Canedo asked doubtfully. "We don't have any papers. They're not likely to let us through, are they?"

"They will if they think we're part of the convoy."

Canedo looked skeptical.

"Sergeant, just do what I say," insisted Frank. "And step on it. It'll work."

Frank stuck his head through the opening to the back and explained the situation to the others. "Push the weapons under the bench," he ordered. "And try not to look nervous."

Canedo drove brazenly down the hill and onto the

bridge, slackening his speed as they neared the guard post where an iron pole hoisted horizontally across the road barred their way. Two Cambodian soldiers approached the truck with carbines at the ready.

Frank took the initiative and pointed up the road. "Convoy. We're with convoy. I'm officer."

The sentries showed no reaction. "Officer," Frank repeated, pointing at the gold bar sewn onto the collar of his fatigues. "Pronto. We go with trucks pronto." He hoped *pronto* was a word of international communication. He didn't know a single word of Khmer, and only enough Thai to negotiate with the massage girls.

The soldiers looked at each other uncertainly, then stepped aside. They raised the gate and Canedo nudged the truck through the narrow opening.

"Good work, Lieutenant." Canedo sighed with relief. "Now what?"

"Now we find a place to pull over for the night. I don't want to chance catching up to them in the dark. If they spot us, we're dead meat."

Canedo looked at him in alarm. "You said it could get rough, Lieutenant, but you didn't say it could get *that* rough. We're just laundrymen, remember. None of us has fired a rifle since basic training."

Frank stifled a laugh. "Sounds like me, Sergeant. But as they say in the Marines, every cook is a rifleman. We're supposed to always be ready to fight."

"Too bad we're not Marines."

"Don't worry, Sergeant. That convoy may attract some unfriendly fire, but if we keep our distance, we'll be fine."

Unfriendly fire. What an understatement. Chapin's B52s

would be more than unfriendly—they'd be downright deadly. He reminded himself that the soldiers with the convoy were traitors, that they had brought this on themselves. Still, he couldn't help but feel some angst for what was about to befall them.

CHAPTER 38

Cambodia
MAY 1, 1970

IN THE MORNING THEY CONTINUED THEIR JOUR-
ney deeper into Cambodia. The convoy was easy to
follow—there was only one paved road. Shortly before
noon, though, the pavement ended and they crawled
along a narrow dirt road, following tire tracks in the
dust. They had donned helmets and flak jackets and held
loaded M16s.

"I think we must be almost there, wherever 'there' is,"
Frank said, consulting a map and eyeing a rise a quar-
ter mile up the road. "This road doesn't go much farther.
Maybe let's pull the truck off here—"

A sharp explosion cut him short, and a geyser of
dirt splashed over the hood. Frank and Sergeant Canedo
leaped from the cab as a spray of machine-gun bullets
ripped through the engine and tore out the windshield,
hurling fragments of jagged metal and shards of broken
glass through the canvas tarp covering the rear.

Frank flattened himself in the dirt and pulled his rifle
close to his side. More weapons opened up, creating a
deafening din. A knot of Cambodian soldiers sprinted
across the road fifty yards ahead and fired into the truck
from their new position. A moment later, the truck burst

into flames. Frank heard screams from the back, soon drowned out by a growing crescendo of gunfire.

Frank saw movement from the corner of his eye and pointed his rifle in that direction.

"It's me, Lieutenant!" shouted Canedo, crawling toward him, dragging a shredded leg. "I'm hit pretty bad, I think."

Frank grabbed Canedo by the shirt collar and pulled him into a drainage ditch beside the road. "We'll be okay here for a while," he assured the sergeant as he tied a tourniquet around his leg. Frank didn't believe his own words, and he knew Canedo didn't either.

"I think the other guys have had it," Canedo said, looking back at the burning truck. There was no sign of Reidy or the others. "Look, Lieutenant, I've had it too. We're not going to last long here, and I'm not going anywhere. You get out of here and I'll cover you."

Frank hesitated, but he knew Canedo was right. He turned and fired a few rounds up the road to keep the Cambodians at bay, then handed the rifle to Canedo. "I won't forget, Sergeant," he said, moved by the man's sacrifice.

"But do me a favor, Lieutenant." Canedo grabbed Frank by the sleeve and pulled him close. "Call my parents when you get home. Joe and Connie Canedo. They live on Ash Street in San Diego. Tell them what happened to me. They have to know."

"I will, Sergeant," Frank promised. "I'll tell them." He wanted to say more but couldn't find the words.

"Go on, Lieutenant. Get out of here before it's too late."

Frank scrambled into the brush, hugging the ground

until he was deep into the jungle, the racket of gunfire receding behind him.

"WELL, LIEUTENANT SCHANIEL, NICE TO SEE you," Colonel Neil said patronizingly as Captain Broderick looked on with a smirk. Frank stood squeezed between the two Cambodian soldiers who had stumbled upon him in the jungle.

Frank decided to say as little as possible. He was about to be killed by Chapin's bombers, but the satisfaction of knowing Neil would die as well gave him some comfort. Still, he wished he'd stayed in Bangkok, that he hadn't gone charging off after the bad guys like a kid playing cops and robbers. Reidy and the men from the laundry were killed on account of him, and he was next.

What happened to the college fraternity boy? he wondered. The guy who never missed a party. The guy who couldn't do ten decent pushups, who was nearsighted—he wore bifocals, for Christ's sake—and color blind. He'd fired a rifle only once before, on the practice range at Fort Benjamin Harrison when he was there for admin school, and the noise had temporarily deafened him. He still found it hard to believe the army had given him a second look, that he wasn't classified 4F.

He had planned on becoming a lawyer, like Ming. In college, he'd studied political science. It would be good preparation for law school, he was told, and if there was an easier major, he couldn't find it. He figured he'd be working as a lawyer in a comfortable, air-conditioned office, with any luck in some high-rise in downtown San Francisco. He would lunch at the Tadich Grill, frequent the bars on Union Street, play Frisbee on the Marina

Green on Sunday afternoons. He would shop for groceries at the Marina Safeway where he worked during college, known as "Dateway" to the young professionals who lived in the neighborhood. He wanted to be one of those young professionals, chatting up the chicks in the vegetable aisle. What the hell was he doing in Cambodia?

"Schaniel, what are you doing here, my friend?" Neil had the same question. He waited patiently for Frank's response, unaware that time was running out, that the bombers were on the way.

"Just out for a ride, Colonel. Got bored with all that paperwork. You know how dull that admin stuff can be."

Frank surveyed his surroundings. They stood beside one of the 558th's trucks, parked with the others in a large, open storage area in a shallow, bowl-shaped valley. The drivers lounged in the shade, seeking relief from the broiling sun, playing cards or napping in the afternoon heat. Cambodian soldiers swarmed over the vehicles, unloading weapons and stacking crates of equipment haphazardly on the ground.

An American soldier trotted up to Neil. "Sir, look at this." He held Captain Diltz's monitor in his outstretched hand. "I found it attached to one of the trucks."

Neil examined the disc carefully, turning it over in the palm of his hand. His expression hardened. "Schaniel, what the hell is this?" he demanded. "Did you plant this thing?"

Frank remained silent.

"Look, you pudgy bastard, your fucking little game is over." Neil was angry now. "You've been playing detective for weeks, and I'm tired of it. Now, what's this goddamn beeper doing in that truck?"

Neil grabbed Frank by the shirt collar and raised a hand to smack him across the face when the distant drone of B-52s broke the afternoon stillness. He dropped his arm and turned toward the sound, then back to Frank. "Anything I should know, Lieutenant?"

"It's too late, Colonel." Frank nodded in the direction of the planes. "Now, it's your game that's over. They've come to finish you off."

Frank slumped to the ground and rested his back against a tire. Neil, bewildered, looked from Frank to the approaching bombers, now visible against the western sky, their wings shimmering in the sunlight. He gave Frank a look of disgust and sprinted to a nearby tent that sprouted a radio antenna through the canvas roof. A generator next to the tent gasped to life.

"MACV, MACV, come in MACV." Neil's urgent call could be heard by Frank and the American soldiers clustered around the trucks—all of them traitors, Frank reminded himself. The soldiers looked anxiously at the bombers growing larger in the distance, their rumble growing louder. Frank counted a half-dozen planes— enough, he thought wryly, to ensure that Ming's team wouldn't have an easy task cleaning up the remains.

"We hear you loud and clear, Colonel," a reassuring voice crackled over the radio. "We were expecting your signal."

Frank couldn't believe that MACV had responded to Neil's desperate call. Even more surprising, he recognized the voice on the radio. It was General Chapin, the commanding general himself.

"What about those B-52s headed our way?" Neil asked urgently.

"Not to worry, Colonel. The bombers have been diverted. Say again, the planes have been diverted."

The deafening roar of the bombers passing overhead interrupted the conversation. Cambodian soldiers scattered and dived for cover. The Americans crouched by the trucks, their frightened, upraised faces nervously stalking the planes. The formation disappeared over the eastern rim of the valley as quickly as it had appeared, the thundering noise subsiding in the distance. Minutes later the deep throb of distant explosions shook the earth as the B-52s released their racks of 500-pound bombs over unsuspecting jungle in Vietnam.

"They've passed," Neil reported with relief, resuming his conversation with Chapin.

"Sorry for the close call, Colonel," Chapin said. "We were notified of your operation only moments ago, by a high-level representative of the White House."

"Roger," Neil replied, his voice subdued.

Confused, Frank pushed himself to his feet. He couldn't help but be relieved the bombers had passed by—he was still alive—but he felt betrayed that Neil was still alive as well. Stumbling to the tent, he pushed open the canvas flap and saw Neil standing beside the radio, the microphone in his hand. A woman sat at a field desk beside him, her back to the door, curls slipping down a slender neck from under a fatigue cap.

Frank froze. Joanna!

The radio crackled again. "Colonel, a company from the First Cav is headed your way." It was Major General O'Malley this time. Chapin would have left the room at the first sign of trouble. "We haven't been able to turn them back."

"What the hell does that mean?" Neil shouted, his relief evaporating.

"Communications breakdown. Can't get through to them. Can you remove your troops from the area? And the Cambodians?"

"No way," said Neil, his anger rising. "Impossible. How the fuck am I supposed to do that?" He didn't wait for a reply. "How close are they? What are their orders? What are they armed with?"

The soldiers milling around the trucks listened with increasing concern as O'Malley described Alpha Company of the First of the Seventh, led by Major Ming Chu and armed with light weapons, sweeping over the border from Vietnam in two dozen Hueys, about to converge on the valley. Their orders? Take out Lon Nol—and Neil and his men along with him.

Frank shook off the shock of stumbling upon Joanna and focused on what O'Malley was saying. Through the confusion he realized what was happening.

"It's Ming," he cried.

Joanna, startled, turned to face him.

"It's Ming," he repeated. "Ming set this up."

Neil, uncomprehending, dropped the microphone and, brushing Frank aside, stepped to the entrance of the tent. Joanna moved just as fast. She grabbed a .45 from the desk and pointed it at Neil's back. Frank shouted a warning. Neil turned, but it was too late—a bullet shattered his left arm.

There were so many questions Frank wanted to ask Joanna. About the *Columbia Eagle*. About the body found in the klong. About earlier, when they lived together in San Francisco, what she saw in him when she could have had any guy she wanted. He wanted to tell her how much those six months meant to him, how much their last time together meant to him, that afternoon in the Siam Intercontinental before she disappeared.

And why did she just shoot Colonel Neil? General O'Malley said they were both traitors, but Frank realized with sudden clarity that he was wrong, that only one of them was a traitor. He flashed on Joanna and Ming talking to the Chinese man with the black eye patch in Golden Gate Park. And he recalled the entries in Neil's personnel file describing the twenty-year career of a dutiful, loyal soldier, a soldier now endorsed by General Chapin himself. He realized in a fleeting second who the traitor was, and it wasn't Neil.

Joanna was wrestling with a jam in the .45, working to slide another round into the chamber. Before she could fire again, Frank drew his own .45 and shot her in the face. Her head disintegrated in an explosion of brain matter and bone and a wash of blood, leaving nothing but the memory of her resolute expression.

Neil held his injured arm tightly against his side and stared in shock at Joanna's blood-soaked body crumpled on the floor. "Schaniel," he said grimly, "I don't know what's going on here, but when this is over, I'll see you rot in hell." Neil lifted the flap and stumbled from the tent. Frank gave Joanna's lifeless body a last, heartbroken look, then followed him out.

The colonel stood a few yards away, speaking with a Cambodian general, a short, pudgy man with hair slicked to one side. Frank couldn't hear the conversation, but Neil must have told him the truth, or at least the truth as he understood it. The general shouted angrily at Neil and shook his fist in Neil's face, then turned and stormed up a slight rise to his command post, his staff trailing after him. He shouted orders and waved his arms to emphasize their urgency. Aides scattered across the encampment, and, within minutes, Cambodian troops in full battle gear began to assemble near the command post.

CHAPTER 39
Cambodia
MAY 1, 1970

COLONEL NEIL IGNORED THE FLURRY OF ACTIV-
ity as the Cambodian soldiers prepared to flee the assault
of the American cavalrymen. He strode over to the trucks
where the men of the 558th were gathered, forty-seven
American soldiers anxiously awaiting his orders. He
stood before them, holding his wounded arm against his
side, blood seeping through his fingers, looking subdued
but not defeated.

"Gentlemen," he said, "get your gear." His voice was
barely audible over the din made by the Cambodians.
"We have a job to do."

The men trotted to their trucks and quickly reassem-
bled, wearing helmets and flak jackets and armed with
M16s. The colonel divided them into two groups, one led
by Captain Broderick, the other by himself. They lined
up in platoon formation, facing the colonel expectantly.

The Cambodian soldiers around them were in a
frenzy, commandeering the trucks and tossing unneeded
cargo onto the ground. They crowded onto the vehicles
and pulled machine guns, mortars, and crates of ammunition up with them.

"The news isn't good, men," Neil continued, ignoring

the ruckus. "There's no easy way to say this. You heard the radio. There's a renegade company from the First Cav—from the First of the Seventh—on their way here to attack the Cambodians. We have to stop them, or the war over here is going to get a lot more fucked up than it already is."

The First of the Seventh was Custer's regiment at Little Big Horn, Frank recalled. Now it was about to attack Neil's men, and this time it looked like the cavalry would win.

Trucks crammed with Cambodian soldiers lurched from the open storage area and converged on the narrow dirt road leading to the southern end of the valley. More soldiers trotted beside the trucks, armed with M16s and with bandoliers of ammunition wrapped around their chests. They were irrationally cheerful, shouting and laughing and waving rifles in the air, a festive show masking their anxiety.

"How do we do that, sir?" Captain Broderick asked. "How are we supposed to stop them?"

"Scare them, maybe. Reason with them. Shoot them, if we have to."

"Sir, they're Americans!" Broderick objected.

"I know that, Captain," snapped Neil. "But we may have no choice. We have to keep them from firing on the Cambodians. They don't know what they're up against. They expected the bombers to have done most of the work for them, but that didn't happen. If we don't stop them, General Lon Nol's men will wipe them out and us with them, and from then on, he'll be fighting Americans, not Communists. If we can slow the First Cav down, the

Cambodians may have time to get out of here, and maybe we can avoid a fucking Armageddon."

The colonel looked at his men with a determined expression. "You men are volunteers. You knew it could get rough when you signed on. God in heaven, I didn't imagine it would come to this, but it has. And now we have to do our duty."

KNOTS OF CAMBODIAN STRAGGLERS FILTERED onto the road, struggling with weapons, cooking pots, bedding, and other essentials of war. General Lon Nol careened by in his jeep, ignoring the Americans, charging after his soldiers down the road leading out of the valley.

The sound of the general's retreating jeep was replaced by the whooshing, slapping sound of approaching helicopters. Major Chu's Hueys slipped gracefully over the eastern rim of the valley and, one by one, tentatively, like cautious dragonflies, settled into a clearing a half mile distant from Neil and his soldiers.

"Let's go, men," Neil ordered. "Captain Broderick, I'll take my platoon to the right. You go to the left, but stay toward the middle of the valley and follow my lead. Take them head on and let them know you're Americans. Shoot only if you have to"—he took a deep breath—"but if you have to, shoot."

Ming's company tumbled from the helicopters and formed a skirmish line. One platoon, rifles at the ready, began to advance toward the American truckers.

Colonel Neil pointed to a shallow creek that meandered from north to south through the middle of the valley, separating the two forces. "Captain Broderick, see that creek? That's where we stop them. If we can't get their attention before then, that's where we make our stand."

Custer again, thought Frank. Another last stand.

Neil's soldiers moved haltingly toward the creek, doing whatever they could think of to identify themselves as Americans. One held up a small American flag. Others waved white T-shirts or pieces of uniform. Broderick's platoon broke into a ragged chorus of "Take Me out to the Ball Game," while shouts of "Chicago," "Hey, First Cav," and "Johnny Bench" rang across the valley.

Frank watched from the knoll vacated by the Cambodian general as the colonel led his men across the valley, like a movie unreeling before his eyes. They kept to open clearings, ignoring the sparse cover afforded by occasional tufts of bamboo. The colonel waved an arm at Ming's soldiers, his damaged arm strapped to his chest. Frank imagined the colonel shouting "Stop," "We're Americans," "We're friends," "Don't shoot," but his words were lost in a crescendo of gunfire as Ming's men opened up with their M16s.

Neil was a hundred yards from the creek when a bullet tore through his right leg and dropped him to the ground. One of his soldiers crawled to his side, slipped the colonel's good arm around his neck, and helped him to his feet. As they struggled forward, Ming's troops faltered, confused by the sight of an unarmed American officer limping toward them. Their fire slackened, but then Ming took the lead and waved them on, forcing them into the fray, not giving them time to question what they were doing.

As Neil reached the creek, a bullet smashed into the chest of the soldier helping him, and Neil fell into the shallow water. The thinning band of soldiers behind him continued to advance, formed into a ragged skirmish line by Captain Broderick. Sickened at what they had to do, they started firing at the soldiers of the First of the Seventh.

Slowly, inexorably, both sides battled forward, finally crashing together in the muddied waters of the stream. They locked in combat, fighting hand to hand like animals. The sound of rifle fire died away, replaced by desperate grunts and screams as the soldiers savagely struggled to kill one another with knives and bare hands.

Suddenly a shell exploded in their midst, hot metal ripping into those still standing. The fighting stopped abruptly, and the dazed and bleeding Americans dived for cover against the stream bank. As shells continued to crash around them, they pressed their bodies deeper into the mud, seeking shelter from the common danger, no longer concerned with distinguishing friend from foe.

Frank jumped to his feet at the sight of the first explosion. By the time the third round hit, he spotted the source—81-mm mortars manned by Cambodian soldiers on the bluffs at the southern end of the valley. Machine guns and small arms joined the mortars, but they were too distant to have much effect.

It's their whole fucking army, Frank realized. Lon Nol didn't take his troops out of the valley—he doubled back to ambush the unsuspecting Americans.

"You assholes," he shouted in rage, shaking his fist helplessly at the Cambodians. "You shitty fucking assholes!"

Frank pulled himself together and scanned the Cambodian position with his binoculars, looking for something—anything—that might help the Americans trapped on the valley floor. He focused on the soldier orchestrating the Cambodian fire and couldn't believe what he saw. Reidy! It was Mike Reidy! He wasn't dead after all. There he was, standing among the Cambodians, marshalling their guns to shell the American soldiers in the valley.

Frank was dumbfounded. Not only was Reidy still alive, he had gone over to the other side. He was like an apparition from a horror film appearing through the mist. An American soldier killing his brothers in arms.

But he wasn't an American, Frank reminded himself. He was Irish. He had his heart set on becoming an American, he said, but here he was killing Americans. Why was he helping the Cambodians? Why had he given up that dream?

Frank's thoughts returned to that afternoon in Golden Gate Park. He'd sat on the grass and watched Joanna and Ming walk hand in hand toward the stage where the band was playing. They joined Mike, who was talking to the Chinese man with the black eye patch standing on the fringe of the crowd. The man looked out of place among the frolicking, tie-dyed hippies—short hair, clean-shaven, the only one in the park dressed in a suit. He nodded at Joanna when Mike introduced her, then smiled at Ming.

Looking back on it now, they seemed secretive, quietly discussing something they didn't want overheard. Was that it? Were Mike, Ming, and Joanna in it together? It was starting to look that way. Mike identified the body in the morgue. Joanna tried to kill Neil. Ming was leading an attack on Neil's troops, and Mike was shelling them all—no better way to make sure the Americans didn't ally themselves with the Cambodians. Were they all

Communist agents? It was hard to believe, but he couldn't come up with a better explanation.

The only hope for the embattled Americans was to get out of the valley, up and over the northern rim where they could conceal themselves in the jungle until American forces came to their rescue. Frank knew what he had to do—he had to help them get away.

Tossing aside his helmet and flak jacket, he unstrapped his pistol belt and let it fall to the ground. He took a deep breath and charged toward the creek where the Americans were pinned down, running as hard as he could, ignoring the bullets that began to whip around him. Soon sweat poured from his body, and his lungs ached for air. No more than two hundred yards to go. Then a hundred yards! Almost there!

He made it, only to crumple into the bloodied water of the creek with a bullet in his right knee. Friendly hands dragged him to the protection of the stream bank, and he lay face down in the mud, gasping for air. The pain from his knee had yet to penetrate his brain, but he knew he would be in for it when the pain finally came.

"Broderick," he gasped. "Where's Captain Broderick?"

A soft, familiar voice answered, muting the sounds of battle around him. "He's down the creek taking care of Colonel Neil."

Frank raised his head and looked at Ming, huddled against the stream bank with the two soldiers who had pulled Frank from the water.

"You bastard, Ming." Frank pushed himself onto his good knee and lunged weakly at Ming. The soldiers gently restrained him.

"It doesn't matter now, Frank," Ming said quietly.

"My job is over. It was important to my people that the Cambodians not become allies of the Americans. After this fiasco, they'll be at each other's throats."

"But you killed Americans, Ming."

"I did what I had to do, Frank, but I don't want to see any more of these men die than you do. And you need me to get them out of here. We're in this together now, whether you like it or not."

Ming crawled along the stream, encouraging the grim, battered soldiers, gathering them into small groups and distributing the wounded for the struggle out of the valley. Barely a hundred were still alive, a mix of Neil's and Ming's units, a third of them wounded. Shells continued to explode around them. A medic hunkered down beside Frank and bandaged his knee.

"Let's go, men," Ming ordered, satisfied with his preparations. "Single file. Keep low." He pulled soldiers one by one from the protection of the stream bank and pushed them up the creek. "Move!" he exhorted. "If we don't move now, we'll all be dead."

Ming led the soldiers along the stream toward the safety of the hills, cajoling them, threatening them, anything to keep them moving. "Keep your heads down! Keep your heads down!" A rear guard kept up a barrage of rifle fire to distract the Cambodians.

They slowly made their way out of the valley. Once they left the stream bed, dense jungle concealed their escape, but it also impeded their progress. Roots grabbed at their boots, thick bushes and vines pulled on their legs. They cut through walls of bamboo and pushed aside clumps of razor-sharp elephant grass.

Frank—exhausted, hobbling on one leg, and numbed

with pain—finally gave up and fell to the ground. "I can't go on," he told the soldiers who had been helping him. "You go on without me."

Worn out themselves and burdened with other wounded, the soldiers stepped over his prostrate form and continued their struggle up the hill. When the last man had passed, Frank relaxed in the damp grass, relishing the solitude. The noise of the battle had faded away. The soldiers from the rear guard had either been killed or slipped into the jungle.

He smiled sardonically at his plight. If he'd only lost some weight, got into a semblance of decent physical condition, maybe he would have been able to escape. Well, too late now. His only hope—that the Cambodians were satisfied with their success and wouldn't put up a chase—was soon dashed. A twig snapped behind him, interrupting the quiet. He remained calm, resigned to his fate.

Ming stooped and pulled Frank to his feet. "Let's go, Frank."

Frank looked at him in surprise. "Ming, I can't," he protested. "I'm done for. I'd just as soon die here anyway, after what's happened." The pain in his leg was excruciating, and weariness weighed him down. He wanted to slump back to the ground and rest.

"What's happened, Frank, is war. Nothing more. Nothing less. You shouldn't feel guilty. I don't feel guilty about using you. I didn't like it, but I did what I had to do."

"You know Joanna is dead?"

"Yes, I figured she was when I didn't see her in the valley." Ming looked off into the distance. "She was a good soldier, Frank. She loved you, but she loved her country even more. Her family has lived in China for thousands of years and she wasn't about to turn her back on them."

"And Mike Reidy—you know that was him up on the hill?"

"Yes, I know. He was doing what he had to do too."

"You and Mike and Joanna were all in this together, weren't you?"

"Well, we didn't plan it that way, but yes, we were, sort of. It was coincidental, really, the way things fell into place. I never would have become involved if you hadn't come to Saigon with the papers from Neil's safe."

"Glad I could help," Frank said.

"Reidy trying to kill us was not part of the plan," Ming said with a wry smile. "But I guess he thought it had to be done, to sever any possible alliance between the Cambodians and the Americans. I probably would have done the same thing if I were in his shoes."

Ming wrapped Frank's arm around his neck and half dragged, half carried him up the hill. They fought their way through the brush and vines, pausing frequently for Frank to rest. Ming stopped once to replace the blood-soaked bandage wrapped around Frank's knee. After two hours of beating through the jungle Ming gently eased Frank to the ground.

"I have to leave you now, Frank. Chapin's people will know to look for you here."

"You told them where to find me?"

"Well, let's just say I left instructions in case things went wrong."

"The rest of the men?"

"They're safe. Just up the hill."

"And Colonel Neil?"

"He stayed behind. He's counting on the Cambodians remembering he was their friend. Captain Broderick stayed with him."

"How are you going to get out of here?"

"Reidy and I made arrangements. We'll be okay. I don't think we would be too welcome back in Saigon."

"No, I suppose not," Frank said, struggling with conflicting emotions. "Goodbye, Ming. And thanks, I guess."

"Goodbye, Frank."

Ming slipped silently into the jungle, the thick, lush foliage closing behind him.

CHAPTER 40
Bangkok
MAY 4, 1970

MACNAMARA'S BAGS WERE PACKED, STACKED BY the door, waiting for the porter to take to the lobby. He was going home. He was tired, fed up with the war, with Southeast Asia, with life in general. But mostly, he was fed up with himself. Frustrated, to put it mildly.

For months, he'd sat in the hotel room and dutifully reported on the events unfolding in Cambodia. Sihanouk takes a long, ill-timed vacation. Lon Nol plots to take over the government while he's away, supported by students demonstrating against North Vietnamese troops in the country. He overthrows Sihanouk and asks the United States for weapons to fight the Communists, but the Americans come through with only a few trinkets, hoping to avoid a political brawl at home.

Then pow! American soldiers invade Cambodia to roust out Communist troops along the border. It all seemed very logical, a natural progression. The prince is out. The general is in. And the general finds new friends.

MacNamara just didn't believe it. Lon Nol couldn't have grabbed power—and certainly couldn't have held on—without American aid. There had to be more to the invasion than met the eye. If not, why would the administration invade Cambodia only weeks after refusing to give Lon Nol more than token military aid?

There was something fishy about the whole thing, and he thought he knew where the smell was coming from—from right under his nose, from that colonel that Reidy was always complaining about. Colonel Neil and his supply depot had to be the key. What could be more ingenious? The colonel uses the depot—there to support the American military in Thailand—to slip military hardware across the border to Cambodia. He's even able to keep Reidy in the dark, the officer in charge of the docks where the arms are unloaded.

MacNamara wished he had paid closer attention during his conversations with Reidy. Neil taking a handful of rifles over the border. Neil sending couriers to Phnom Penh. It should have been obvious, but it was too late now. He couldn't find Neil. He couldn't find Frank Schaniel, Reidy's friend from college. He couldn't even find Reidy. They were all gone, as if they had vanished from the face of the earth.

He had no choice but to write the script as the powers-that-be wanted it written. Maybe the truth would come out one day, but it would take someone smarter than him to figure it out. He would write what they wanted him to write—not a word more than he could confirm—and then he'd be done with the hot, humid, corrupt, godforsaken place. He'd had his fill of Southeast Asia.

Dateline: Bangkok, Thailand
May 4, 1970
By Robert A. MacNamara

Four days ago, thousands of South Vietnamese
forces, supported by U.S. war planes and artillery

and accompanied by U.S. advisers, swept across the border into Cambodia in a major operation against Vietnamese Communist sanctuaries. The forces reached a Viet Cong stronghold in the Parrot's Beak area of Cambodia, where 375 enemy soldiers were reported to have been killed by ground fire on the first day.

The following morning the president announced he was sending U.S. troops into Cambodia to attack the "headquarters for the entire Communist military operation in South Vietnam." He stated in a television appearance that the action was not an invasion but a necessary extension of the Vietnam War designed to eliminate major Communist staging and communications areas. He said that the U.S. troops will be withdrawn once their objectives have been accomplished.

Ending his press conference, the president said, "I would rather be a one-term president and do what I believe is right than be a two-term president at the cost of seeing America become a second-rate power and accept the first defeat in its proud 190-year history."

Later that morning, about 2,000 American air cavalrymen moved in helicopters across the border after B-52s, helicopter gunships, and artillery softened up suspected enemy positions in their path. The American troops reportedly penetrated 20 miles inside Cambodia to attack the headquarters of the Communist high command.

Yesterday, two students and a professor at Steven L. Davis State College died in a volley of

National Guard gunfire during continuing student protests against the Cambodia incursion. The
deaths marked the third day of protests on university campuses throughout the United States.
Elsewhere, 37 college and university presidents
urged the president to "demonstrate unequivocally
your determination" to end military involvement
in Southeast Asia.

On the political front, Sens. Bill Waite and
Brian Forbes announced they will offer an amendment to the pending military procurement bill to
cut off funds for continued U.S. military action
in Southeast Asia unless there is a congressional
declaration of war. In a news conference, the senators stated that the "invasion of Cambodia marked
the turning point in the war." Sen. George Hinman
vowed to vote against all foreign aid bills, which
he claimed had been "subverted" around the world
for military purposes.

The porter came to the room and picked up the bags.
MacNamara took a last look around—the bare floor
marred by broken tiles, the soiled bedspread, the faded
wallpaper peeling from the wall, the window that looked
out at nothing worth seeing. He wouldn't miss it, not a
bit. Picking up his typewriter, he followed the porter out
the door.

He had just enough time to meet Ceci at the embassy
to pick up her visa and make it to the airport for their
flight to San Francisco. It had taken him two months of
wheedling and coddling and cajoling and threatening

to get the visa, and even that wasn't enough—he had to marry her to get her home. He smiled. It was the best thing that ever happened to him, making the whole sordid stay in Thailand worth the sacrifice.

CHAPTER 41
Washington, D.C.
MAY 5, 1970

FRANK RECLINED ON A SOFA ON THE BOEING 727 an hour out of Saigon on his way to the States, his wounded leg propped on a pillow.

John Lynch entered the compartment with two cans of cold beer. "Well, Lieutenant, looks like you're being well looked after. How are you feeling?"

"Getting better, but my leg hurts like hell." He sighed heavily. "And to tell you the truth, Mr. Lynch, I feel a lot worse about what's happened than I do about my leg."

Lynch handed him a beer. "It's not your fault, Lieutenant. The fortunes of war and all that."

"That's what Major Chu said. Still, if I hadn't butted in, all those men from the 558th—and those guys from the laundry—would still be alive. There wouldn't even have been an invasion of Cambodia. It's incredible, isn't it? Unbelievable. Ming really won big, didn't he?"

"Yeah, there's no denying it. Still, if it makes you feel any better, it wouldn't have made any difference in the long run. Chapin was determined to invade Cambodia even before he learned of Neil's operation. And you flushed out Chu—you can take credit for that. And Tsai and Reidy. Think of the damage they could have done if they hadn't been uncovered."

Frank snorted. "What could've been worse?" He took a pull on the beer. It was depressing, thinking about the mess in Cambodia and the hand he had in it. "Do you think they'll ever get Chu and Reidy?"

"Well, officially, they already have. They appeared on a list of KIAs from the invasion. And, Lieutenant, that's how it happened. Understand?"

"Yeah, I understand. They were my friends, but I don't feel anything for them now." Frank was comfortable speaking openly with Lynch, having worked closely with him the last few days in Saigon. "Joanna's a different case. I can't get her out of my mind. I thought she was just for fun, but there was more to it, I know that now. I think I was in love with her, but I was too fucking insecure to admit it—worried she'd dump me for some rich guy."

"They've confirmed she was a Chinese agent," Lynch said, resting a hand on Frank's shoulder to soften the news. "Turns out Chu is too. Reidy, who knows? It looks like he wanted to divert weapons to the Irish Republican Army, but how that got mixed up with the Weather Underground and this Cambodia thing I don't know. They say people from County Clare aren't too bright—maybe that's the problem. They'll trace him eventually, but for now he's pretty much a mystery."

Frank had taken an immediate liking to Lynch when they met at MACV headquarters. He was a big bear of a man, his disheveled appearance and forthright, friendly manner incongruous with his position as national security advisor to the president. He had taken charge as soon as the small, weary group of survivors was airlifted from Cambodia to Saigon, barking commands like a hardened combat veteran, even ordering the generals around. He had brought Frank into his confidence to help sort out the mess.

Frank was relieved to be heading home. He had half expected to end up in a stockade in Vietnam, closeted away where he couldn't cause any more trouble. He had Lynch to thank for getting him out of the country before he became a permanent resident. Lynch was a good man to have on his side.

Frank slept almost the entire way to the States, wakened occasionally by an attentive nurse—Cate Sullivan, an army colonel—who fed him hot soup and changed his bandages. Shortly before they landed, she gave him a shave and helped him dress in an ill-fitting suit scrounged from a closet in the forward cabin.

Frank gave the nurse an appreciative once-over. She was one of the few round-eyes he'd met since leaving the States three months earlier.

"Ma'am, how did you pull this duty? Seems a bit beneath a nurse of your rank."

"I'm not a nurse, Lieutenant," she said, smiling sweetly. "I'm a veterinarian. For the last year I was the chief vet in Vietnam. I was waiting at Tan Son Nhut for a ride home when they shanghaied me into this duty. I guess they figured nursing you couldn't be any harder than taking care of the scout dogs, and I kind of liked the idea of flying home on Air Force One."

"Well, you're the most attractive army colonel I've ever seen."

She gave him a wry smile. "Careful, Lieutenant. I'm old enough to be your mother."

Lynch looked in on him as the plane descended through the murky evening to Andrews Air Force Base near Washington.

"You look great in the president's suit," Lynch said.

"Geez, I didn't know it was his." Frank self-consciously smoothed the fabric. He was sitting awkwardly on the sofa, his leg supported on a stool. "Colonel Sullivan had to slit the pants to get my leg in."

"Don't worry about it," Lynch said, smiling. "I'm sure the president won't miss it."

"What happens now?" Frank took a sip from the beer Lynch handed him. "Do you know where I'll be going?"

"Well, to a hospital, would be my guess. Then you have another year in the army, don't you? I'm sure they won't send you back overseas. Maybe I can pull a few strings. Where would you like to go?"

"San Francisco, I guess. I have friends there from college. Maybe I could start night law school before I get out."

Lynch looked at him appraisingly. "You know, it may not be all smooth sailing, Frank. There's bound to be questions about what happened. Nobody knows about you yet, as far as we can tell, but that doesn't mean they won't find out."

"Yeah, I figured this might not be the end of it. Before we left Saigon, I read about those college kids getting killed protesting the invasion. I guess there's quite a stink about it back home."

Lynch reached into his briefcase and handed Frank a sheaf of papers. "This is a copy of the president's official statement on the 'incursion' and some press clippings. I want you to go over them when you get a chance."

"Why?"

"Only a few people know what really happened, Frank. The two of us, three or four officers at MACV, and a couple of Neil's friends at the CIA. Everybody else thinks Cambodia went down just as the president said it did. As far as the world is concerned, we went in for one purpose—to cut the North Vietnamese supply lines to the South."

"But how can you keep it secret? Between the men in the 558th and that company Major Chu brought in, there must be a hundred men who came out of that valley alive."

"They're confused. They have no idea what really happened. They've been debriefed and strongly impressed with the need for secrecy. And even if one of them talks, no one will be able to make sense of it. The press could never put it all together."

"What about the president?"

"Even he doesn't know the whole story. MACV had been planning an incursion into Cambodia for some time and for some very sound strategic reasons having nothing to do with Neil's little army. And MACV has never told the president about Neil. As far as the president knows, everything he said in that statement you're holding is the truth."

Frank felt a shiver of fear. He turned to the window and watched the runway lights blink white and blue in the dusk. The plane banked sharply and began its final approach.

"I'm the weak link then—is that what you mean?

Other than you and MACV and maybe the CIA, I'm the only one who knows the whole story. And I'm the only one with nothing to lose by telling it."

"The country sure has a lot to lose," Lynch said, choosing his words carefully. "There's enough turmoil over this Cambodia thing as it is. If anybody finds out that the real reason we invaded Cambodia was to destroy a friendly army—a blunder so immense even you and I can't wrap our heads around it—the administration would be thrown into chaos. The country could implode."

Lynch hesitated. "And not to scare you, but there are some people who would go to great lengths to make sure that doesn't happen, to make sure the story is never told. The Army and the CIA, to name two."

"You don't have to threaten me," Frank said quietly. "I can't see how my talking would do anybody any good. My friends over there are dead or gone. Hell, I'd just as soon forget the whole thing."

"Good," Lynch said. "I knew you'd see it that way. If anybody asks, by the way, you were injured in an accident at Korat. Your records don't indicate you were ever anywhere else."

"What kind of accident?"

"A tennis accident. You play tennis, don't you? That officers' club at Korat is supposed to have some of the nicest courts in Southeast Asia."

Frank laughed. "Who's going to believe I was shot on a tennis court?"

"You weren't shot. You ran into the net post."

"Jesus, Mr. Lynch, couldn't you come up with something better than that? Sounds pretty lame to me."

"It'll do. Just stick to the story if anybody asks."

—

PART THREE
The Investigation

CHAPTER 42

San Francisco

MAY 6, 1970

FRANK WAS TAKEN BY AMBULANCE TO WALTER Reed Memorial Hospital, the Army's flagship medical center in Washington. It was a busy place, filled with hundreds of soldiers wounded in Vietnam. Two days later, after surgery on his leg and still on a stretcher, he was loaded onto a small Air Force hospital plane for a flight to San Francisco.

"You must be some kind of bigwig," observed the nurse, Captain Geraldine Stewart, as she straightened the blankets on his stretcher. "You have the whole plane to yourself."

"What about those guys?" Frank nodded in the direction of two men in the forward compartment. They were dressed in civilian clothes, but Frank could tell they were military: close-cropped hair, short-sleeved white shirts, narrow black ties. They were sitting stiffly in their seats, smoking cigarettes and flipping through *Popular Mechanics* magazines.

"Why, they're with you," Captain Stewart replied sweetly. "You're being well looked after."

Frank looked at the men with renewed interest, remembering Lynch's warning. The Army wasn't taking any chances that he might talk to the wrong people.

HIS WOUND HEALED RAPIDLY AT LETTERMAN Hospital at the Presidio. Within a week, he was walking a few short steps with the support of a walker, and soon was negotiating the hospital corridors on crutches. By the end of the second week, he was making brief forays into the city, his leg still swathed in bandages.

Classmates from college dropped by, sometimes taking him on afternoon outings to Sausalito or Stinson Beach. Bim Coyle brought him up to speed on the prospects for the school's basketball team, predicting, as he did every year, that they would make it to the NCAA regionals. Joe Scheid talked about working for his father in the family hardware business while wishing he was training thoroughbreds at Golden Gate Fields instead. Skip Schafer finished his first year of law school and was clerking for a downtown firm—he had the job Frank wanted.

They asked about Mike Reidy, at first. He hadn't seen Mike in a couple months, he told them, deflecting any further inquiries. When they asked about Ming and Joanna, he feigned ignorance, telling them he hadn't been in touch with either of them since leaving for Thailand.

But he couldn't forget them. They were once like family, and he couldn't get them out of his mind. He found himself avoiding the neighborhood where he had shared the apartment with Joanna, and he kept away from Golden Gate Park, afraid of unwelcome memories of that last afternoon, when he was still full of innocence and exuberance and looking forward to a government-paid holiday in Thailand.

And the two men who shadowed Frank wouldn't let him forget. They were like a persistent itch, a constant reminder of Cambodia. He wasn't afraid of them—he knew they were only there to keep an eye on him—but he couldn't go anywhere without them trailing along.

As the weeks passed and the vigilance of his two minders didn't let up, he became concerned about what they might do if they thought he was talking to somebody about Cambodia. The attention they paid to Eileen McClellan underscored the danger. She came to visit him in the hospital, partly because of their brief dalliance before he left for Thailand, but mostly, he suspected, because, like so many others, she felt guilty—guilty that he'd been injured in Southeast Asia and she hadn't been the least bit inconvenienced by the war.

Eileen had been no more than an acquaintance in college. In their senior year she was editor of the college newspaper, and now she held a minor staff position with the sports section of the *Herald*, a second-rate afternoon rag that, miraculously, still boasted a wide circulation. She took a keen interest in his injuries, which he tacked up to the natural inquisitiveness of a reporter.

"Looks pretty serious for a tennis accident," she remarked, examining the red, ragged wound that peeked out of the bandages. "Must have been quite a serve."

Frank doubted many of his friends believed the tennis-accident story. Like everyone else, they assumed anyone injured in Southeast Asia was wounded in combat. Eileen took it a step further, though, focusing on the inconsistency between the injury and his cover story.

"Yeah, it was a freak accident, all right. Caught the leg just wrong. They had to cut it up to get the bone set right."

Eileen looked skeptical. She was about to ask another

question when a nurse interrupted to announce the end of visiting hours. Frank wondered if the timing was coincidental or if his army guards had sent her in to cut the conversation short. Eileen kissed him lightly on the cheek and promised to stop by again. Frank found himself hoping she would; she had been in the back of his mind since their night together, and he was starting to think maybe it was more than a one-night stand.

The next evening Eileen telephoned. "Say, Frank, I just wanted to let you know that I had a visit from some friends of yours."

"What friends?"

"Couple guys from army security. You don't have to worry about a thing. I'll keep my mouth shut. I'm a firm believer that national security trumps the public's right to know."

He guessed his bodyguards overheard Eileen ask about his wounds and became concerned she might try to make something of it. She was a reporter, the worst kind of friend he could have.

"What did they say, Eileen?"

"Oh, just national security and all that. You didn't have to send them over, Frank. I mean, I'm a sports reporter now. I couldn't care less about what happened over there. That's not my beat."

Frank pretended to be clued in to the story his keepers had fabricated. "That's great, Eileen. I knew you could be counted on. They just wanted to be sure, is all."

Eileen was quiet a moment. "Of course, if there's anything you want to talk about, I could put you in touch with the right people."

"No, nothing, Eileen. But thanks. It's best if you just forget about it."

LYNCH CALLED THE NEXT DAY. "THERE'S GOING to be a congressional investigation. I guess you heard."

"Yeah, it was on the radio this morning. It sure doesn't look like it's going to blow over."

"Nobody has contacted you, have they?"

"You mean from the Oversight Committee? No, I haven't heard from anyone."

"What about your friend Eileen McClellan?"

"Jeez, leave Eileen out of it," Frank replied testily, then caught himself—he should be more respectful to the national security advisor. Still, Lynch was as responsible as anyone for getting him into this mess, and now he was interfering with his personal life.

"She's a sports reporter, for Christ's sake," he continued. "I think she was skeptical of the tennis accident story, but that's no surprise. I told you it wouldn't fly. Your guys made it worse by trying to intimidate her."

"Is she going to let it drop?"

"Look, Lynch, I hardly know the girl." No more "Mr. Lynch," even if he was one of the most important men in Washington. "She asked some questions about my injuries, and your two goons were all over her. If she was a better reporter, it would have only fueled her interest. Anyway, she doesn't know anything."

"She can add two and two," Lynch persisted. "She has doubts about the tennis accident, and she knows it must have happened about the time of the invasion."

"Lynch, you're paranoid. There's hundreds of thousands

of guys in Vietnam. It would take a real stretch to connect my leg to some sinister plot in Cambodia."

"Sinister plot?" Lynch's voice rose an octave. "It wasn't sinister, and it wasn't a plot. Don't talk like that."

"Jesus Christ, calm down, will ya? I didn't mean anything by it."

Lynch took a deep breath. "You're right. I am a bit stressed. The investigation is consuming the White House. Everyone's wondering who knew what and when did they know it. The president's making it worse. He thinks the hearings are an opportunity to 'vindicate his strategic policies.' If he only knew."

"Well, don't worry about me. My lips are sealed."

"Okay, kid," Lynch said, sounding relieved. "Keep your chin up. And keep your mouth shut. We're in a perilous situation, and we have to stick together to weather the storm."

Frank hobbled down the corridor to the hospital gift shop and bought a copy of the *Herald*, carrying it to the cafeteria and settling into a corner with a mug of coffee. The front page ran another article on the killing of the college students at Davis State. Parents of the students were clamoring for a criminal investigation of the National Guard. The governor wanted to wait for the National Guard to complete its own investigation, confident they would do a "thorough job." Frank laughed—the only "thorough job" the National Guard would do would be to pin the blame on someone else.

In Washington, the shooting at Davis State was treated as a local matter, but the invasion of Cambodia, which sparked the campus violence, was of national concern. Senator Steve South, ranking minority member of the Military Oversight Committee, announced that he would conduct hearings on the invasion and ordered his staff to start an investigation.

The newspaper reported that senators complained the invasion was misconceived, ill timed, and unsuccessful, and that the president exceeded his authority by ordering American troops across the border without their approval. They were incensed they had not been consulted. They didn't attribute the president's actions to any ulterior motives, but argued the invasion was a dangerous miscalculation and they could have stopped it if they had been told.

Frank turned to the sports section and found Eileen McClellan's byline on the third page, over an article on high school baseball. It amused him that the national security advisor was worried that a novice journalist who wrote about high school sports might blow the whistle on the Cambodia invasion.

The next day, Frank received orders to the Naval Hospital in San Diego. He called Lynch to complain. "What gives, John? I thought you were going to use your influence to see that I stayed in San Francisco for the rest of my time in the army."

"Sorry, Frank. MACV thought it would be safer to have you a little more out of the way until the investigation is over."

"You're not still afraid of Eileen McClellan, are you?"

"No, it's a combination of things. Anyway, San Diego's a nice place, especially during the summer."

"But I was going to start law school at USF."

"You'll have to put it off, Frank. You're still in the army, remember, subject to orders and all that. But call me if you find San Diego unbearable, and I'll see what I can do."

"I've heard that before," Frank said caustically.

That afternoon, Eileen stopped by the hospital, wearing a light summer dress and sporting a blue ribbon in her strawberry-blonde hair. His heart sped up when she walked in, but he was careful not to show it—he didn't want to scare her off.

"How's the tennis star?" she asked playfully.

"I'm doing fine, thanks. Nice of you to come by."

"I was on a story out this way. Thought I'd look in to see if there's anything you need."

Frank swung his legs off the bed and pulled himself to his feet on his crutches. He led Eileen to the day room at the end of the hall. They sat on a bench next to the window and looked out over the bay. Alcatraz Island lay in the distance; Frank wondered wryly if he would end up there one day.

"I'm fine, Eileen, really. But tell me, how are you? Aren't you tired of writing about high school baseball?" He regretted the comment when he saw the hurt look on her face and touched her gently on the shoulder. "Hey, I'm sorry. I didn't mean it the way it sounded."

"No, it's okay, Frank. I know what you mean. 'Why's a talented girl like me wasting her time with high school sports?' Well, you may be right, but I keep telling myself I have to start somewhere, that it's only a matter of time and experience before I'll be handling the big stuff. Anyway, I'm lucky to have a job in journalism at all, especially on a big city newspaper, even if it is the *Herald*—otherwise, I'd be an English teacher at some podunk high school."

"I'm sure you're right. And I'm sure it'll work out."

"It used to be worse. First, I was doing the police beat, fires and things like that. Only I was mostly doing research or getting coffee for the veteran reporters. Then I was on the rewrite desk, editing articles from Vietnam and Laos and Cambodia, articles that didn't mean anything to me about places I'd never heard of. At least now I get to write my own stories. The *Herald* may not be the *Chronicle*, but it still has a hundred thousand readers."

An uncomfortable silence fell between them. Frank studied Eileen's face until she looked away in embarrassment. She wasn't a beautiful girl, he decided, but she was attractive in a refreshing, freckle-faced sort of way. He guessed she spent a lot of time sorting through her thick, curly hair.

"How come we never got to know each other in college?" he asked.

Eileen smiled self-consciously, the pain of Frank's earlier comment forgotten. "Because you were a right-winger—fraternity, ROTC, that sort of thing. In fact, I didn't like you much." She caught herself. "I don't mean you personally, but the whole ethic you and your friends stood for. Parties, drinking, sorority girls. Short hair and Madras shirts. Converse shoes and white socks. Everything was a joke. Everything had to be a good time. I thought you guys were seriously out of step with what was going on in the real world."

"So why bother with me now?"

Eileen was quiet for a moment. "Well, now's different, I guess. The real world caught up with you." She indicated Frank's leg, still swathed in bandages. "And you suffered the consequences."

A new thought came to Frank. "Eileen," he asked

impulsively, "can you get away for a few days? I'm being transferred to a hospital in San Diego. Why don't you drive me down?" He rushed the words before he lost his nerve.

Eileen hesitated. "I don't think I can, Frank. I have some vacation coming, but I have to give them notice."

"Aw, come on, Eileen," he pressed. "Tell them it's for a wounded veteran. How could they say no?"

"And besides, I hardly know you." Eileen blushed. Neither had mentioned their night together, but he knew what she was thinking.

"That's why it's such a good idea. We'd have a chance to get to know each other better. You might even start to like me instead of just feeling sorry for me."

Eileen mulled it over for a minute, then shrugged. "Okay," she said, grinning. "It sounds wild. My friends will think I'm crazy, but I'll see what I can do."

CHAPTER 43
Santa Barbara
JUNE 16, 1970

FRANK STAGED HIS DEPARTURE FROM THE HOSPI-tal to throw off his watchers. With the Senate hearings scheduled to start in a few days, he thought they might get jumpy if they knew he was traveling with a news-paper reporter. He made a reservation to fly to San Diego on a commercial airline and left early to make the flight, watching through the rear window of the taxi as a dark-green military sedan pulled out behind him.

Frank directed the driver to the Imwalle Lodge, bet-ting his tail would assume he was stopping for a last drink, a farewell toast before heading to the airport. He entered the dimly lit bar as the army sedan pulled up across the street. The two men inside made no move to follow him in.

Frank clumsily gripped his duffel bag against a crutch and worked his way across the room, smiling disarmingly at the waitress. He pushed a shoulder against the back door and stepped into the bright sunlight of the park-ing lot where Eileen was waiting in her Volkswagen. She stowed the duffel bag and crutches in the back seat.

"Do you think they're suspicious?" she asked as they pulled out of the lot. He had told her he was under intermittent surveillance, but concocted a yarn about an investigation of stolen equipment from Mike Reidy's warehouse in Thailand that had nothing to do with him. It was a weak cover story but with a grain of truth, and Eileen seemed to accept it. She remembered Reidy from college and had no trouble believing he was caught up in something nefarious.

"I don't think so. But let's not wait around to find out."

They stretched the one-day trip into three. The first night they stayed in a small inn in Carmel, Eileen insisting on separate rooms. They ate dinner at the Kevin the Falconer Inn, a restaurant owned by Rick Poe, an aging actor who once starred in rough-and-tumble cowboy movies and now made Carmel his home. After dinner they sipped brandies in front of the fire—Carmel could be chilly even in the middle of summer.

"This town brings back a lot of memories," Frank said, gazing into the fire. "The last time I was here I was with Kathy McKee, a college girlfriend who went to Lone Mountain, the college for rich girls." He gave Eileen a forlorn look. "She dumped me."

"She dumped you? Here?"

He had her interest. "Yeah, she dumped me. She was mad about something. I don't remember what, exactly, but I remember it was my fault. I just didn't think it was that big a deal."

"What happened?"

"Well, after dinner, we strolled down to the beach. It was early evening. There was this amber glow over the water, the sunset mixing with the evening fog. The tide was out. We walked along the beach a ways, then Kathy stooped and picked up a stick." He took a deep breath; as much as he loved telling the story—his college pals knew it by heart—it still hurt.

"Go on." Eileen was all ears.

"She took the stick and wrote 'Goodbye Frank' in the wet sand."

Eileen tried to stifle a laugh. "Sorry, Frank. I know it must have been a shock."

"We never exchanged another word. Ever. We walked silently to the car, and I dropped her off at her parents' house."

"Wow. That's quite a story."

"Here's the worst part. Her parents live on the Seventeen Mile Drive in Pebble Beach. They're rich! If I hadn't pissed her off, I would have been set for life."

Eileen insisted they walk down to the beach to visit the scene of the crime. The tide was out, just like that evening with Kathy McKee. Eileen picked up a piece of driftwood and wrote "Hello Frank" in the sand. Frank laughed. "Thanks, Eileen. That makes me feel a lot better."

The second night they stayed at the Biltmore in Santa Barbara. The hotel was way out of Frank's price range, but he still had some money saved up from Thailand—he hadn't spent all his pay on Laurel, just most of it. The hotel was so expensive that Eileen acquiesced in their taking a single room.

Frank called Lynch from the hotel lobby.

"Where are you?" Lynch shouted. "We have people crawling all over San Francisco looking for you."

"Don't worry, John. I just wanted to be by myself for a while. I got tired of your goon squad following me around."

"Look, Lieutenant, this is serious business. I want you to tell me where you are. You're technically AWOL, you know."

"I'm not AWOL and you know it. I have travel orders. I'm not due in San Diego for another couple days."

"Is that McClellan girl with you?"

Frank was not surprised Lynch knew about Eileen—they seemed to know everything. "Yes, she is. But not as a reporter. Anyway, I won't talk to her about 'you know what.'" Frank took a perverse pleasure in playing on Lynch's fears. "I just wanted to get away."

"Frank, I want you to come in. Eileen McClellan may know more than you think. She edited some articles about Cambodia. We can't afford to have you out there by yourself. We can't protect you."

"Protect me from what, John?" His amusement at Lynch's discomfort turned to irritation. "What are you talking about?"

"Let me be candid, Frank. A lot of powerful people could be hurt if 'you know what,' as you put it, gets out. That 'goon squad' you're so fond of was there to keep you quiet—sure, I admit it—but they were also there to protect you from less disciplined elements of the government who might prefer to see you made permanently quiet."

"Lynch, that's crazy." It was ludicrous to think that his life could be in danger, that somebody could be out to kill him. "This fucking thing has gone on long enough. I'm Frank Schaniel, a dumb-shit second lieutenant in the army. A nobody. Even if I was inclined to 'spill the beans,' nobody would listen to me. I'm not important enough that anyone needs to keep me quiet, so how about you all just leave me alone, okay?"

Frank slammed the phone down and walked slowly back to the room, annoyed with himself for losing his temper. Lynch was just trying to help, he knew. Maybe he shouldn't have been so quick to reject his assistance. If Lynch was right—if people were looking for him for the wrong reasons—he might regret it.

"What's wrong?" Eileen asked, reacting to his dour look. "Bad news?"

Frank forced a smile. "No, everything's fine. We can take as long as we want to get to San Diego."

Frank sat wearily on the bed and let his crutches fall to the floor. Eileen pulled down the covers and gently pushed him back onto the sheets. She kissed him on the lips, then unbuttoned his shirt and helped him out of it. His pants were another matter, but after a few false starts she managed to pull them over the thick bandage that still encased his knee. She slipped out of her own clothes and snuggled into his arms.

FRANK WOKE WHEN THE MORNING SUN SPILLED over the balcony and into the room. Eileen lay on her stomach, stretched naked across the bed, her head scrunched into a pillow. Frank brushed his fingers lightly across her back, eliciting a reluctant moan. She stretched and squinted at him through sleep-filled eyes, then moved closer and draped an arm across his chest, laying her head on his shoulder.

"You're wonderful. You know that, don't you?" she said.

"Yeah, that's what they all say. I'd have thought a reporter would come up with something original."

Eileen punched him playfully in the side. "You're not

supposed to say that. You're supposed to tell me how wonderful I am."

Frank kissed her gently on the lips. "You are. Wonderful, I mean."

"That's all? That's all I get for jeopardizing my job and spiriting you out of San Francisco on a moment's notice—from under the nose of the United States Army? For having conspired with you to evade the law without even a hint of remuneration?" Eileen pushed Frank away in mock disappointment, a pout contorting her lips. "Maybe you should go back to that Kathy girl."

"Okay, okay," Frank said, laughing. "You're right. You're more than wonderful." He paused. "Especially in bed."

Frank rolled off the bed and lurched toward the bathroom, ducking the pillow Eileen threw after him. He stooped and pulled a toothbrush from his duffel bag, spilling the contents onto the floor.

"I hope your leg falls off," Eileen called as he closed the bathroom door.

Frank sat on the edge of the tub and let the warm water cascade over his head and shoulders, careful to keep his bandaged knee dry. His thoughts turned to Cambodia. He still couldn't fathom the role he'd played in what had become a national tragedy. It wasn't his fault, he told himself for the umpteenth time. It wasn't his fault the Army and the CIA didn't talk to one another. If they had, those soldiers in the valley and the kids at Davis State would still be alive.

He reminded himself that he could have been killed too. Having dodged death in Cambodia, he wasn't going to let the investigation drag him under. The committee hearings would eventually blow over, and Davis State wouldn't be on the front pages forever. He just had to be patient. He would never be able to forget Cambodia, but he wasn't about to let the memory derail the rest of his life, a life that he now hoped to share with Eileen.

Eileen was sitting on the bed when he stepped out of the bathroom, a damp towel wrapped around his waist. She was leafing through the papers Lynch had given him on the flight from Vietnam.

She looked up at him curiously. "How come you have these?"

Frank gently pulled the papers from her fingers and tucked them back into the duffel bag. "You're a little nosy, aren't you?"

"They were lying on the floor," she said defensively. "I picked them up."

"They don't mean anything. You're acting like a reporter. They're some clippings I cut out, that's all."

"No, they're not. Some are, but there's also a Xerox of a talk the president gave about Cambodia. Where'd you get that?"

"Eileen, don't worry about it," he said irritably. "It's nothing."

"You were there, Frank, weren't you? In Cambodia. That's where you hurt your leg, wasn't it? Not in Thailand. And it wasn't a tennis accident, was it?"

He sat on the bed and considered how much he could tell her without getting into the secret stuff. If he didn't tell her at least part of the story, her reporter side would take over, and that would be worse.

"Yes, it was Cambodia," he said reluctantly. "I was there. I was wounded. But I can't talk about it."

"Why can't you talk about it? The Cambodia thing is all over the news. That cat is out of the bag. Why can't you talk about your part? Were you there on a secret mission or something?"

"Yes, sort of. At any rate, I'm not supposed to say anything. Especially to reporters."

Eileen looked hurt. "That's all I am, after last night? A reporter?"

Frank took her into his arms. "You're more than a reporter to me, Eileen. A lot more. No matter what happens, I want you to know that. But I can't tell you about Cambodia. I can't tell anybody. It's not that I don't want to. I wish I could. I wish I could just to get it off my chest."

"Okay, Frank, I trust you. But if you're in trouble of some kind, you have to tell me."

"I will. I promise."

They made love again, more gently this time, aware of how precarious their relationship was. Dark clouds hovered over them, and they resolved to savor every moment, no telling when the storm might break.

CHAPTER 44
San Diego
JUNE 18, 1970

FRANK AND EILEEN CHECKED INTO THE SURF-rider, a motel on the beach in San Diego with a Mexican restaurant on the bottom floor that advertised itself as "world famous." The morning overcast had burned off, and it was a warm summer afternoon. College kids were out in force celebrating the end of the school year. Frank and Eileen sat on the boardwalk and watched the passing bicyclists and skaters and the bikini-clad girls walking hand in hand with their college boyfriends.

It was time for Frank to report to the Navy medical center in Balboa Park, where he would be an outpatient for a few months, closeted away by Lynch and his cronies. Eileen handed him the keys to the Volkswagen with a warning not to screw it up, and he reluctantly pulled himself away from the sunshine and pretty girls, leaving Eileen relaxing on the sand.

He stopped at Sam's Market across from the roller coaster to pick up a copy of the *Los Angeles Times*. The hearings had started that morning, and the first session appeared to have been fairly dull. Linnea Arrington, a constitutional law scholar from Harvard, shared her opinion of the limits of the president's power to send troops into Cambodia without the consent of Congress. Thomas

Henderson from the State Department spoke next, lay-ing the groundwork for the balance of the testimony—the topography of the Parrot's Beak region, the political cli-mate of Vietnam and Cambodia, the relative strengths of the military forces in the area. He confirmed that North Vietnam was increasingly using Cambodian territory to funnel arms and soldiers into the South.

It appeared to Frank that the president won the opening round. The committee would have to come up with some pretty strong stuff to undercut his decision to interdict the Ho Chi Minh trail. Cutting off supplies and reinforcements for Communist troops in South Vietnam would save American lives and maybe shorten the war. His failure to consult with Congress wouldn't be enough to sway the opinion of the American public against him.

Frank scanned the related articles on the inside pages, one of which listed upcoming witnesses. Most were from the State Department or the Army—no apparent surprises—but a name at the bottom of the list caused his heart to skip a beat: Canedo, David C., Sergeant, U.S. Army.

Frank found a phone booth outside the hospital and dialed Lynch's private number. "John, what's going on? Where the fuck did they find Canedo?"

"Nothing to worry about, Frank. We can take care of it."

The nervous tenor of Lynch's voice belied his words. Frank knew Lynch wasn't as tough as the press made him out to be—he just hoped he was tough enough to get them through the hearings without anyone going to jail.

"What do you mean, 'We can take care of it?' He's going to identify me. I thought he was dead." Frank felt a spasm of guilt. After what Canedo had done for him in Cambodia, he should be celebrating that he survived.

"So did we, but he made it back, although he was shot up pretty bad. He's been recuperating at an army hospital in Japan. He apparently contacted the committee on his own when he read about the hearings in *Stars and Stripes*."

Frank heard metallic clicks on the line. He wondered if someone was trying to trace the call but chalked it up to paranoia.

"But don't worry, Frank," Lynch continued. "We can put you under wraps. They can't subpoena you if they can't find you. We'll put you up in some nice resort for a few months until all this blows over."

Frank thought of Eileen, waiting for him at the motel. He didn't like the idea of leaving her just as they were getting to know each other, and he didn't want to be imprisoned in some resort, no matter how nice it was.

"John, I'm not so sure. Maybe it's time to 'fess up' anyway. We may be digging the hole deeper by covering things up. No sense making it worse than it already is."

"Frank, we have to keep it quiet," Lynch said, pleading. "For the sake of national security. What would our allies think if they knew we were duped by a couple spies in our own army—or worse, tripped up by our own bureaucratic infighting? We can't let this get out, Frank. We have to protect the president."

"How would this hurt the president? He didn't know what was going on, did he?"

"That's the point. Some people would use that against him, maybe even to try to force him from office. They'd say he wasn't paying enough attention to Cambodia. That he allowed himself to be talked into approving an invasion of a neutral country, an invasion that was a pretext to cover up some illicit CIA plot. That now he's covering up the cover-up."

"Isn't that what we're doing? Covering up the cover-up?"

"Don't talk like that, Frank. We did what we thought was in the best interests of the country, both of us. It didn't work out so well, but our motives were pure. There's nothing to be gained by dragging the president into it."

Frank heard the metallic clicks again. Maybe it wasn't paranoia. "I have to go, John," he said. "I'll be in touch."

"No! Don't hang up!"

"I have to go, John. Sorry."

He replaced the receiver and mulled over their conversation. Was Lynch right? Was he protecting the president by keeping quiet? Or was he protecting himself? Maybe it didn't matter. Maybe the country had a right to know the truth no matter who was hurt.

The story would come out anyway with Sergeant Canedo's testimony. But, on second thought, he realized there were limits to what Canedo could tell the committee. He didn't know the worst of what happened that day—he was wounded before they got to the valley. He couldn't implicate him in anything more than following Neil's trucks across the border. The others Canedo could identify were either dead or missing. Still, he could expect a call from the committee, and he would have to decide what to do. Lynch's idea of keeping out of sight wasn't going to cut it.

He needed to talk things over with someone he could trust, someone impartial, someone without an axe to grind.

He reflected on his conversation with Eileen that morning and decided to confide in her when he got back to the motel. She would have a fresh perspective, maybe some suggestions on how to deal with the investigation.

He walked up the steps to the hospital, his leg healed enough that he managed with a single crutch for support. He located the admissions desk and laid his orders on the counter.

"Okay, Lieutenant," the orderly said as he skimmed the document, "we'll check you in and schedule an appointment with Dr. Pramuk in a few days. My guess is he'll put you on physical therapy. Other than that, you're on your own. You need quarters?"

"No, I'd rather rent a place, if I can."

"That's okay with us. We'd have to give you a bed on one of the wards, and they're pretty full right now, mostly Marines medevac'd from Vietnam. How about call tomorrow, and we'll tell you when to report for the intake paperwork. We'll have a housing voucher ready for you as well."

The orderly turned and dropped Frank's orders in front of a young clerk-typist who gave them a cursory glance before sliding them into a tray at the side of her desk. Then something caught her eye, and she retrieved them for a closer inspection. She looked up curiously at Frank.

"Anything wrong?" Frank asked, mildly alarmed.

"Oh, no, Lieutenant," she replied self-consciously. "I thought your name rang a bell, but I guess not. We don't see that many Army people here. Most of our patients are Navy or Marine Corps."

Frank turned back to the orderly. "Need anything

else?" He didn't want to linger, worried the clerk may have been told to keep an eye out for him.

"No, that'll do it, Lieutenant. If you need some money, take your records to Disbursing Clerk Gambee in the finance office down the hall. She'll give you an advance and straighten it out with the Army later."

The clerk called to him as he turned to leave. "I remember what it was, Lieutenant." She sounded relieved to have an explanation for her behavior. "There's a message for you. It's pinned to the bulletin board in the lobby."

Frank found his name printed on a folded piece of paper among the notes tacked to the cork board inside the front entrance. A name and telephone number were printed on the inside. He was to call a David Franklin at the office of the Senate Military Oversight Committee in Washington.

Well, that's it, he thought. There's no way to avoid the committee now.

He glanced outside to see two men walking rapidly toward the entrance. They weren't the goons who followed him in San Francisco, but he recognized them just the same. One was Captain Broderick, formerly with the 558th, looking uncomfortable in civilian clothes. The other was Colonel Michael Ira Neil, dressed in an ill-fitting suit and tie, walking with the help of a cane, one arm in a sling. Frank was momentarily paralyzed at the sight.

Christ, the man's indestructible. He's taken two bullets, and he's still going strong.

It couldn't be good for him that Neil and Broderick had shown up at the hospital. If Colonel Neil's involvement with the Cambodia fiasco ever came out, it would look bad for the president, but it would look worse for Neil and the Army. Like Lynch, Neil would want to keep a lid on it. Maybe he was one of those extremists Lynch had warned him about who wanted to make sure the lid stayed on permanently.

Brushing off a wave of panic, Frank looked at the note in his hand. If nothing else, he had to return Franklin's call. He turned and headed toward the finance office, clumsily swinging down the hall on the crutch. He glanced over his shoulder as Neil and Broderick pushed through the glass doors and walked up to the orderly at the reception desk. He ducked into the finance office before they saw him.

"Yes, sir, may I help you?" Disbursing Clerk Gambee was the only person in the room.

"I need to drop off my finance records, Miss Gambee." Frank laid the brown envelope on the desk. "Say, I don't feel so good. You mind if I get some air by the window while you're doing the paperwork?"

"Be my guest, Lieutenant." She looked up at him sympathetically. "I'll go through these real quick so you can get out of here."

Frank pushed open the window and glanced back at Gambee, who was engrossed with his records, her back to him. He sat and swung his legs over the sill, then pulled the crutch out and dropped on his good leg to the grass a few feet below. He hobbled across the lawn to the parking lot. Out of the corner of his eye, he saw Broderick burst out of the hospital entrance and chase after him, Colonel Neil close behind.

Frank had a fifty-yard head start, but his wound slowed him down and he couldn't maintain the lead. Broderick closed to within thirty yards by the time Frank reached the Volkswagen. He threw the crutch into the back seat and climbed awkwardly behind the wheel, fumbling in his pocket for the key.

Broderick caught up with him as he started the engine. "Lieutenant, you're to come with us," he said, resting his hands on the door and breathing heavily through the open window. "Orders from Department of the Army."

"Oh yeah? Can I see them?"

"Look, Lieutenant, we're with the Army Security Agency now. We have orders to take you in, so I'm giving you an order to get out of that car."

Frank shrugged. "Okay, Captain, if you say so."

Broderick backed away as he swung the door open, but instead of getting out, Frank slammed the car into gear and pressed his foot to the gas. As the Volkswagen lurched forward, Colonel Neil jumped in front of it and pulled a gun from the waistband of his slacks. Frank jerked the wheel and sideswiped the colonel, sending him sprawling to the ground. When he looked back, Neil was lying prone on the asphalt with Broderick hovering over him.

Two bullets and run over by a car—maybe now he'd seen the last of Colonel Neil.

CHAPTER 45
San Diego
JUNE 18, 1970

EILEEN WAS SITTING ON THE BEACH, READING A book, when Frank returned to the motel. He dropped to the sand and rested a hand on her bare leg in silent greeting.

"Hi there, fella," she said, brushing her fingers lightly through his hair. "How goes it?"

"Fine, Eileen. All squared away at the hospital." He gave her a halfhearted smile. "Everything's fine."

Eileen was silent for a moment. "I was hoping you wouldn't say that, Frank. I don't think everything's 'squared away,' and I don't think everything's 'fine.' I think you're in trouble of some kind. And I wish you'd tell me about it. Maybe we can help."

Eileen looked away and stared into the distance. A few bathers splashed in the surf. Farther out, a surfer sat on his board, waiting patiently for the perfect wave.

"What do you mean by that, Eileen? Who's 'we'?"

"I called Chuck Fox, my editor, Frank. He had two messages for you. One was from John Lynch, who, last I heard, was the president's chief of staff or something. The other was from a David Franklin. You're to call him, and he says it's important."

"What'd Lynch want?"

Eileen gave him a look that said he'd better be careful, that he had a lot of nerve asking her questions when he was so tight-lipped.

"He told Fox to tell me to tell you that you can come in, that the pressure's off."

"What did he mean by that?"

Still annoyed, Eileen pulled a slip of paper from the pocket of her shorts. " 'Tell Lieutenant Schaniel the pressure is off,' " she read. " 'I'm going to testify.' "

Frank looked at Eileen with a raised eyebrow. "I suppose your editor put you on the story?"

"He tried. I quit."

"You what?"

"I quit, Frank. If we're going to be together, I can't be investigating you at the same time. You could never completely trust me if I was still connected to the paper, even if I told you I wasn't working on the story."

Frank gently stroked her cheek. "You're quite a woman, Eileen. I'm glad you're on my side."

"But, Frank, now that I'm not a reporter, I want you to tell me what this is all about."

Frank had already decided to do just that. He needed advice, and she was the only one he could turn to. He told her the entire story, beginning with Reidy walking across the bar of the Chao Phraya Hotel his first day in Thailand. Eileen sat transfixed, interrupting only occasionally to clarify a detail or two. He spoke for half an hour, concluding with his narrow escape that afternoon from Neil and Broderick in the hospital parking lot. When he finished, the sun was setting over the ocean, throwing golden rays into the pink clouds on the horizon.

They fell silent to watch for the storied green flash, the

final bursting reflection of the sun as it disappeared over the Pacific. They didn't see it. "Probably because I'm color blind," Frank said with a laugh.

"Are you going to go back? To testify?"

"Well, it doesn't matter now, I guess. That's what Lynch was saying. For whatever reason, he's decided to tell the story himself. Hopefully they won't need me, although that's probably wishful thinking." Frank squeezed Eileen's hand. "But either way, I feel a lot better about it. Now we can relax. I won't have those army goons on my back anymore."

Frank walked back to the room to call David Franklin while Eileen stayed on the beach to watch the sunset fade into night. He hesitated before placing the call. It would be easier now that he didn't have to buck Lynch, but he could still be in for a grueling experience.

"Mr. Franklin? This is Lieutenant Frank Schaniel. You left a message for me to call?"

"I sure did, Lieutenant. Where are you?"

"San Diego."

"Lieutenant, I'm minority counsel for the Senate Military Oversight Committee. As I'm sure you know, we're looking into the Cambodia incursion. We understand you were there."

Frank took a deep breath. "Yes, I was there." There was no turning back now.

"We need you back here, Lieutenant. You know Sergeant Canedo. He told us quite a story, but the big pieces are still missing."

"Yeah, I bet. But I understand John Lynch will take care of that."

"We were hoping he would too. He caught a sudden

case of guilty conscience, and I think you had something to do with it, Lieutenant. He thought you were quite the hero in this affair. Part of the reason he came forward was to take the pressure off you."

"How about that." Touched by Lynch's concern, Frank regretted being so rude to the man. "I thought Lynch's skin was too thick to get sympathetic about anything. When will he testify?"

"He won't be testifying. He was killed in a traffic accident two hours ago."

Stunned, Frank sat down heavily on the bed. "He was what?"

"He was driving over here from the White House when he ran off the road. Single car accident. May have been a heart attack."

Frank thought of Neil and Broderick accosting him at the hospital. "You sure it was an accident?"

"No, we're not sure, but the police have nothing at this point that indicates otherwise." Franklin paused. "Lieutenant, we need you here, and we need you quick. Can you catch a plane tonight? Tomorrow at the latest? I would send a military aircraft, but I don't have the authority, and it would complicate things anyway with the Army circling the wagons. I'd just as soon not let them know you're coming to Washington."

"I'll see what I can do, Mr. Franklin, but there are people out here looking for me. I ran into Colonel Neil, literally, and Captain Broderick was with him." Frank recounted the altercation in the hospital parking lot.

"Unfortunately, Lieutenant, we can't help you. We don't have the resources and can't ask the military or the FBI or anybody for assistance. We don't know who's involved. You have to get back here on your own. The good news is the Army seems to be keeping this confined to a very small group. If we're lucky, Neil and Broderick are the only assets they have in San Diego, and maybe you've sidelined them."

"When do you want me?"

"Get here as soon as you can. I'll put you on the stand on Monday. Call me at the office when you arrive. Or call me at home. My number's in the phone book."

The conversation was interrupted by static and a metallic clicking sound. "We'd better hang up now," Franklin said. "Call me when you get here." The phone went dead.

Eileen walked in the door as Frank replaced the receiver. "How about dinner, Lieutenant? I'm starved. We could try that place downstairs and find out why it's world famous." She saw the worried expression on his face. "What's wrong? I thought everything was okay now that John Lynch will be testifying."

"Lynch is dead."

"Oh, God!" Eileen sat down on the bed beside him and took his hand in hers. "How did that happen? What will you do now?"

"He died in a car accident. Or at least they think it was an accident." He was silent for a moment. "And now I have to go to Washington."

"I'll go with you."

"No, you won't," he said firmly. "It may be danger-ous. And it definitely won't be fun."

"I don't care. I want to be with you." She put her

hands on his shoulders and turned him to face her, looking him squarely in the eye. "And I'm a reporter. I want the story."

Frank chuckled and kissed her lightly on the cheek. He took her into his arms and held her tight, afraid to let her go, afraid to face what he had to do. He would return to Washington, and he would tell his story. He owed that much to Lynch, who ruined his own career—maybe lost his life—to take the heat. And he owed it to the men who died in Cambodia.

"Okay, let's go to dinner," he said. "The last supper. How about we go to Saska's instead, that steak place on the boulevard. I'm going to need some protein to get through this."

They walked hand in hand down Salem Court to Mission Boulevard. The sidewalk was lined with old beach cottages, clapboard shacks built in the 1920s and fitfully improved over the years with a hodgepodge of additions. Paint peeled from shingled walls, losing the fight with the salty sea air. It was a little too early in the season for the Arizona refugees from the desert heat to have arrived, and college students sat on the patios drinking beer and enjoying the last few days of their winter leases.

"Eileen, maybe we could live in a place like this," Frank suggested, "when all of this is over and I'm out of the army."

Eileen gave him a calculating look. "Is that a proposal?"

They came to the boulevard, the passing traffic inching along, the summer beach crowd heading home. Beachgoers walked along the street, now bundled up against the evening chill.

"Well, what would you think of that? If we got married?"

It was still early for dinner, and Saska's was half-empty. They took a quiet booth and ordered sirloin steaks—locally grown on the family cattle ranch, according to the menu—and shared a bottle of Mondavi wine.

"So, what do you say?" he asked.

"I'll have to get back to you," she said, looking down at her bare ring finger, making sure he followed her gaze. "Maybe I'll leave you a note in the sand."

CHAPTER 46
San Diego
JUNE 19, 1970

THEY LEFT THE CAR IN THE AIRPORT PARKING lot and walked to the terminal. Eileen carried a small satchel containing Frank's uniform and their spare clothing. He walked beside her, supported by a crutch, wearing blue cotton slacks and a loose-fitting rayon shirt covered with a colorful pattern of palm trees.

"You look like you're coming back from a Hawaiian vacation," Eileen said cheerily, "rather than going to 'meet your destiny.'"

Frank playfully poked her leg with the crutch. "No jokes, Eileen. This is serious beeswax."

The terminal was crowded. Vacationers and businessmen impatiently jostled each other in the ticket lines. Frank and Eileen nervously waited their turn at the American Airlines counter, scanning the terminal for anyone who may have noticed them. They had delayed entering the terminal until the last minute to minimize the chance of being recognized, and now the flight to Washington was about to depart. The clerk—Carrie Jo Koonce, her name tag read—carefully counted the bills Frank laid on the counter, then began to methodically write out the tickets.

"Miss Koonce, do you think you could speed it up? The plane's about to take off."

"Well, that's not my fault, mister." She looked up at him disapprovingly. "You should have given yourself more time. I issue hundreds of tickets every day, and I can't get excited about yours just because you're late."

"Okay, okay," Frank said. "Didn't mean to upset you."

"And it's not Miss Koonce—it's Mrs. Koonce."

She finished issuing the tickets and handed them to Frank. "Next time you'll know better."

Frank and Eileen walked rapidly down a long hallway to the boarding area, joining a queue of passengers at the boarding gate. Two men stepped out of an alcove. Frank froze—Neil and Broderick! They weren't sidelined. They were still in the game.

Frank ducked out of the line and pulled Eileen with him, but it was too late—Neil spotted them and drew a .45 from under his coat. As Frank pushed Eileen back up the corridor, he heard the first report. A bullet grabbed at his sleeve and buried itself in the wall. He dropped to the floor and dragged Eileen down with him, squeezing her against the wall for protection, but Neil's shots were lost in a cacophony of gunfire and screams.

Frank raised his head and looked down the hallway. Captain Broderick was sitting on the floor, his back to a wall, holding a wounded arm. Neil stood partially protected by a doorway, exchanging gunfire with a security guard wearing dark glasses and a baseball cap pulled low over his face. Frank took a second look. The guard looked like Mike Reidy, but that was impossible, a trick of the eyes.

The other passengers in line had also dropped to the floor, some wounded, their screams adding to the din. Neil and the security guard were the only ones still standing. Neil leaned on a cane and fired steadily from a gun poking out of the sling supporting his injured arm. A smear of blood suddenly appeared on the security guard's shirt and he tumbled backward as if shoved by a strong gust of wind. Neil dropped his gun and grabbed his left shoulder, blood seeping through his fingers and dripping to the floor.

That's the third bullet. Surely, he's out of action this time.

Scrambling to his feet, Frank stumbled back to the terminal lobby, pulling Eileen with him, as security guards and police streamed the other way. He hoped to cash in their tickets—they needed the money to fund their getaway—but Mrs. Koonce stood comatose behind the American Airlines counter.

"Carrie Jo, I don't suppose you could refund our tickets, could you?"

She stared at him blankly, immobilized by the noise and commotion in the boarding area. Then she recognized Frank, and her eyes narrowed. "I told you it was Mrs. Koonce."

The terminal quickly filled with panicked, screaming passengers rushing for the door. Frank and Eileen gave up on Mrs. Koonce and, keeping their heads down, joined the throng and ran into the street. Police and firemen pushed into the terminal, and ambulances with lights flashing nosed through the crowd.

"Now what?" Eileen asked, catching her breath.

"Well, we can't go back for your car, that's for sure. They'll be looking for it. We've gotta keep moving. Let's put a few blocks between us and the airport, then I need to find a pay phone. I know someone who might help."

They walked three blocks to India Street and ducked into Filippi's, a pizza grotto in Little Italy, and took a booth in the back. Frank found a pay phone by the restrooms and flipped through the pages of the phone book. He ran his finger down a column of names. Canedo, Joseph. Ash Street. He dialed the number.

"Mrs. Canedo? This is Lieutenant Schaniel. I'm a friend of your son's."

"Yes? Is David all right? He called just the other day. My husband's working in the garden. Can you call back later?"

"No, Mrs. Canedo, I'm out of time. I need help and have no one else to turn to."

A HALF HOUR LATER A GLEAMING 1963 CHRYSLER four-door sedan pulled up at the curb. Joe and Connie Canedo looked around expectantly from the front seat. Frank and Eileen stepped out of a recessed doorway and slipped into the back.

Connie Canedo turned to look at them. "We know who you are. We spoke to David."

"Mrs. Canedo, I hate to put you in a jam, but we need a place to stay tonight," Frank said, "and we need a ride to the Los Angeles airport in the morning." He hesitated, embarrassed. "And we need to borrow some money."

"David said we should help you. He said you saved his life, put a tourniquet on his leg. We thank you for that."

"He asked me to call you if I made it home, tell you what happened to him. I couldn't bring myself to do it, kept putting it off. I'm glad he's okay."

She smiled. "We'll go home now and get you some dinner. I made some fresh tamales. You can sleep in David's room."

She turned to look at them again. "Are you married?"

"No, we're not, Mrs. Canedo."

"Then one of you will have to sleep on the couch."

FRANK CALLED DAVID FRANKLIN FROM KENNEDY Airport the next evening. "Mr. Franklin? It's me, Lieutenant Schaniel. I'm in New York."

"What happened? Your picture's splashed all over the papers."

"I know. I saw them."

Frank peered furtively from the phone booth, watching the passengers as they walked past, looking for any sign he'd been recognized. Eileen sat in a chair across the aisle, positioned to observe anyone approaching the phones. She was peeking over the top of an open newspaper, trying to look inconspicuous.

Frank smiled. She's Miss Marple, right out of an Agatha Christie novel.

"Lieutenant, what happened at the San Diego airport?"

"It wasn't me. I mean, I was there, but I didn't shoot anybody. I think it was the security guards. They must have opened fire when they saw Neil pull out a gun. It was a real bloodbath."

"They say Lieutenant Reidy was there. He was one of the security guards."

"No, I don't think so. I noticed the guy. He fooled me

for a second too, but it wasn't him. I mean, how could it have been Reidy?"

"Maybe he has an interest in your testifying. If he is who they think he is, he's interested in getting American troops out of Vietnam any way he can. He could be thinking your testimony would help with that." Franklin was quiet for a moment. "Or maybe he was there to help a friend get out of a jam—a jam he helped put him in."

"Well, I suppose it could have been him, but I don't think so." It was too surreal to believe, a mini version of the battle in Cambodia, now with Reidy trying to kill Neil at the San Diego airport.

"Mr. Franklin, what'll I do? You still want me there?"

"We sure do. Your testimony is more important than ever. Can you find a place to lay low for a couple nights and be here at one o'clock Monday?"

"I guess so. Where do you want me?"

"Meet me on the Capitol steps. I'll arrange for some people to help if there's any interference. Once we get you inside the building, you'll be fine. Those army boys can't touch you here."

"Okay, Mr. Franklin. I'll see you Monday."

"Lieutenant, I know how tough this is. Everyone's looking for you—the Army, the press, probably the FBI. I wish I could help, offer you asylum or something, but that's not possible. We don't have anybody we can rely on, anybody we can trust."

"I understand. We'll make it. We made it this far. Tell Sergeant Canedo I owe his parents three hundred dollars. They funded our escape."

"Be careful," Franklin warned again. "Lynch's death is looking less and less like an accident."

Frank hung up and signaled to Eileen, who stood and led the way through the terminal to the taxi stand. He followed a few steps behind, walking as steadily as he could without a crutch, which would have been a sure giveaway to anyone looking for him.

"Did you kids hear what's going on out in California?" the cabbie asked as he pulled away from the curb. "Big shootout in some airport. They think Commie spies did it. Can you believe it? Right out of some spy thriller or something! Now they're looking for some army guy. A turncoat. Jeez, who'd believe it? I didn't think that sort of stuff happened anymore."

Frank and Eileen slipped lower in the back seat, Frank taking Eileen's hand as they exchanged weary smiles.

CHAPTER 47
Washington, D.C.
JUNE 22, 1970

THE TAXI PUSHED THROUGH THE LUNCHTIME
traffic on Constitution Avenue and slid to a stop in front
of the Capitol, the white-columned portico looming above
them. Frank paid the driver and helped Eileen out of the
car. Men in suits and ties and women in short summer
dresses walked at a brisk clip up and down the steps.
Three men stood by themselves on the sidewalk.

One of them detached himself from the group. "Lieutenant Schaniel?"

Frank eyed him cautiously. "Yes?"

"I'm David Franklin." He stuck out his hand. "Happy
to finally meet you."

Frank shook his hand. "You too. I hope I'm still happy
when this is over."

Franklin motioned to the men with him. "Chris
Cooke and James Ryan, two lawyers from the office. The
best security force I could muster. They're here for show.
They won't be much help if the shit hits the fan."

As they started up the steps, a green sedan screeched
to a halt at the curb. Two military policemen scrambled
out and started after them. Frank turned and watched as
Neil slowly climbed out of the car behind them, his left
arm strapped to his chest.

Frank laughed mirthlessly. No surprise there. Nothing seemed to stop the guy. He should have killed the bastard with the Volkswagen!

"Lieutenant Schaniel!" shouted one of the MPs. "You're under arrest."

But Franklin was too quick. He pulled Frank and Eileen into the building a few steps ahead of the MPs, who were barred from entering by Capitol police, and led them to a large office adjoining the hearing room. The first person Frank saw was Sergeant Canedo, seated in a wheelchair looking out the window, one leg in a cast propped on a pillow, an arm wrapped in bandages.

Frank laid a hand on Canedo's shoulder. "Sergeant, I've seen you looking better, but it's still good to see you."

A self-conscious grin spread across Canedo's face. "Hey, Lieutenant. Guess I opened a can of worms, huh?"

"Yes, I guess you did. But somebody had to speak up. You can be proud you had the guts to do it."

"I didn't know that Mr. Lynch. These guys think he was going to tell what happened in Cambodia when he was killed."

"I'm sure he was. He had a lot of guts too, I think. But he was a little late to the party, like me."

A young clerk rushed into the room, flushed with excitement. "Did you hear the news? The president's asked for some television time. Rumor is General Chapin is out."

Franklin looked sharply at Frank. "Your appearance here has apparently shaken up a few people."

Frank was doubtful. "Maybe, but they don't even know what I'm going to say."

"Oh, I think they have a pretty good idea. I had a long

talk with John Lynch the night before he died. They have to assume he told me everything."

"How much does the president know? Did he say?"

"A lot. The president apparently wasn't told the real purpose for the invasion, that it was to disrupt Neil's little arrangement with Lon Nol. But he knew shortly after it happened—the CIA director filled him in. I think that's what convinced Lynch to come to us. He suspected Fish and the president would try to hang the whole thing on him and he wasn't about to take the fall."

"You think the president can weather this?"

"Hard to say, but I don't think he'll be thrown out of office for trying to squelch a bad story. Too bad, though. This war might be over quicker with someone else in the White House." He looked at Frank appraisingly. "You ready? You're due on the stand at two o'clock. We can't take a chance on somebody getting to you before you testify."

"Okay," Frank said, taking Eileen by the hand. "Let's go."

THE HEARING ROOM WAS PACKED. REPORTERS shouting questions crowded around Frank as he entered, and photographers jockeyed for position. He was ushered to a chair at the witness table facing a forest of microphones. Eileen sat in the first row of seats behind him while three senators took their places on the raised dais, ignoring the hubbub in the room. The chairman's chair remained vacant.

Frank turned to look at the crowd and was greeted by a sea of blinding flashbulbs. He spotted Colonel Neil sitting by himself in a corner, looking wan and tired. Neil returned his gaze with a grim but confident half smile, unnerving Frank. How could he even be there? After the shootout at the San Diego airport, they should be looking for Neil as much as they were looking for him. And why would he *want* to be there, knowing that Frank was about to blow the whistle on his whole operation.

Back in uniform, Neil wore more medals than Frank could count, a veritable smorgasbord that crawled up his chest and disappeared under a lapel. Frank straightened in his seat and smoothed his own uniform. One lonely ribbon was pinned above the coat pocket, the National Defense Service Medal, given to every soldier just for showing up. If credibility was measured by military decorations, he was screwed.

A scrawny, sunken-chested senator with thinning brown hair and a permanent scowl on his face banged a gavel on the table.

"Lieutenant, we've already had a long morning," he wheezed, "and these hearings, in my opinion"—he turned with exaggerated courtesy to his colleagues—"have been unduly prolonged as it is. I'm told by a friend of mine, a general officer in the United States Army—General Edward Dewey Chapin, to be exact—a man of unquestioned integrity, that you, sir, are a spy. And I have been told by counsel for the minority, Mr. Franklin here, that you are not a spy, that you are, in fact, a patriot, and that you have a story to tell that we should hear." He paused dramatically. "So why don't you just tell your story, and we'll decide for ourselves."

The senator stuck a large, unlit cigar into his mouth and began to work it back and forth as he leaned back in his chair and surveyed the room. When his gaze settled on Frank, the room turned deathly still.

"Well, Senator," Frank began, "it started a few months ago, in Bangkok. I was in the bar of the officers' club, and my friend Lieutenant Reidy walked in. I remember he was grinning—"

Frank was interrupted by the entrance of a tall senator with an ample paunch and jowly cheeks followed by a phalanx of aides. He squeezed behind the seated senators and sat heavily in the empty chair at the center of the table, pulling the microphone toward him and bunching the green felt cloth against his bulging stomach.

"Young man," he said, "I think maybe we've heard about enough from you today."

He turned to the senator who had been conducting the hearing. "Senator South, do I understand correctly that counsel for the majority did not have an opportunity to interview this young man before you put him on the stand?"

"Well, that's true, Mr. Chairman, but I thought you—"

"And do I also understand that the police are looking for him this very minute, and that he may have perpetrated a murder three days ago?"

"Well, I don't know about that, Senator Weber, but—"

"I think I can assume, Senator South, because of the unusual circumstances surrounding the appearance of this witness and because of the unusual precautions of your minority counsel"—he nodded accusingly at Franklin—"that we shall be treated to some testimony perhaps vilifying our military, perhaps defaming our president, and all without any effort to corroborate the testimony in advance, all of which seems highly irregular."

"Mr. Chairman, I can explain—"

"Well, no need, Senator. Perhaps we can take care of

4

this right here and now. If this man speaks the truth, we shall hear him out. However, out of deference to those who may be the subject of his testimony, and perhaps of his calumny, we should at least inquire first into his credibility—his *bona fides*, so to speak."

Senator Weber turned to Frank. "Lieutenant, is it true you are a friend of one Ming Chu, a Chinese agent?"

"Well, yes, sir. He and I—"

"And Joanna Tsai, a suspected agent?"

"Yes, I knew her, but—"

"Is it also true you were present at the San Diego airport on Friday when two officers of the United States Army were shot, presumably by Chinese agents?"

Frank was starting the perspire. "Well, I was at the airport—"

"This is all a very interesting coincidence, isn't it, Lieutenant? You're chummy with foreign agents, and you were part of an ambush of military officers on an official assignment."

The chairman turned to Senator South. "Senator, I believe this man's testimony is premature, to say the least. He may have some pertinent information on the incident at the airport, information that may be critical to the police investigation. I propose we delay his testimony until he has been properly vetted. That will not only assist the authorities in their investigation of the shooting in San Diego but will also allow us an opportunity to evaluate his credibility. I think that's a more sensible plan. Is that acceptable to you, Senator?"

"Well, of course, Mr. Chairman, although I would prefer—"

"Well, good then." Senator Weber turned and smiled

paternally at Frank. "Lieutenant, you just go on now with these army people waiting in the rear of the room, and we'll see you back here in a few days. I believe your testimony will be only tangential to the matter at hand, and we have some more important areas to look into in the meantime."

The two military policemen who had attempted to arrest Frank on the Capitol steps approached down the aisle. Frank glanced at them nervously, then turned back to the senator. "Mr. Chairman, I'm afraid if I go with these men, I may not be around to testify in a few days."

"Lieutenant, no need to worry," Senator Weber assured him. "They're aware of this committee's interest in your continued well-being. They'll take better care of you than your own mother. As we say in Okeene, they're not about to rile the wagon master."

The chairman rapped his gavel on the table to adjourn the hearing. The military policemen took Frank by the arms and escorted him back down the aisle to where Neil was waiting by the door, that same confident half smile on his face.

"I told you I'd get you, didn't I?" Neil whispered, making no effort to hide the malice in his voice.

CHAPTER 48
Washington, D.C.
JUNE 22, 1970

MACNAMARA DETACHED HIMSELF FROM THE
group of reporters crowding after Frank and approached
Eileen, who was left standing by herself in the front of the
room. "Come with me, Eileen," he said quietly. "I think I
can get you and Frank out of here, get you both to safety."

Eileen eyed him suspiciously. "And you are?"

"I'm a friend. I work for the *Herald*. I was in Thailand
when Frank was there. I wrote articles that you edited."
He smiled. "With a heavy hand, I might add."

"Robert MacNamara?"

"Yes, that's me. The guy whose articles you mutilated
all those months."

"What do you have in mind?" she asked, still wary.

"I think we can catch up with Frank before they
can get him out of town, maybe snatch him away from
those MPs."

"Okay, I guess," Eileen reluctantly agreed, having no
better alternative. She followed MacNamara out of the
hearing room and down the Capitol steps. He pushed
through the crowd on the sidewalk and flagged down
a taxi.

"Dulles Airport," he ordered. The driver nodded and

swung away from the curb and into the traffic on Constitution Avenue.

"Why the airport?" Eileen asked. "And what about Frank?"

"If my suspicions are correct, Frank isn't in the hands of the Army at all. I think Neil's with the CIA, not that it makes much difference. And I think he plans to slip Frank out of Washington as quickly as he can." He smiled reassuringly. "At least that's what I've been told, and by a very reliable source."

A half hour later they pulled up to the main entrance of the terminal. The driver dropped the flag and turned to MacNamara with an outstretched hand. "That'll be six bucks, mister."

MacNamara handed him a ten. "We need to wait here a couple minutes, okay?"

The cabbie looked at the bill and shrugged. "Wait time is ten cents a minute. This'll pay for a few, I guess."

Five minutes later a green sedan slid to the curb behind them. The two MPs got out, followed by Schaniel and Neil.

David Franklin stepped out of the terminal and blocked their way. "Going somewhere, Colonel?"

Neil was startled by Franklin's sudden appearance, but recovered quickly. "Don't interfere, Franklin," he warned, "or you're going to be in big trouble."

" 'Big trouble,' Colonel? That's the best you can come up with? I think you're the one who's going to be in 'big trouble.' What are you doing at the airport? You're supposed to be on your way to Fort Belvoir with this man. I don't think the Army even knows you're here."

Neil moved to brush Franklin out of the way, but Franklin stood his ground. Neil turned to the MPs for help, but instead of confronting Franklin, they released Schaniel and stepped aside. MacNamara got out of the cab and took a bewildered Schaniel by the arm, leading him into the terminal with Eileen at their heels, leaving Franklin on the sidewalk to deal with Neil.

"Frank, I'm Bob MacNamara, a friend of Mike Reidy's in Bangkok," he said as they walked to the ticket counter. "I'm a reporter for Eileen's newspaper."

"Yes, Mike spoke about you. Nice to meet you, I think."

MacNamara bought three tickets for San Francisco. The plane was about to take off, and they hurried down the corridor to board.

"How'd Franklin manage those two MPs?" Frank asked once they were settled in their seats.

"He had help from some army friends. I don't know what line he fed them, but he can be a pretty persuasive guy. The MPs were under orders to release you to Franklin if Neil did anything other than take you to Belvoir."

"Franklin knew all along this was going to happen?"

"Well, let's just say he was prepared for the possibility."

"So what do we do now? Neil's people will be looking all over for us."

"I don't think they'll be looking in San Francisco, at least not yet. We'll be there before he can get his guys organized."

"And after we're there?"

"That's up to you."

"Any suggestions?"

"Well, Franklin figures if you aren't able to tell your story to the committee, second-best is to tell it to the press. That's where I come in."

Frank looked up to see a Chinese man in a dark business suit walking down the aisle. Ming Chu settled into a seat directly across from him.

"Ming, I don't believe it," Frank said, shaking his head in wonder.

"It's me, all right." Ming smiled. "Seems I'm always around when you need help."

Frank laughed mirthlessly. "Thanks for nothing, Ming. If it wasn't for you, I wouldn't be in this mess."

"Frank, we share the same goal again. Last time it was to get out of the valley. This time it's to give you a chance to tell your story."

Frank nodded toward Bob MacNamara, who was sitting next to the window on the other side of Eileen. "This *Herald* reporter has already taken care of that."

"Major Chu," Bob interrupted, leaning forward in his seat, "I'm as surprised as Frank to see you. But you're right—getting Frank's story out serves your interests as well as his, or at least David Franklin's. Franklin thinks the country has the right to know the truth no matter the consequences, and I suspect you think one of those consequences may be to shorten the war."

"That's right, Mr. MacNamara. And maybe I can help you get the story out. What's your plan?"

"I was going to suggest Frank and Eileen spend a few days with me in an isolated cabin I know of in Marin County, north of San Francisco. It's in Bolinas, the middle of nowhere, owned by Sam McCullagh, a friend from college who can be trusted to keep his mouth shut. Eileen and I will write the story, and after the *Herald* publishes it, Frank should be able to come out of hiding."

"Sounds good to me," Ming said. "Need any protection while you're at it?"

MacNamara grimaced. "That's probably not such a good idea, Major—you being a Chinese agent might undermine our credibility."

"Yes, I suppose you're right," Ming said with a weary smile.

"Ming, whatever happened to Mike Reidy?" Frank asked. "Is he all right?"

"He's dead." Ming spoke without emotion. "At the San Diego airport."

Frank was stunned. "You mean, that *was* him?"

"Yes, it was. He was there to make sure you got to Washington."

"Who was he, really?"

"Well, ostensibly, he was with the Weather Underground, a group willing to go to any lengths to throw a wrench into the cogs of the American military machine. But I think his real goal was to divert American weapons to the Irish Republican Army. They're starting trouble again in Northern Ireland, and apparently have allied with the Weather Underground to further their goals."

"How did Mike expect to accomplish that?"

"It looks like he *did* accomplish it. Those weapons stolen from his warehouse, the thefts he was always complaining about? Well, he was the one who stole them. He figured he could cover his ass by raising the alarm himself, that Neil would never authorize an investigation."

"Pretty clever. I take back all those County Clare jokes. Maybe they're not as dumb as people say."

"Certainly Mike wasn't—he stayed two moves ahead of everyone else."

"And you, Ming? How do you fit into all this?"

"I'm Chinese, Frank. Always have been and always will be. Reidy and I linked up as a matter of convenience. Foiling Neil's plans served both our purposes. China supports the North Vietnamese in this war and doesn't want Cambodia helping the other side. And the Weather Underground wants the war over no matter who comes out on top. You know the old saying—the enemy of my enemy is my friend."

"How'd you and Reidy get out of Cambodia? Let me guess—it was Vincenzo, right?"

Ming responded with an ambiguous nod. "I'm not saying Vincenzo helped us get away, and if he did, it doesn't mean he sides with the Communists. He helps everyone. That's how he stays in business. *Andare d'accordo andare avanti*—go along to get along."

Ming ordered a bottle of champagne from the stewardess and filled four plastic flutes. He raised his glass to Frank. "To your success."

Eileen downed her champagne in one gulp and held her glass out for a refill. "I can't wrap my head around this," she said wearily. "I'm living a story, not writing one, with no idea how it will turn out."

"We'll get through this one way or another, Eileen," Frank assured her, taking her hand in his. "Things will work out just fine—you'll see."

He turned back to Ming. "Ming, I can't let you go,

you know. I'm still a lieutenant in the army. I have to turn you in to the authorities."

"Well, I can understand that, Frank. But you have bigger problems, don't you? They're looking harder for you than they are for me. They want you more than they want me. And I think they want you dead."

Frank glanced at Eileen, hoping Ming's words didn't unsettle her any more than she already was. "I suppose you're right, Ming," he said. "We may need your help, Chinese agent or not. Maybe you'll save my butt again, then slip off into the jungle."

Frank slumped back and stared unseeing at the back of the seat in front of him. His emotions had run the gamut. His thoughts were on Mike Reidy, who died saving his life. But Reidy was now part of a fog, with Laurel and Joanna and Neil and the soldiers from the laundry, and with John Lynch—with everyone involved in the affair. Their faces floated in the ether, all part of a shattered mosaic he couldn't fit together.

He knew he should miss them, at least the ones he'd been close to, especially Joanna and Mike. But he felt nothing—no sympathy, no compassion, not even pity for himself. He wasn't sure he cared if the Cambodia debacle ever got out, if the deaths of his friends were ever explained. He felt empty, nothing left to give.

He turned to Eileen, who was trying to dull her senses with a third glass of champagne. He *did* care about Eileen, though. He was in love, and he had to get her out of this mess. Ming and Bob MacNamara were right, he decided. Their only chance was for him to tell the story, no matter the consequences.

He looked out the window and idly watched a Navy jet flying parallel to the airliner about a half mile distant, a stream of vapor trailing behind it, its aluminum fuselage shimmering in the sunlight. An array of silver missiles hung under the wings, reminding Frank of the B-52s that came close to dropping their bombs on the Cambodian valley. He shook his head—everything reminded him of Cambodia. Would it ever get better?

CHAPTER 49
San Francisco
JUNE 22, 1970

FRANK SAT BOLT UPRIGHT AND STARED OUT THE window. It was a Navy jet, all right, an F-4 Phantom. And the missiles strapped to its wings were as real as the jet itself, as real as the pilot who banked the fighter ever so slightly toward the 727. Frank imagined the pilot's finger hovering over a red button, ready to unleash a missile to pierce the fragile hull of the airliner and explode among the passengers.

Frank reached over and grabbed Ming's arm, spilling champagne on Ming's lap. He pointed out the window where the jet was slowly closing on them. He could read the tail number on the fuselage and see the pilot's head in the cockpit window. Frank imagined the pilot's face screwed up in concentration. What type of person was he? What type of person would shoot down an unarmed passenger plane? Was he a fanatic, a patriot who followed orders without question, or a dupe, convinced that destroying the airliner was necessary to the defense of the country?

The thought of the pilot about to press the red button galvanized Frank into action. He sprang from his seat and limped quickly up the aisle, hustling a stewardess ahead of him to the cockpit. There was no way the 727 could outmaneuver the Phantom, but they had a chance

if the captain would follow his instructions. He ordered
the stewardess to call the captain on the intercom, then
grabbed the microphone from her hand. She backed
up and cowered in a corner, intimidated by his menacing look.

Frank took a deep breath to calm his nerves and spoke
into the mike. "Captain, see that plane off your starboard
side, the Navy jet? I have reason to believe it intends to
take aggressive action."

"Who is this? What kind of action?"

"Captain, there's no time for that. He's going to shoot
us down, do you understand? It doesn't matter who I am
or how I know. Just do what I say, okay? You can't afford
not to. You're responsible for the passengers on board this
plane, and they won't be around much longer if you don't
do exactly what I tell you."

Frank paused to let the words sink in, but not long
enough for the pilot to argue. "Call the San Francisco
tower, Captain," he ordered. "Immediately. Right now.
Tell them a Navy jet is tracking you and that you are
concerned about its intentions. And—this is important—
identify the plane."

Frank craned his neck to look out the porthole. "It's
an F-4 Phantom. Tail number NL 104. U.S. Navy. Got
that? Send it now."

The fighter leveled off close enough for Frank to make
out the features of the pilot who was staring intently
out the cockpit window. He could even read the pilot's
name painted on the fuselage in block letters: LT. Darrell
"Condor" Gary. Frank hoped Lieutenant Gary was trying to determine if there were passengers on the airliner,
maybe having doubts about his orders. Another couple

minutes while he made up his mind might be enough to save them.

The F-4 pilot suddenly looked down at his console, turned for a last look at the 727, then abruptly banked away, disappearing a moment later into the cumulus clouds in the distance. Frank breathed a sigh of relief. He had counted on the fighter backing off once it was identified. If the passenger jet went down, it would be impossible to keep the Navy involvement a secret.

Frank smiled apologetically at the stewardess and returned to his seat. They were safe for now, but it would be a different story when they landed in San Francisco. If Neil's people were prepared to shoot down an airliner to keep him quiet, they wouldn't think twice about killing him when he stepped off the plane. He had to come up with a plan, a way to get through the airport without being caught, a way for them to lose themselves until it was safe to surface.

Frank pulled a diagram of the 727 from the seat pocket and studied the layout of the cabin. "Ming, how's this sound?" he said, whispering across the aisle. "They'll be waiting for us when we get to San Francisco, but what if we're not on the plane?"

Ming looked skeptically at the diagram. "You mean bail out before we get there? What do we use for parachutes?"

"No, we wait until we're on the ground. Then we jump out of an emergency exit and run for the fence. They won't be expecting that."

"And for good reason. It's impossible. We'd break a leg dropping to the ground—you've already got a bad one—or the wash from the engines would blow us under a wheel."

"What if we use an emergency slide? And what if the captain thinks there's an emergency and shuts down the engines?"

"Well, even if it works, won't they catch up to us before we can get very far?"

"Maybe, but if we time it just right, we won't be too far from that industrial area on the north side of the airport. They'll have to come after us by car, and they can't drive through the fence—they'll go around on the frontage road next to the freeway. Maybe that'll give us time to get away."

"How do we get over the fence?"

Frank laughed self-consciously. "Well, I haven't figured everything out yet. Maybe there's a gate. Or maybe we can climb over. We'll cross that bridge when we come to it."

The plane dipped over the hills east of San Francisco Bay and began its approach to the airport. Frank turned to Eileen and Bob and explained the plan. They nodded in agreement. "It seems a bit wacky," Bob said, "but I don't have a better idea."

Frank and Ming moved to the forward emergency exit, just aft of the cockpit. Ming took up a position near the intercom. The stewardess kept her distance. A face appeared in the window of the cockpit door, but Frank knew the pilots wouldn't interfere—their first concern would be to keep the kooks out of the cockpit.

They braced themselves as the aircraft touched down on the tarmac. The pilot braked and reversed the thrust of the engines, slowing the plane amid the roar of the turbines, then revved them enough to maintain forward motion. The plane reached the north end of the runway and turned left onto the apron that paralleled the fence.

Frank had never been so scared, not even when the Thai soldier was shooting at him on the highway outside Kanchanaburi or when the Cambodians were shelling the valley. But he felt like he did then—confident, working a plan, ready for action. He was not the same man who had looked at what he thought was Joanna's body covered by a white sheet in the Bangkok morgue.

He signaled to Ming, who reached for the intercom and punched the button for the cockpit, keeping the stewardess at bay with an outstretched arm. "Emergency," he said into the microphone. "It's an emergency. Stop the plane. Stop the plane now."

As the plane slowed to a stop, Frank lunged for the handle of the emergency exit, shoved the door open, and watched the emergency chute unfold to the ground. The first officer stepped cautiously into the cabin, but Ming blocked his way.

"Don't interfere," Ming warned. "Just let us go and nobody will get hurt."

The officer looked from Ming to Frank, then calmly folded his arms across his chest and leaned back against the bulkhead to watch what developed.

"Okay, let's go," Frank ordered, pushing Bob toward the chute. "You go first, Mac. When you get to the bottom, help Eileen. Ming and I will be right behind."

MacNamara took a quick look out the door, then dropped onto the slide, the others following close behind.

Frank led them across fifty yards of concrete to the fence, hobbling as fast as he could on his bad leg. A large maintenance truck was parked next to the fence, the driver squatting on the ground and working on a light fixture, his back to them. He hadn't noticed the plane stalled on the runway or the small group approaching across the apron.

"Hey, buddy, we need some help," Frank called as they came up to him. "Some trouble on the plane back there."

Surprised, the man stood and turned around, looking quizzically from Frank to the plane. He pulled off his earmuffs and was about to respond when Frank knocked the breath from his lungs with a blow to the solar plexus. The man doubled over, and Frank sent him sprawling to the ground with a chop to the back of his neck.

Frank looked at the others and shrugged sheepishly. "Had to do it. There wasn't time for niceties."

He climbed into the truck and started the engine. He backed up a few yards, then lurched forward and slammed the truck into the chain-link fence, flattening it under its weight.

"Okay, let's go!" Frank shouted. He stepped from the truck onto the far side of the fence and turned to help Eileen as she scrambled over. "Eileen, I'm sorry about all this," he whispered before the others caught up. "I'm sorry I got you involved."

"It was my own choosing, Frank," she said, panting from the exertion. "Don't blame yourself. I'm here because I want to be with you."

They found themselves in the employee parking lot of an aircraft maintenance facility. In the distance they could hear the wail of sirens approaching from the direction of the terminal. Frank turned to the others. "Anybody know how to hot-wire a car?"

They shook their heads.

"Let's look for one with the keys in it," Eileen suggested. "There's always someone who leaves their keys in the car."

They fanned out across the parking lot. "Here's one!" shouted Bob a couple minutes later. They piled into a late-model, four-door Buick sedan. Frank backed out of the stall and pulled into the street, heading toward the Bayshore Freeway.

"Anybody got any ideas?" Frank asked. "Do we go north or south?"

"South," Bob said. "They'd expect us to go into the city. No way we can get through to Bolinas now."

Frank took the ramp leading to San Jose just as a police car whipped past in the opposite direction. "You better duck down," he told he others. "They'll be looking for four people, not one."

Frank found a golf hat in the glove compartment and pulled it low over his face, hoping to look like a typical golfer on his way home from a day on the links. He had changed out of his uniform on the plane and was wearing his Hawaiian shirt.

Once they were on the freeway, Bob spoke from low in the back seat. "Now what? Anybody know a place to hide out?"

"My parents live in Cupertino," Eileen suggested. "They'd be happy to put us up."

"I doubt it," Frank said, suppressing a laugh. He saw the hurt look on Eileen's face and turned to her apologetically. "I mean, I'm sure they would take us in, but it wouldn't be very fair to them, would it? Anyway, the police would think of that right away."

They found a forlorn, beaten-down motel on O'Rourke Boulevard in the skid row section of San Jose, thirty miles south of the San Francisco airport. Trash, discarded furniture, and rusted shopping carts littered the street, and heroin addicts and alcoholics sprawled in nearby doorways. They concealed the car between two dumpsters behind the building.

Eileen checked them in, taking two rooms. "I don't think we have to worry about the manager," she said. "He doesn't speak English. I'm sure he can't read the newspapers, and if he watches the news, he won't know what they're saying. And the last thing he wants is to attract police attention to this place. I know flea traps like this from my time on the police beat—there's more illegal stuff going on here than you can shake a stick at."

"Let's get some rest," Frank suggested. "Tomorrow's going to be a big day."

Bob laughed nervously. "It can't be any bigger than today. A congressional hearing. You're arrested. We escape to San Francisco. The plane almost gets shot down. We steal a car. And now the police are after us."

"Well, keep good notes, Mac," Frank said with a wry smile, trying to lighten the mood. "It'll add some excitement to the story you're going to write."

"As if we need any more," Bob said.

CHAPTER 50

San Diego

JUNE 23, 1970

"WHERE TO?" FRANK ASKED. THEY SAT IN ONE OF the motel rooms, eating bacon sandwiches Eileen had picked up at a neighborhood diner. Early morning sunlight filtered in through the closed curtains. "Any ideas?"

"I know a place," Bob offered, balancing a cup of coffee in one hand and a sandwich in the other. "My girlfriend's parents have a house in the mountains east of San Diego. They're in Indiana now, visiting her." He caught himself. "I mean, my ex-girlfriend, Lisa Viera. I'm married now—but not to her. That's why it should be safe for a few days. It would take them a while to think of it."

"Good idea," Frank said wearily, "but we're not in San Diego."

"We can drive down," Eileen suggested. "The farther we get away from the Bay Area, the better."

"They'll be looking for the car," Ming said.

"How about we fly down?" Bob said. "There's no reason they'd be watching the San Jose airport."

"That may not be a bad idea," Frank said, mulling it over. "They wouldn't expect us to get back on a plane."

They finished their breakfast and headed for the airport. Frank drove, the others huddled low in the back seat, and pulled into a remote corner of the parking lot. They pooled their cash and sent Eileen in to buy the tickets, then filed into the terminal and filtered one by one onto the plane, taking seats well apart from one another. Frank breathed a sigh of relief when the aircraft taxied down the runway and took off over the bay.

In San Diego they regrouped in the terminal coffee shop to discuss their next move. MacNamara looked around anxiously. "Somebody might recognize us," he warned. "Remember, Frank, your picture was all over the papers yesterday. Probably all our pictures are in today's editions."

Frank gulped his coffee. "I just wish we could have a minute of peace. I'm beginning to enjoy this game in some perverse way, but I'm ready for a half-time break." He looked at Eileen. "I guess you're getting a bit tired of it too, aren't you, Eileen?"

"Frank, quit worrying about me," she said testily. "I'm fine. I'll be able to keep up with you boys, so let's just leave it at that, okay?"

Ming intervened before tempers flared. "We're all tired, but Mac is right—we have to keep moving before somebody spots us."

Ming went out and hailed a cab. The others followed a moment later and slipped into the back seat.

"Where to?" the driver asked.

Ming turned to Bob for directions. Bob grimaced in frustration.

"We can't take a cab to the house," he whispered to Frank. "It's too far, forty miles maybe. And this guy would know where we were."

Frank leaned forward and spoke over the driver's shoulder. "We're going to rent a car. Aren't there some rental places on Pacific Highway?"

"Sure there are, mister. But there's some right here at the airport too. You don't need a taxi for that."

"No, that's okay. We'd rather get one away from the airport. Cheaper that way."

"Suit yourself, mister."

The cab pulled away from the curb. "Far West Rent-A-Car? That sound okay?"

"That sounds fine."

Frank counted the last of their pooled funds. He figured they had enough to rent a car, but no more. A credit card would leave a paper trail for their pursuers to follow.

The taxi dropped them off in front of the rental car agency. Frank watched it disappear in the traffic before he spoke to the others.

"Wait for me on the corner by that coffee shop," he said, pointing to a Denny's up the block. "I'm going to rent a car from the place across the street. Maybe we'll be a little harder to track that way."

Frank limped across the street and walked into the office. He filled out the necessary forms, using MacNamara's driver's license for identification, hoping the discrepancy in descriptions would confuse anyone on their trail. He selected a standard-size sedan and picked up the others on the corner.

MacNamara bought a newspaper from the dispenser outside the restaurant. "Says here we're all spies," he reported, scanning an article on the first page, "or at least that's what the Army's saying. Ming here is a Chinese Communist, a colonel in their army, no less. The rest of us are connected to the Weather Underground. There's a manhunt on, but they're concentrating on the Bay Area."

"Good," Frank said. "Maybe we've outfoxed them."

They drove a mile north on Pacific Highway, then turned east onto Interstate 8, following MacNamara's directions.

"Anybody got any money left?" Frank asked. "We're down to our last few bucks."

They searched their pockets and came up empty.

"The way I see it," Frank said, "we need some cash. We need food, maybe some gas. We need a tape recorder for Mac and some emergency funds in case we have to make another run for it."

No one spoke. They looked at Frank expectantly.

"How about we knock over a liquor store," he suggested, eliciting a snigger from MacNamara in the back seat.

"No, I mean it, Mac. It'll be no big deal compared to what we're supposed to have done already—the invasion of Cambodia, people getting killed at the airport. Hell, compared to that, a liquor store ought to be a piece of cake." He turned to MacNamara. "Look, Mac, we have to do something. If we don't get some money, they'll catch us for sure."

MacNamara looked dubious.

"Really, it won't be as bad as it sounds," Frank continued. "We'll turn off in El Cajon. Find a liquor store. Ming, you'll take the wheel. Mac and I will go in for the money."

"We don't have a gun," Bob said, hoping to derail the plan. "Don't we need a gun?"

"Nah. We'll just bluff it through."

Frank left the freeway at Magnolia Avenue and turned east onto Main Street. They found a liquor store on the outskirts of the town, far enough off the beaten track that there were no cars in the parking lot.

"Perfect," enthused Frank. "I just hope they have some money. It might be slim pickings from the looks of the neighborhood."

Frank pulled to the side of the building, hiding the car from view. He and Bob got out and Ming slipped into the driver's seat. They moved quickly to the front of the building.

Bob suddenly grabbed Frank by the arm. "Frank, I can't do it. I'm sorry, but I've never done anything like this before."

Frank pulled his arm free and looked at him in disbelief. "What are you talking about, Mac? We have to get some money. We have no choice."

"I know," Bob said, averting his gaze. "It's just that I've not done anything wrong yet. I mean, you haven't either, but they say you have—the shooting at the airport, that stuff in Cambodia. I'm a reporter, Frank. I just can't get that involved. If I do, I lose my objectivity. At least, that's what my editor will say." He took a deep breath. "I'm sorry. I just can't do it."

Frank glanced around the parking lot and peered furtively through the window. The store was empty except for the clerk, who was standing next to the open cash register counting the day's receipts. He was a pudgy, middle-aged man with thin, stringy hair wrapped over a bald pate. Ill-fitting glasses slipped down his nose.

"Okay, if you can't, you can't," Frank said, not taking his eyes off the clerk. "I've gotta move quickly before someone comes. Wait in the car. I'll be back in a minute."

Frank walked into the store. The bell above the door jangled, startling him, but the clerk didn't look up, engrossed with the small pile of bills lying on the counter. Frank stepped behind the counter and, before the clerk had time to react, jammed his fist into his solar plexus and slammed his face down on the counter. The man slumped to the floor, unconscious.

I'm getting good at this, Frank thought. First the guy in San Francisco, now a liquor store clerk. Not that there's any pride in it. Just something that had to be done.

He pocketed the money lying on the counter, then grabbed the bills in the cash register, lifting the tray to get to the larger bills underneath. He jammed the cash into his pocket and ran out of the store, jumping into the back seat next to Eileen. Ming drove away in a spray of gravel.

Frank counted the stolen money, just over two hundred dollars. "Not bad for my first heist," he said, holding up the cash triumphantly. "I had to knock the guy cold, but I got the money."

"You sound like you enjoyed it," Bob said, turning to look at him.

"Sorry," Frank said, giving him an apologetic look, "but I had no choice."

Eileen squeezed his hand. "We know you wouldn't have done it if you didn't have to, Frank."

But Bob wouldn't let it go. "No, I mean it, Frank. This is the second guy you beat up in so many days. It's not right."

Frank looked out the window and took a deep breath, collecting his thoughts. He couldn't afford to lose his temper—too much was at stake. "Mac, they're trying to kill us," he said quietly. "This is war. There's collateral damage in war, and that's what these guys are—collateral damage. It couldn't be avoided."

"You sound like the president," Bob said. "He's willing to do whatever it takes to win this thing in Vietnam, no matter how many innocent people get hurt."

"I'm beginning to understand his perspective. I was almost collateral damage in Cambodia. Lesson learned. I'll do whatever it takes to bring Neil and his CIA handlers down. If innocent people have to get hurt along the way, that's just the way it is. It's for the greater good."

Frank leaned forward and tapped Ming on the shoulder. "Ming, we need a secondhand store to buy a tape recorder for Mac."

Ming pulled over at a pawnshop a few miles up the road. "You sure we shouldn't just head out of here?" he asked. "Now the local police will be after us."

"No, they won't," Frank said confidently. "The guy in the liquor store never saw me."

Frank purchased a small Sony tape recorder and some blank cassettes, then stopped at the gun case. A semiautomatic rifle caught his eye. "How much is that?" he asked the man behind the counter.

"Sixty-seven dollars."

"That much?"

"It's a good buy," the clerk said with a wink. "It'll get you all the rabbits you want."

Frank purchased the rifle and three clips of ammunition, plus a .38-caliber pistol for backup. He filled out the registration forms using a false name and address. An extra ten dollars helped the clerk overlook the lack of identification.

Frank stowed the tape recorder and weapons in the trunk of the car and took over the driving from Ming. They continued east into the mountains.

"We need anything else?" Frank asked.

"Food," Eileen replied. "I'll do the cooking if you guys do the dishes."

"It's a deal," Frank said.

"Are there pots and pans and things like that in the house?" Eileen asked Bob.

He nodded. "Yeah, everything's there. It's their regular home. They're retired, spend about half the time here and the other half with Lisa in Indiana."

"How about a telephone?" Frank asked.

"Yeah, they've got a phone."

Frank turned to Ming. "Do you think Mac should call his editor from there or from a pay phone?"

Ming thought for a moment. "Probably from the house. There won't be any operator involved that way. Even if they've tapped the newspaper phones, they won't be able to trace the call if Mac doesn't stay on the line too long."

They stopped for groceries in Alpine, a small town in the foothills of the Cuyamaca Mountains. Eileen did the shopping, returning with three large bags of groceries.

"Well, there goes the rest of our money," observed Frank. "Looks like we'll have to knock over another liquor store."

Bob grimaced, and Frank held up his hands defensively. "Hey, just joking, Mac. No more liquor stores, I promise. My life of crime has come to an end."

They turned off the highway at Descanso Junction and followed the road along the Sweetwater River, a shallow stream that disappeared for long stretches beneath the gravel riverbed. They passed an old Catholic church, partially obscured by a thicket of willow trees. Cattle grazed languidly in the meadows, oblivious to the passing car, the only vehicle on the road. The sun had set behind the hills, and evening began to descend over the valley.

"It's a little spooky up here," observed Eileen. "Seems awfully quiet."

"Not too many people live here anymore," Bob said. "There used to be a resort, but it burned down years ago. Most of the people left. Those who stayed are either ranchers or retired."

They passed the remnants of what was once the Coveney Grove vacation cabins. A solitary, fire-scarred stone chimney stood like an icon among the oak trees, a grim reminder of the long-abandoned resort. The swimming pool was empty and littered with leaves, the chain-link fence surrounding it rusted and broken.

The road terminated at a washed-out bridge. Following Bob's instructions, Frank turned onto a dirt road and pulled over next to a dilapidated horse stable that was once part of the resort. A brush-covered, granite cliff loomed above them, rising five hundred feet into the evening sky.

"The house is a quarter-mile back from the top of that cliff," Bob said, "but we have to drive about three miles around to get to it. That's the only way in or out, other than a hiking trail from the house directly into this valley." He pointed up the river. "Comes out where you see the river disappear into those trees. It's an old Indian trail used by horseback riders when the resort was open."

They drove up the steep, rutted road. Frank swung the car from side to side to avoid the potholes and gullies carved in the gravel by the winter rains. The road leveled off in a meadow spotted with tired-looking oak trees, then climbed the shoulder of a ridge into a broad, shallow valley.

The house stood above them on a promontory overlooking the valley. It commanded a sweeping view, with good visibility in all directions except directly behind it, where the ground rose sharply to the top of the bluff that overlooked the stables. The last rays of the dying sun reflected from the windows.

Frank drove slowly up the long drive to the house, loose gravel crunching under the tires. They climbed out of the car and stood in silence, listening carefully to the sounds of the evening, crickets chirping in the bushes and lizards rustling in the weeds. The first few stars appeared overhead in a clear, blue-black sky. The house loomed in front of them, dark and foreboding.

Frank shivered involuntarily. "Let's get moving," he whispered. "Ming, you put the car in the garage. We'll take the groceries in and get set up."

MacNamara led the way up the walk. He groped beneath the wooden steps for a key, then unlocked the front door and pushed it open on squeaky hinges.

Frank shook his head in mock exasperation. "That's all we need. On top of everything else, a haunted house."

Frank and Eileen followed Bob into the living room. A narrow doorway led to the kitchen. To the left was a bedroom and bathroom, to the right a large bay window that overlooked the valley. No lights were visible in the darkness.

"We'd better not turn on any lights yet," cautioned Frank. "They'll really stand out up here."

Frank and Bob fumbled with the blinds, securing them well enough to risk lighting an oil lamp resting on the kitchen table. The light was dim and flickering.

"We'll have to make do with the one lamp," cautioned Frank. "Anything brighter might be seen through the blinds."

Eileen unpacked the groceries and served hot soup and cheese sandwiches. "Sorry for the limited fare, boys," she apologized. "Didn't want to chance cooking anything more extravagant in the dark."

They decided there was no need to post a lookout. "If they're on our tail this soon, we're finished anyway," Frank said. "Let's get some sleep—it'll be *another* big day tomorrow."

Ming and Bob rigged beds on the living room floor with cushions from the furniture, and Frank and Eileen settled into the single bedroom. Frank loaded a magazine into the rifle and propped it against the wall. Eileen looked at the rifle apprehensively.

"Don't worry, Eileen. We're not going to need it. Just best to be ready. It's my Boy Scout training—be prepared."

He slipped into the bed and took Eileen into his arms.

CHAPTER 51
Washington, D.C.
JUNE 24, 1970

CIA DIRECTOR SHAREE FISH STOOD BEHIND HER desk and stared out the window. Summer. Hot and muggy. She wished she was at her vacation home on the Virginia shore with her husband, but a number of matters kept her in Washington, and heading the list was how to distance the CIA from the Cambodia fiasco. So far, the damage was limited to the Army—General Chapin was about to be relieved—but if she didn't get on top of it, they would soon connect the CIA to Colonel Neil and Premier Lon Nol. Worse, if they found out Chu was her CIA plant in MACV headquarters—a double agent—she would be thrown to the wolves.

She took a deep breath. This was no time to lose focus. When she was appointed to the job, they said a woman wasn't up to it, that it wasn't ladylike to be involved in the unseemly world of espionage. She had silenced her detractors by dint of hard work and massaging the right egos, but she hadn't been tested by anything like Cambodia.

The CIA would weather the storm—she wasn't overly worried about that. They would bury enough of the details in the name of national security that no one would be able to get to the bottom of it. It was *her* neck she was worried about. She'd struggled by hook and by crook to make her way in a man's world—screwing a few of those men on the way up—and she wasn't about to be taken down by a misstep in Cambodia.

She returned to her desk and mentally reviewed the list of people who could do her harm. John Lynch was the only other senior administration official who knew about the operation, and he was dead. A good man, Lynch, for whom she had some affection, but it had to be done. It wasn't her fault that he caught a case of honesty, that he felt the need to clear his conscience. He should have kept his mouth shut. She was sorry he was dead, but he may as well have killed himself.

Only three other people could link the CIA to Cambodia. Colonel Neil was one, but he showed no inclination to turn state's evidence—his career was on the line too. Lieutenant Schaniel was another, but Neil was on his trail; with any luck he'd catch up with him before more damage could be done. And then there was Captain Broderick— she would deal with him herself.

She'd come a long way from Columbia Falls, Montana. The youngest of six girls, she was raised by loving parents who worked hard but struggled to put food on the table. They lived in public housing and subsisted on commodities handed out by the government. Her father ran a local bar but barely managed to stay in business, what with he and his buddies drinking most of the profits. Without money for college or prospects for employment in their small town, after high school she joined the Navy and soon impressed her superiors enough to shag a slot at the Naval Academy. After a few years as a junior officer learning the ropes, her career blossomed, helped along by marrying one of the richest men in Virginia. Now she was at the pinnacle of what even her detractors acknowledged was a remarkable career. She wasn't about to let this Cambodia thing end it early.

There was a perfunctory knock on the door, and her assistant showed Captain Broderick into the room. He was dressed in a civilian suit and tie, his arm in a sling.

"Have a seat, Captain," Fish said, indicating a chair. "How's the arm?"

"It's fine, Director Fish. The bullet went right through, didn't hit any bone. It's little more than a flesh wound. I can live with it."

"I understand the Army wants to talk to you."

Broderick squirmed in his seat. "They want me to come to the Pentagon tomorrow," he said, a worried expression on his face.

"How long have you been in the army, Captain?"

"Eight years. I should make major soon."

Fish gave him a sympathetic look. "Captain, to be blunt, my guess is your army career is over. Whatever else happens, they'll decide they don't have any more use for your services, and that's a shame. You've served honorably, above and beyond the call of duty. It's not right that you should get tossed out on the street."

"You think they'd do that? Throw me out?"

"Rumor is they're going to get rid of Chapin because of what happened. If they can boot a four-star general, they can boot you. They won't want anyone around who's linked to the Cambodia debacle. It's an embarrassment."

"I suppose you're right, Director Fish." He looked disconsolate.

"But we may be able to help," she said, tossing him a lifeline. "Ever thought about joining the CIA? You'd get credit for your army service and could retire with a good pension after another twelve years here."

"No, ma'am, I hadn't given it any thought." He was only half listening, distressed at his imminent dismissal from the service. "The army's my career, my home. I've never thought about doing anything else."

"We could use a man like you," Fish continued. "You're resourceful. You've got a lot of experience on the operations side. You had substantial CIA training before you went to Thailand. Your instructors gave you very high marks, I might add." She was exaggerating a bit, but Broderick was too preoccupied to be suspicious. "I was thinking we could make you a deputy in the operations section. That would put you in upper management. You'd make a lot more money than you're making now."

"Gosh, I don't know, Director Fish."

"Let's consider it done. I'll have you transferred to the CIA by close of business."

Broderick was stunned, but Fish didn't give him a chance to object. "I want you to meet someone, Captain." Fish motioned toward a corner of the room where a man sat in the shadows, having slipped in unnoticed while they were talking.

"This is Gordon Jennings, Captain," Fish said. "He's from our black ops section. One of the best. He's going to give you a hand."

Jennings stared at Broderick through cold, unfriendly eyes. He was dressed entirely in black—black shirt, black coat, black pants, even a black tie—and his pale face appeared to bob untethered in the dim light. He was slightly built—he didn't fit the mold of what one would expect a CIA operative to look like—but his expression said it all: anyone who fucks with me is in for a big surprise.

"Give me a hand with what?"

"Your first assignment. Colonel Neil is back in San Diego trying to chase down Lieutenant Schaniel. I want you to go out and help him. We're keeping this confined to as few people as possible, and Neil's going to have to rely on the local police. You're his backup, just like in San Diego last week. Jennings here will clean up any mess."

"I was hoping I was done with Colonel Neil. He's brought me nothing but grief."

"I guarantee this will be the end of it. Jennings will fill you in. I've arranged for a plane at Andrews. You can take off within the hour."

"Yes, ma'am," Broderick said, realizing he was being dismissed. He stood to leave. "And thank you, ma'am, I guess."

"No need to thank me, Larry. I can call you Larry, can't I? Now that you're a civilian? I believe you will be quite an asset to the CIA. We're honored to have you on board."

COLONEL NEIL SAT QUIETLY AS UNDERSHERIFF Patrick O'Toole of the San Diego County Sheriff's Department examined the warrant.

O'Toole looked up. "Colonel, is this the same guy I've been reading about in the paper? The one involved in the shooting at the airport? The guy that escaped from custody in Washington?"

"One and the same, Sheriff. He's a very dangerous man. We need to catch him before he causes any more harm."

"Why aren't the feds giving you a hand?"

"No jurisdiction. It's a federal warrant, but the airport shooting was a local affair, and whatever happened in Washington happened in Washington. Anyway, the FBI doesn't have the manpower here to track him down, and they don't have the familiarity with the territory you guys have."

"What do you need?"

"Well, I could use the help of your intelligence people. Check on taxi cabs, hotels, anywhere they might get a lead on where this guy could have gone. We don't know what happened to him and his friends after they left the San Diego airport yesterday afternoon. Once we've pinned them down, I think three squad cars and six deputies should be enough to take them into custody. Your deputies will need automatic rifles, just in case, and a sniper rifle. And we may need some specialized communications equipment."

O'Toole laughed. "That's a tall order."

"Yes, but the job shouldn't take long. They're not professionals, and they're on the run. I don't think they have any contacts here they can rely on. There's a Chinese guy with them—he should stand out. They'll screw up, probably already have. I would guess we'll have them in custody within twenty-four hours."

O'Toole leaned back in his chair and mulled it over.

"Okay, I'll put a team together. Sergeant Paul Tuomainen will be in charge. He's one of our best."

"Thanks, Sheriff O'Toole. The government appreciates your cooperation. You can be sure there will be accolades out of Washington when this is over."

"And expenses? We don't have the budget for this. Think we can get reimbursed?"

"I'll see what I can do."

CHAPTER 52
Descanso
JUNE 24, 1970

THE MORNING DAWNED BRIGHT AND CLEAR, and the warm sun dissolved the sense of apprehension that shrouded the house the night before. Their spirits rose as the sun moved higher in the sky, and by the time they sat down to the bacon and eggs Eileen laid out on the kitchen table, they were joshing with one another and making light of their circumstances.

Ming found a pair of binoculars in a cupboard and took what he jokingly called the "first watch." He settled comfortably into a wicker chair in a corner of the kitchen with a view to the ocean forty miles away, a blue haze in the distance. By walking to the other side of the room, he could surveil the brush-covered rise behind the house. He retrieved the rifle from the bedroom and propped it beside the chair.

Bob led Frank to a covered patio a short distance from the house and pointed to a cleft in a ridge a mile away. "That's where the trail is," he explained. "It goes to the stables where we stopped the car last night, about a two-mile hike." He looked at Frank. "Hopefully, we won't need it, but it's the only back door out of here."

Bob and Eileen discussed how to write the story, and how to make sure it would get printed. "I don't trust that editor, Eileen," Bob said. "Fox always chopped my stuff to pieces, the stuff I filed from Thailand. Hell, I never knew what it was going to look like until I saw the paper."

Eileen laughed. "You're just mad because he rewrote your stories. He did that mostly because he thought you speculated too much. And he did it to everybody. Anyway," she said with a mischievous grin, "it wasn't him. It was me."

"But what do you think, Eileen? Can we trust him to print the story?"

"I think so. If nothing else, Chuck is a newspaperman. He knows a good story when he sees one, and this one's a blockbuster. I don't think he can be pressured into burying it. We can expect the Army or somebody has already been to see him, explaining the importance to 'national security' that he sit on it, but I don't think he'll listen. I think he'll print it. He'll smell a Pulitzer." Eileen shrugged. "Anyway, who else have we got? We have to rely on somebody."

Bob picked up the phone and dialed a number in San Francisco. "I'm calling Miles Stanich," he explained as he waited for an answer. "That hippie guy on the night shift. I shared a desk with him when I got back from Bangkok. I'll make arrangements through him to talk to Chuck later today."

He held up his hand for silence. "Hello, Miles? This is Bob MacNamara."

On the other end of the line, Miles Stanich reached over to the nightstand and picked up the alarm clock. "Hey, man, you know what time it is? It's only nine o'clock. Shit, man, I only got off work a couple hours ago. Where are you, anyway?"

"Look, Miles, no time for that now. And I can't tell you where I am."

Stanich pushed himself up from the bed and rubbed the sleep from his eyes. "Eileen with you, man?"

Bob looked at Eileen. "Yes, she's with me. We're okay, Miles. Listen, do me a favor, will you? Tell Chuck Fox I'm going to give him a call later today. Tell him I don't want to call in on the office phone, so I'll call him at noon at"—he paused to think of a safe place—"the Tadich Grill, that restaurant down on California Street. Got that? Noon at Tadich Grill."

"Whatever you say, boss."

"Thanks, Miles. And Miles, one more thing. Don't tell anybody, okay?"

Bob replaced the receiver and turned to Eileen. "Well, we better get started. We have a lot of work to do."

"How do you want to structure it?" she asked. "Put together a series of pieces in chronological order?"

"Yeah, I think that would be best. But we better start with a broad overview, a summary of what's to come. Maybe that's not the best way to go from a journalistic point of view, but it might buy us some security. Once we get the essentials on the table, there won't be any reason for them to chase after us anymore. It'll be too late."

"That may or may not be the case," interjected Frank, who was sitting at the table listening to their conversation. "They may be all the more anxious to find us after the first installment, before you can do any more damage."

Bob thought a moment. "How's this for an idea? We'll do an overview but put in enough sources that it can be independently confirmed. That way, somebody else can flesh it out if they have to."

"That should work," Frank said. "If the series can be finished without you, there wouldn't be anything to be gained by keeping us quiet."

"So, who can independently confirm it?" Eileen asked.

"Well, Sergeant Canedo, for one," Frank replied, "although he only knows a piece of the story. And there's David Franklin, for another, but he has it second or third hand from John Lynch. Then there's those army officers at MACV—Chapin, O'Malley, and a couple others—although I don't imagine they'd be willing to talk."

"Anybody else?" Bob asked.

"Well, all those guys from the First of the Seventh, and the truck drivers with the 558th, but I don't know their names, and they wouldn't know the whole story anyway. Besides, the Army will keep them quiet."

They exchanged uneasy glances. Outside of the military, only Frank and Ming could put all the pieces together, and the Army would deny everything.

"They didn't have a course on how to do this at Occidental College," Bob said. "Maybe I should have studied criminal justice instead of English."

"Do the best you can, Mac," Frank said. "We'll just have to make sure nothing happens to us."

Frank rose from the table and joined Ming, who had moved to the garden outside the kitchen. He held the rifle loosely in his hand.

"You think it's a good idea to be carrying that around?" Frank asked, nodding at the rifle. "Somebody might see it and wonder what's going on here."

Ming laid the rifle against a granite boulder. "I feel foolish with it anyway. We foreign agents are supposed to use our heads, not guns."

Frank leaned back against the boulder. "Ming, Mac is going to have to interview you, you know. You willing to talk?"

Ming looked out over the valley. "Yes, I've thought about that. I have nothing to lose. They already know who I am, and they can't tie me to anybody in the United States. Joanna's dead. Mike Reidy's dead. My parents will suffer, but they've never known about my other life, so there's nothing the government can do to them."

"What are you going to do after we get out of here?"

Ming smiled. "You mean *if* we get out of here, don't you?" He paused in reflection. "Go back to China, I guess. Actually, 'go back' is a misnomer—I've never been there. It'll be a new experience."

"How come you've stuck around this long, Ming? You could have bugged out once we landed in San Francisco. In fact, you never had to get on that plane in the first place."

"Just trying to finish a job, Frank. I owe that much to Joanna and Mike. Anyway, it's too late to change my mind—you've spent all my money. This is one international spy who can't afford a ticket home." He smiled again. "Maybe I'll knock over a liquor store."

"Don't you have any contacts here who can help?"

"Careful, Frank. That's one thing I won't talk about."

"Well, there's one thing I've gotta know—it's been bugging me for months. Who was the Chinese guy with the black eye patch in Golden Gate Park, that last afternoon we were together with Joanna?"

"That I can tell you. His name is Tom Zung. He's a radiologist at the UC San Francisco medical center."

"Another Chinese agent?"

"Yes and no. He's not a spy. He's a messenger, trusted by both the Chinese and U.S. governments to deliver messages to the other. Direct communications are a bit difficult these days."

"What'd he have to do with Cambodia?"

"Nothing. He's just a go-between, a mailman. He doesn't know any secrets, doesn't get involved in operations. The only thing he knows is how to read X-rays. That's why the government tolerates him—he can be a helpful back channel, and he's not a risk."

"Which brings us back to our problem, Ming. I'm still in the army. How can I let you go?"

"Frank, let's continue to let it ride for now, okay? You need me for the time being. Mac still has to interview me, and I can shoot a rifle if it comes to that. Let's take it one step at a time."

Frank rested his hand on Ming's shoulder. "Okay, Ming. Another bridge we'll cross when we get to it."

CHAPTER 53

San Diego

JUNE 24, 1970

COLONEL NEIL WAS FAVORING HIS RIGHT LEG, HIS left arm strapped to his chest. It took a big effort to push himself out of the passenger side of the squad car. He winced when he turned back to speak to Sergeant Tuomainen.

"Wait for me here," he said. "I'll only be a minute."

He walked slowly into the garage of the cab company. Justin Savarese sat over a cup of coffee at a grimy table in the lunchroom, listlessly turning the pages of a two-month-old, grease-stained *Spiegel* catalog. He looked up when the colonel walked in.

"You the one that wanted to see me?"

"That's right, Mr. Savarese." Neil eased himself into an empty chair. "I understand you picked up four people yesterday afternoon at the airport. Three men and a woman. One of the men was Chinese. You remember where you took them?"

"Sure do," he replied confidently. "Far West Rent-A-Car. Over on Pacific Highway. Thought it was strange they didn't just rent a car at the airport."

BOB AND EILEEN SAT AT THE KITCHEN TABLE, outlining the story as best they could with the information they had, beginning with Neil and the 558th Supply and

Service Company and ending with their narrow escape from the San Francisco airport. They pieced together the details Bob knew from his time in Bangkok and what Eileen remembered from the account Frank shared with her on the beach in San Diego. There were still some gaping holes.

"Well, time to get to work," Bob said. Taking the tape recorder, he went in search of Frank.

NEIL CAME UP EMPTY-HANDED AT THE RENTAL car agency and limped out to the sidewalk. His leg bothered him more than the shoulder wound, which was of more recent vintage. The pain in his shoulder had diminished to a dull throb; the pain in his leg was sharp and unpredictable, shooting into the nerves that ran up his back.

He stood on the sidewalk and watched the passing traffic while Sergeant Tuomainen waited in the squad car. "Where to now, Colonel?" he asked through the open window.

Neil noticed the coffee shop down the street. Tuomainen followed his gaze. "Want me to check out Denny's? Ask if they've seen them?"

"No, don't bother. They wouldn't have taken a break this close to the airport."

Neil walked to the rental car agency across the street. Tuomainen did a U-turn and waited at the curb while the colonel talked to the clerk and thumbed through the rental records from the previous day.

MACNAMARA RANG THE TADICH GRILL EXACTLY at noon. He asked for Fox and waited while the maître d' went off to find him. He pictured the man carrying the phone across the tile floor, weaving through tables covered with white linen and set with silver and crystal. He would plug the phone into the wall jack where the editor sat, hopefully alone, in a wood-paneled booth in the corner.

Fox would be perturbed that he had to pay for such an expensive lunch. Keep your expenses down, he constantly harped. He'd played football for USC, a big man with a big appetite, but he was more into bean and cheese burritos than Alaskan halibut. MacNamara smiled mirthlessly at the modest payback for all the articles Fox had chopped up.

"It's me," MacNamara said when the editor came on the line. "Can you talk?"

"I suppose so," Fox replied. He glanced around and focused on the two men who had followed him into the restaurant and were sitting at the bar. "I'm being followed, but I suppose there's no way they can tap the line."

"I'll be quick," MacNamara said. "I'm doing a series on this Frank Schaniel thing. I want to phone in the first installment tonight at six. It'll be a blockbuster. Can you do it?"

"Well, we'll take a look at it," Fox replied guardedly. "Other than this Schaniel guy, you have anybody to confirm the story?"

"Ming Chu's with us, that Chinese agent the senator identified at the hearing."

Fox wasn't impressed. "He is, is he? Anybody else? Anybody without an axe to grind?"

"Look, Fox," MacNamara replied irritably. "We'll give you what we've got. You judge for yourself, okay?"

"You know I'll do just that, Mac." He paused. "Are

you at least going to write the story as their version of events, rather than the last word on what really happened? I'm already getting heat from the Defense Department. They say they want to 'fill us in,' make sure we don't go off halfcocked without all the facts."

"I could do it that way if you want."

"I think that would be best. Call the story into the city desk. I'll have a team in to check the lines and make sure they're clean."

"Chuck, I'll do what I can," Bob said, wiping perspiration from his brow. "It may not measure up to your normal journalistic standards. I mean, who else is there to confirm it? The Army won't talk. The CIA won't talk. It's important you print it, though. At least print something. Otherwise, they'll keep looking for us to keep us quiet."

Fox was silent for a moment. "Well, that's another problem, Mac. We've gone on the hook before without independent confirmation, you know that, but here you and Eileen are involved in the whole thing. She's sleeping with Schaniel, from what I hear. How objective can you guys be?"

"Okay, Chuck, you do what you want with it," MacNamara snapped. "I'll call it in at six. You can print it or you can shove it up your ass."

MacNamara slammed the phone down and looked up at the inquisitive faces gathered around him. He turned his palms up in a gesture of helplessness. "Well, nobody said it would be easy."

NEIL RUBBED THE STUBBLE ON HIS CHIN WITH the flat of his hand. His suit was wrinkled, and he was tired and dirty. He sat patiently in a room in the El Cajon

Valley Hospital. Bernie Giesing, the clerk from the liquor store, lay on the bed beside him. Giesing's eyes were blackened and his nose was swathed in bandages.

"Did you get a good look at him, Mr. Giesing?" Neil asked.

The clerk shook his head. "Never saw nothin'," he whispered through swollen lips.

"A kid on a bicycle saw a man run out of the store. Can you tell me what he was wearing?"

"I tell ya, I never saw nothin'. Didn't see what hit me. All a blur."

The colonel got up without another word and left the room, Sergeant Tuomainen trailing after him.

WITH EILEEN'S HELP, BOB FINISHED THE FIRST installment—the overview—banging out the final copy on an old portable Remington they found in a closet. At six o'clock sharp he placed the call to the newsroom.

Chuck Fox was all business. "Okay, Mac, let's get started. They tell me this line is clear, but let's make it quick, just in case. I'm putting Miles Stanich on the extension. He'll type whatever you give us. I'll listen in. Okay?"

"Okay," Bob said, and began dictating from the copy he held in his hand. He could hear Stanich typing furiously at the other end of the line.

When he finished, the editor spoke. "Sounds good, Mac," he said. "I'll see what we can do with it. What about the end though? That stuff about the Navy jet and people waiting for you at the airport. You sure about that?"

Bob realized his mistake. He was so involved in the story he hadn't been as careful as he should have been to sift fact from conjecture.

"We had some people at the airport," Fox continued. "They didn't see anything unusual, just the normal contingent of security people who were alerted when the pilot called in a disturbance on the plane. The First Infantry Division wasn't there or anything like that, and there's no reports of an errant military jet. You may have seen a Navy plane out the window, but there's no way to prove it was ill-intentioned."

"Yeah, you're right," Bob admitted, embarrassed. "I guess we can't confirm there was anything amiss. How about drop the last couple paragraphs?"

"I already have," Fox replied caustically. "Anything else I should drop?"

"Yeah, drop dead." Bob banged the phone down again, the second time he'd hung up on his editor. He immediately regretted it—he needed Fox on this. He should be more respectful, not sour him on the story. If Fox didn't print it, they were toast.

NEIL STOOD IN A TELEPHONE BOOTH OUTSIDE the El Cajon pawnshop, listening as the father of Mac-Namara's former girlfriend described the house and the valley it overlooked. He asked a few perfunctory questions, then replaced the receiver and returned to the waiting squad car.

CHAPTER 54

Descanso

JUNE 24, 1970

THEY SHARED A SENSE OF RELIEF ONCE THE FIRST installment was behind them. To celebrate, Eileen prepared a spaghetti dinner and broke out a bottle of burgundy she'd secreted in one of the grocery sacks. They relaxed around the table, engaging in idle banter, the wine adding to the tranquility of the evening. They quietly watched darkness descend over the valley, sharing the camaraderie of reluctant fugitives, the danger making the evening all the more poignant.

Ming looked idly out the window, admiring the sunset, listening to Bob chat about his new wife and the total unexpectedness of his marriage and how happy he was to have found her. Bob reminded them that Ceci had a hand in knitting the story together—she'd confirmed John Lynch, Colonel Neil, and the Cambodian charge d'affaires had met in a hotel room in Bangkok not long before the invasion.

Suddenly, Ming sat bolt upright.

"A light," he said, startling the others. "There's a light down the valley."

They followed his gaze to see two lights wink out in the distance.

"It's headlights," Bob said. "Has to be down on the

road, about where it turns out of the meadow and winds up toward the house."

"Who could it be?" Eileen asked.

Nobody answered. They didn't have to. They all knew who it was, even Eileen. Frank reached over and doused the lamp, throwing the room into evening gloom.

"Well, we better do something," Ming said. "They could be close."

"Let's open up all the windows," Frank said, assuming command. "Maybe we'll hear something even if it's too dark to see. Ming, you take the rifle."

He turned to Bob. "Mac, gather up your tapes and keep them with you. They may be our ticket out of here."

He looked at Eileen with a disconsolate expression. "Eileen, I'm sorry about this, I really am. You'd better stay in the bedroom, out of the way."

Frank pushed the .38 into his waistband and helped Ming organize the house for their defense, should it come to that. They upended furniture and shoved a sofa against the wall below the bay window. When they finished, they looked out over the valley but could see nothing in the darkness. Frank stretched out on the living room floor and stared at the ceiling, listening attentively to the crickets and other nocturnal sounds coming through the open windows. Ming knelt on the floor, his chin resting on a windowsill, staring into the night.

Bob came into the room with a paper sack holding the recorder and cassettes. He sat on the floor in a corner, his back against the wall, and watched the evening stars emerging over Ming's shoulder.

Eileen opened the bedroom door a few inches. "Can I come out?" she asked plaintively. "It's lonely in here."

The others laughed quietly, breaking the tension. Eileen settled on the floor next to Frank, snuggling close and draping an arm across his chest.

He smiled. "We'll be fine, Eileen," he said. "We'll make it out of here, I promise."

Frank wished he was as confident as he led Eileen to believe that things would turn out okay. A few months earlier he was a carefree lieutenant on the fast track to discharge. Since then, he had lost some friends and some new acquaintances—he thought of Lynch—and had fallen in love. He'd been shot and arrested and was now on the run from some very determined people. He'd learned he was a lot tougher than he thought he was at the beginning—when he was just an admin officer—but he wasn't sure he was tough enough to get them out of the shit pile they were in now.

Bob wasn't any more confident than Frank that things would turn out well. His life had taken an ironic twist. In Bangkok, he had plenty of time to write his articles but never had enough to say. Now he had the story of a lifetime, and it might not get published. Worse, he could end up in jail for consorting with fugitives—or dead, if Neil had his way.

"I hear something," Ming whispered over his shoulder. "Down there below the house."

Frank crawled to the window and looked out. He could make out only formless shapes, some darker than others, brush and granite boulders and patches of bare gravel. He focused on one spot to see if he could pick up movement in his peripheral vision but saw nothing. Then he heard a scrape, as if something made of metal brushed against a boulder. He looked in the direction of the sound and thought he saw a dark spot merge with another, but he couldn't be sure. His heart was pounding.

The shrill ring of the telephone pierced the silence. Nobody moved. Frank continued to stare out the window, frozen by the unexpected sound. The dark spot moved a few feet closer to the house.

The telephone was insistent. Frank pushed himself to his feet and walked into the kitchen. He picked up the receiver and placed it tentatively to his ear.

"Schaniel," Neil said matter-of-factly, "if any of you want to come out of there, now's the time. Turn on the porch light, walk out slowly and down the stairs, hands above your heads. You've got three minutes." The phone went dead.

NEIL SAT SIDEWAYS ON THE DRIVER'S SIDE OF Tuomainen's squad car, his legs sticking out the open door, his feet resting on the gravel. He placed most of his weight on his left hip to take the pressure off his injured leg. The car was parked on the road down the valley, where Ming had spotted the headlights. A line from the phone in Neil's hand looped up to a nearby telephone pole.

FRANK TURNED TO THE OTHERS, NOW GROUPED behind him in the kitchen. "It's Neil. He says if anybody wants out of here, they have to go now."

They looked at each other uncertainly.

Bob broke the silence. "Well, do we trust him? Or are we out of options anyway?"

"Well, I can't go, that's for sure," Ming said, forcing a smile. "Code of honor among us spies." He nodded toward the unseen men in the darkness. "If they get hold of me, I'll wish I was dead anyway."

"So what do we do?" Bob asked.

"Let's do this," Ming suggested. "Exercise all our options, so to speak. What say Eileen goes out the door? She hasn't done anything, shouldn't be in any danger. Frank, you and Mac take the tapes and hike over the ridge on that trail Mac pointed out." Ming patted the rifle he held in his hand. "I'll stay here and cover your departure."

Frank considered the plan. "You think we'd make it to the trail? They don't have us surrounded?"

"Who knows? But you're resourceful, we've all seen that. Just keep low and go slow. Feel your way out. Put some distance between you and the house, hunker down for a few hours until the sun comes up, then take the trail to the stables. They can't possibly be watching everywhere."

Frank looked out over the dark valley. "I hope you're right."

"It won't be easy with your bad knee," Ming said, "but I don't see any other way out."

With no second thoughts, with no goodbyes other than Frank's quick peck on Eileen's cheek, they put the plan into action. Eileen stepped to the door. "We're coming out," she called, flipping on the overhead light. She opened the door and stepped onto the porch. A spotlight from a squad car on the road switched on and isolated her in its glare.

Frank and Bob slipped out the bedroom window. They lay flat on the ground for a moment, then rose to a crouch and worked their way across the yard and into the rocks below the patio. Hampered by Frank's injured leg, they slowly wormed their way into the thick brush, moving as quickly as they could away from the house.

Twenty minutes later the phone in the kitchen rang again. Ming ignored it. He propped the rifle on the windowsill in the living room and aimed at the rocks and brush below the house. He pulled the trigger and flame spouted from the barrel. The noise was deafening in the quiet valley.

Frank looked over his shoulder. Ming's initial burst was answered by three or four automatic weapons. There was an explosion and the house caught fire. A spire of flames reached into the night sky, extinguishing the stars.

NEIL WATCHED THE HOUSE BURN FOR A FEW MINutes, then slipped behind the wheel of the patrol car and turned back down the road, leaving Tuomainen to catch a ride with the other deputies. He drove slowly through the darkness, the headlights casting eerie shadows from the brush and trees that hugged the road, and pulled over by the old bridge next to the abandoned stables. He lit a cigarette and settled back to wait.

DAWN WAS BREAKING WHEN FRANK AND BOB walked into the valley and turned down the river. The brush gave way to a meadow, broken by oak trees and an occasional clump of sage. It was quiet and peaceful, belying the violence of the night before.

Neil watched through binoculars as they came toward him, then pulled a high-powered rifle from the back seat and laid it carefully across the roof of the car. He pulled the rifle butt tight against his right shoulder and sighted through the scope.

The car radio crackled. "Colonel Neil, you there?"

He put the rifle aside and reached into the car for the microphone. "Yeah, what is it, Tuomainen?"

"You see them anywhere?"

"No, I don't, Sergeant. They must have got away."

"Need any help?"

"No. They're gone, and they're not armed anyway. I'll be okay."

"Uh, Colonel, there's some news came over the radio."

"What's that, Sergeant?"

"You know that talk the president was going to give? Well, he gave it. He said General Chapin is going to be court-martialed for what happened in Cambodia. Blamed the whole thing on the general."

Neil replaced the mike and picked up the rifle, sighting down the barrel as Schaniel and MacNamara walked out of the trees. He pulled the trigger twice in rapid succession, the sound of the shots reverberating from the sides of the valley. Frightened birds rose from the grassy meadow into the sky.

Neil caught movement in his peripheral vision. Startled, he turned to see Broderick step out of the brush behind the stables, another man by his side.

"Captain Broderick, what are you doing here? I thought you were in Washington."

Broderick didn't respond. He continued to walk silently toward the colonel.

Neil nodded in the direction of the river. "Captain, we got them. We're in the clear."

Broderick held a long-barreled .22-mm Ruger pistol loosely at his side.

"What's the gun for?" Neil asked. "That peashooter's not going to be much help out here."

Broderick was ten feet away when he raised the pistol and shot Neil between the eyes. He watched Neil collapse onto the road, then dropped the pistol and turned to Jennings.

"Well, I did it. I did what she asked." He looked back at Neil's body crumpled in the dirt. "I hope I never have to do anything like that again."

Jennings bent down and picked up the pistol. "You won't," he said and shot Broderick in the head.

CHAPTER 55
San Francisco
JUNE 25, 1970

MILES STANICH SAT AT THE TYPEWRITER, PUT-
ting the finishing touches on the story, Chuck Fox
watching over his shoulder. The telephone on the desk
rang. Fox picked it up and put it to his ear without taking
his eyes from the page.

"Yeah?"

He listened briefly, then replaced the receiver. Blood
drained from his face, and he rested his bulk on the edge
of the desk. Stanich looked up at him expectantly.

"That was the police," Fox said. "Bob MacNamara
was killed earlier this evening. Traffic accident down the
Peninsula."

"Holy shit," said Stanich. "That's unbelievable. The
guy just got married."

"Well, that's it for the story," Fox said in resignation.
"We can't use it now. No notes, no tapes, no independent
confirmation, no reporter even." He shrugged helplessly.
"We've got nothing, Miles. We've got nothing."

He leaned over and pulled the sheet of paper from the
typewriter and tore it into pieces, dropping them into the
wastebasket beside the desk.

EPILOGUE
Del Mar
NOVEMBER 1974

EILEEN SAT ON THE BEACH WITH HER TOES IN the sand, a pile of English papers at her side waiting to be graded. She watched her son splash around in a puddle of water, a plastic bucket in one hand and a shovel in the other. It was getting late and the sun was setting, but she wasn't ready to leave, not yet. Her routine was to wait for the green flash when she brought Leo to the beach—if she saw it, maybe Frank saw it too.

She had to laugh. She was an English teacher now, the refuge of a failed journalist. Frank would laugh too, she used to make such fun of the idea. But she liked her new life—teaching at a nice high school, living near the beach, watching Leo grow up. She hoped he would be like his father.

Frank was dead, she knew that. They never gave her a satisfactory explanation, nor did they have to; it wasn't like she was Frank's wife. To them, she was a nobody, and they made sure she understood that. If something happened to her, she would be missed by her parents and a few friends, but they would make sure it looked like an accident. No one would ask any questions.

They kept an eye on her. Every so often they would make themselves known, just to remind her to keep quiet.

A man would be standing on the sidewalk watching her apartment. A black car would drive slowly by, stopping for a moment in the middle of the street. A parent who was not a parent would show up at parent-teacher night and leave before she could engage him in conversation.

She never told them about Leo, never wanted them to know she had something of Frank's that she needed to protect. But they knew. They had to know. And because of Leo, they knew she would never break her silence.

What they didn't know was that she and Leo weren't alone. Two or three times a year she was visited by a slim, middle-aged man, always dressed in a stylish suit with a carnation pinned to his lapel. He would show up unannounced, sometimes at the door of her apartment, sometimes in the school parking lot, once at the grocery store.

Each time he slipped her a bag of cash, and each time he would say the same thing. "It's from Frank's friends," he said, a European accent shaping his words. "They're looking out for you." And that was it. He would walk off without another word.

He never introduced himself, never gave her a chance to ask questions, but she knew who he was, recognized him from Frank's description. Vincenzo Bartolotta, the fixer. And she knew where the cash came from—Ming Chu.

The story of the Cambodia incursion was buried by White House scandals and the president's resignation and the end of the war and the POWs coming home. There were hints in news articles from time to time, but no one seemed to want to dredge it up—except for the man Vincenzo brought with him on one of his visits, and who later would come by on his own.

He was a slightly built, middle-aged Chinese man dressed in a rumpled suit, with thinning hair and a black patch over one eye. He never spoke to her, just handed her an envelope of documents each time. At first, it was a few news clippings about the Cambodia incursion and the confrontation with Lon Nol's troops. Later, some government cables that alluded to a connection between the CIA and Lon Nol. Then transcripts of conversations and phone calls between the CIA and the White House, even some notes handwritten by John Lynch, the national security advisor. It was the corroboration Bob MacNamara had been looking for, and she used it to give Frank the credit he deserved.

The sun set, but she didn't see the green flash. She smiled. Probably because Frank was color blind.

THE SAN FRANCISCO HERALD
Nov. 10, 1974
By Miles Stanich

Two days ago, advance copies of a book about the 1970 Cambodia incursion reached government officials. The book asserts that the incursion—which led to the deaths of thousands in Cambodia and unrest on U.S. college campuses, including the killing of two students and a professor at Steven S. Davis State College by the National Guard—was a plot hatched by John Lynch, then the president's national security adviser, now deceased, and Sharee Fish, the director of the Central Intelligence Agency.

The book was written by Eileen McClellan, the

girlfriend of Frank Schaniel, a young army lieutenant who played an unwitting part in the affair and disappeared before he could testify to Congress. The incursion, she reports, was sparked by the CIA's misguided attempt to enlist the aid of a new Cambodian government in the American fight against Communist forces in Vietnam.

Yesterday morning, Sharee Fish called a press conference to deny the book's allegations, saying the CIA had no involvement in the Cambodia affair. By early afternoon, however, she had tendered her resignation and left CIA headquarters. She was arrested by federal authorities at her residence later in the evening.

Neither the military aid to Cambodia nor the incursion was authorized by Congress, as required by law. The efforts of Congress in 1970 to get to the bottom of the affair petered out, and its investigation ended without pinning down the details or assigning responsibility. McClellan's book appears to complete the record.

"I'm impressed with her research," said David Franklin, counsel to the Senate Military Oversight Committee that investigated the incursion. "We went to great lengths to piece the story together, but either came up empty-handed or were unable to corroborate the information we developed."

Other knowledgeable sources pointed out that the book's allegations would be difficult to refute. The text is accompanied by 251 detailed footnotes and 50 pages of cables and transcripts supporting the story. One reporter likened it to the Pentagon

Papers—chapter and verse about what occurred, too complete for the participants to credibly deny.

Steve Amundson, a Washington reporter for the *New York Times*, said he smelled a Pulitzer. "I've never seen anything like it. It's a bombshell. If the president hadn't already left office, this would bring down the government."

The book sheds light on the death of John Lynch in what was initially thought to be a single-car accident while he was on his way to meet with congressional investigators. One transcript suggests that his death was ordered by CIA Director Fish. McClellan was not able to explain the mysterious disappearances of a number of other figures embroiled in the affair. In addition to Schaniel, they include Army Colonel Michael Ira Neil and Captain Laurence G. Broderick, who apparently led the unauthorized CIA-directed operations in Cambodia. Also missing is Robert MacNamara, a reporter for this paper who was working with Schaniel to assemble the story before he disappeared.

Eileen McClellan was also a reporter for this paper at the time of the Cambodia incursion and is now a high school teacher in Southern California.

McClellan ties in a side story that has long been the subject of speculation. In April 1970 an American munitions ship chartered by the U.S. government to carry bombs to Southeast Asia was hijacked by two "hippies" and taken to the Cambodian port of Sihanoukville. McClellan's book includes evidence that the hijacking was orchestrated by the CIA to deliver weapons to the Cambodian military.

In an interview, McClellan said she hoped the book would spur an investigation into the disappearance of Schaniel and MacNamara.

"Frank Schaniel is the hero of this story," she said. "He tried to stop the plot before it unfolded, and he tried to blow the whistle once it was over. We need to find out what happened to him. He deserves to be remembered."

Made in the USA
Columbia, SC
18 August 2021